D0104332

the ex-wife
CANDICE DOW

GC

GRAND CENTRAL
PUBLISHING

NEW YORK   BOSTON

This book is a work of fiction. Names, characters, places, and incidents are the product of the author's imagination or are used fictitiously. Any resemblance to actual events, locales, or persons, living or dead, is coincidental.

Copyright © 2013 by Candice Dow
Discussion Questions © 2013 by Candice Dow
All rights reserved. In accordance with the U.S. Copyright Act of 1976, the scanning, uploading, and electronic sharing of any part of this book without the permission of the publisher is unlawful piracy and theft of the author's intellectual property. If you would like to use material from the book (other than for review purposes), prior written permission must be obtained by contacting the publisher at permissions@hbgusa.com. Thank you for your support of the author's rights.

Grand Central Publishing
Hachette Book Group
237 Park Avenue
New York, NY 10017

www.HachetteBookGroup.com

Printed in the United States of America

RRD-C

First Edition: January 2013
10 9 8 7 6 5 4 3 2 1

Grand Central Publishing is a division of Hachette Book Group, Inc. The Grand Central Publishing name and logo is a trademark of Hachette Book Group, Inc.

The Hachette Speakers Bureau provides a wide range of authors for speaking events. To find out more, go to www.hachettespeakersbureau.com or call (866) 376-6591.

The publisher is not responsible for websites (or their content) that are not owned by the publisher.

Library of Congress Cataloging-in-Publication Data
Dow, Candice.
 The ex-wife / by Candice Dow. — 1st ed.
     p. cm.
 ISBN 978-0-446-17954-6 (trade pbk.)
1. African American women—Fiction. 2. Women radio talk show hosts—Fiction. 3. Atlanta (Ga.) —Fiction. I. Title.
 PS3604.O938E9 2013
 813'.6—dc23
                                                  2012012896

R0427398282

ACKNOWLEDGMENTS

Writing is my first love and it has always been true to me. I couldn't ask for a greater gift. The ability to pour my heart and soul out through the written word is truly a blessing. It is my voice and it allows me to affect and influence others. That means more to me than words can describe. To my readers, thank you for allowing me into your lives and for reaching out to let me know you're anxiously awaiting my next work. Your support and encouragement are priceless. Thanks to all the book clubs that support me. To the ladies of OOSA, you are the best and I truly appreciate your love and support. Quana Frost, your continued support means the world to me. Thanks to Carleen Dickerson for taking notes during her exotic vacations so I have something to write about.

Thanks to my family for your love, guidance, and support. As always, thanks to my friends, my good-good girlfriends...this book is dedicated to you. Every girl needs at least one good girlfriend! It is key to survival. Having good friends requires being a good friend, but the investment has great rewards.

Love always,
Candice
Follow me on Twitter: @candicedow

ayana

For early April the weather was warm, the sun beaming through my windshield forcing me to run my AC as if it were midsummer. I pulled up to a condominium development in Buckhead, not far from Lenox Square Mall. Using my hand as a sun visor, I checked the address on the building. My producer Quentin had referred me to his celebrity real estate agent friend, whom I was meeting for the first time. I'd done some online home browsing but this was the first place I was seeing in person. Quentin had told me this guy sold million-dollar homes, but his slogan was "Nothing too big or too small." He was Cameron Small, of Small Realty Group. His slogan was catchy enough for me to give him a try.

A silver Audi A6 pulled up a few parking spaces away at exactly two thirty. I assumed it was Cameron's. After the driver got out of the car, I stepped out and headed in his direction.

He shook my hand. "Hi, Ms. Blue. Pleasure to meet you."

"Cameron, the pleasure is all mine. Call me Ayana, please."

"And you can call me Cam. Everyone else does," he said, smiling. I smiled back, mesmerized by his charisma. My entire body overheated. Could it just be the temperature?

He blushed almost as if he were reading my mind. It seemed like an eternity before he continued: "So the spot is in the building here."

Quentin hadn't given me any details about Cam aside from his being the best Realtor in Atlanta, but at that moment I wanted to know everything. Was he married? Did he have kids? Was he heterosexual?

Cam was wearing jeans and a black fitted T-shirt with black Prada sneakers. He carried a leather backpack. I estimated that he was about five foot eleven; he wasn't short, but I had the feeling that he wasn't quite six feet. He walked ahead of me as we climbed the stairs to a second-floor garden condo. I was not feeling the place, but I was definitely feeling the swagger of the guy in front of me. I watched his strong mocha arms as he rolled the code on the lockbox. The key fell out of the box and he unlocked the door. When we entered the condo, he said, "First order of business, I'll need you to sign these forms."

He handed the forms to me as we stood next to the countertop in the empty unit. He hovered over me as he told me where to sign and why I was signing. His face was clean-shaven with a nice dark mustache. His hair was cut low in a temple taper. He looked and smelled crisp: a light cologne mixed with Irish Spring soap. I inhaled the scent of him; his vibe was smooth and jovial, almost familiar.

"A'ight. Cool. Now that the business is taken care of, we can get to the fun part. We're going to visit every condominium complex in Buckhead. Cool?"

I said, "I'm really not the type that needs to see everything. I want to see the three best condos in my price range, preferably two-bedrooms with a den, and I can make a decision."

He stopped in the middle of the living room and laughed. "So Ayana Blue is not picky."

"Is there something about me that makes you think that I am?"

He shrugged. "I shouldn't say this, but most women are picky. Usually when men come to me, they see one or two places and they are ready to put a contract down. Women, on the other hand, can spend two, three, sometimes even six months looking at everything on the multiple listing because they have something in their mind that they're looking for and they don't stop until they get it. Nature of the business though."

"So are you as patient and friendly with these women after month three?"

He laughed. "Of course. I earn a living from referrals. I'm as eager to show the sixtieth place as I am to show the first place. If I'm showing, I'm still in the game, and that's all that matters to me. As long as I put food on the table and clothes on my son's back, you know?"

Why did my heart sink? Just because there was a son

didn't mean there was a wife. He didn't have on a ring, but that didn't mean anything either.

"How old is your son?"

"He's eight."

I had been so wrapped up in work that my flirtation was rusty. I entered the master bedroom and looked at the bathroom before I decided to pry further.

"What's your son's name?"

"Caron."

"He lives with you?"

He took a deep breath. "We have joint custody."

"So what's that like? Do you do week by week or do you have certain days and she has certain days?"

"Our schedule is not so formal. I guess, if anything, it's more like I get certain days and she has others, but not always the same days. You know?"

Would I be real pressed to ask which days he's most likely to get his son? I needed to know how his parental schedule would interfere with dating and he wasn't giving me enough information. We had toured the condominium and were scheduled to see another. Though it was clear that he wasn't in a relationship with his son's mother, it still wasn't clear whether there was a wife or a girlfriend in the picture. For fear of pressing too hard, I figured I should back off. Maybe I should have just come out and asked if he was single and ready to date. Instead I said, "Not sold on this place. We can go to the next one."

"Cool, you wanna just hop in the car with me?"

I shrugged and we headed to his car. He opened the door for me. *That was quite gentlemanly.* I smiled and thanked him. As we drove to the next place, he opened up a little more.

"I'm glad you're decisive, Ayana."

"Why is that?"

"I usually schedule showings like these in late evening or early in the day."

"What do you mean, 'like these'?" I asked, using my fingers for quote marks.

"I just mean residential real estate. That's all."

"Oh, I thought that was some type of snobbish way of saying your pro bono properties."

He smiled. "No, Ayana. Selling properties like this is how I got where I am. I never disrespect the game."

"That's good to know," I said flirtatiously.

"And during the week I pick my son up every day so I like to schedule around that."

"Wow. Every day?" I asked with my dating hope fading.

"Yeah, I usually have him from four to six or seven."

"Really?"

"She's a hairstylist and doesn't usually get out of the salon until that time."

"His mom? Your wife? Your girlfriend?" I jabbed that question in quickly so I could get the info I needed to either stop or continue flirting.

He laughed and looked at me. I couldn't help laughing too. That was tacky, but I wanted to know.

"No girlfriend," he said, still shaking his head in disbelief before he continued. "His mom. My soon-to-be-ex-wife. We're in the middle of a divorce."

"Ooh," I said, with screeching brakes.

"It's a nasty one."

That was a double *ooh*. We pulled up to a high-rise building. As we hopped out I shifted into counselor mode. "Divorces are never fun. I think that two adults who realize they are going in opposite directions should agree to disagree and come to an understanding as to how they are going to handle the family business apart. But unfortunately, emotions get the best of us and it becomes a battle."

"Exactly."

We caught the elevator to the top floor. This unit was a penthouse condo with a loft and den. As soon as we entered, it felt like home. He looked at me and knew that we had struck gold.

He said, "Don't get too excited. We have others to see."

This place had a concierge, a twenty-four-hour doorman, a fitness center, and a meeting room. It offered everything I needed and more. The floors were mahogany. The kitchen shone with granite countertops and stainless steel appliances. Both of the bedrooms were large and called master suites. The loft overlooked the family room. There was a bump-out eat-in kitchen and a formal dining room, as well as a wraparound patio off the family room and kitchen. I imagined having my girlfriends over for our Friday night chats. It was as if the architect knew me personally and had designed the floor plan just for me.

"I told you that I was simple. Didn't I?"

"Now simple is one thing, but it's my job to make sure you've seen at least three to five options before you put a contract on anything."

"If that means I get to hang out with you for a little while longer, that's cool."

We both burst out laughing. *Why did I even let those words come out of my mouth?* I really wasn't interested in dealing with a man in the middle of a nasty divorce.

"Ayana, you are cooler than Quentin made you out to be."

"What did he say about me?"

"Honestly?"

"Yeah, honestly. Even if it does hurt my feelings."

He looked directly in my eyes. "He said that he's never met a woman quite like you. He said he didn't even know God created women like you."

Cam nearly brought tears to my eyes. I had known Quentin respected me but to hear it from someone else was flattering.

"Aw. He really said that?"

"He said you're amazing and the man that snags you would be a lucky son of a bitch."

I felt almost bashful hearing these things about myself.

"But you're not settling down anytime soon. Things are going too good," he said.

"Cam, no one should ever be too busy for love."

He smiled. "On that note, when can I take you to dinner?"

I appreciated his direct approach. While I had baited

him, I was shocked that he had bitten almost immediately. I certainly wasn't going to turn him down.

"I love to eat."

"And I love a woman that likes to eat. Is this evening too soon for you?"

It was, but I wasn't going to let him know. Some men only ask once and I didn't want to make him think I wasn't interested. It had been nearly a year since my last date and this was all so sudden. I felt that I needed to get my mind right. Reluctantly I shrugged. "Of course not."

"Is seven a good time for you?"

"Perfect."

Cam took me back to my car and we agreed to meet at Copeland's on Piedmont.

Cam had sleepy eyes and they were so sexy under the dim lights. Over dinner I discovered that he had simply married the wrong woman for the right reason. They were young and fresh out of college. He believed he was in love and she was passionate and exciting, but he grew professionally while she stayed the same or even regressed over the years. Before long they were worlds apart. Surprisingly, that wouldn't deter him from remarrying. He wanted to do it again with the right person. He said that he believed in marriage, that when he looked at all the men he respected, they were married and he wanted the same thing. He loved to cook and travel. He gave me a rundown of his family structure. He respected his mother and more important he loved his late father.

His parents had been in their mid-forties when he was born, but he claimed their maturity had made him the man he was.

A part of me wanted to wait until I got the full report from Quentin in the morning to fall for him, but I *really* liked him. I was imagining that I could be with this man. This is the one thing I tell people not to do, but sometimes advice without emotion is unrealistic. I adored his zest for life, how much he wanted to know about me, and how straightforward he was about what he was looking for in a relationship. His taxi light was on and he was practically jumping up and down saying, "I'm available." From what Quentin had told me, this man was pretty wealthy, but there wasn't a pretentious bone in his body. For me pretentiousness was the biggest turnoff of all and the one thing I had found to be common to all the men I met in Atlanta. Not him though. He was real. He was open. He was different.

Good conversation made the hours pass rapidly. The staff began to clean the restaurant around us as we sat absorbed in each other. Ten o'clock arrived too soon and I didn't want the night to end, but it was time to go.

After we left the restaurant and headed to the parking garage I was tempted to ask him to come back to my place, but I felt that it was too late. My car was a little distance from his, so he offered to drive me to it.

When I sat in the passenger seat, he looked at me. "Ayana, it's been a really long time since I was out on a date."

"So you're telling me that a man like you isn't swarming with women?"

"Nah, not at all. I'm picky for one. Number two, I'm all about drama-free living."

"I see."

"Yeah, but this is different. I like what I see." He laughed. "I like it a lot."

"Me too, Cam," I said before I could catch myself.

He leaned over and kissed me. His masculine hand touched the side of my face. His tongue twirled slowly in my mouth and my vagina began to throb. It seemed like we were connected. Our lips were locked and neither of us pulled back. He wanted more of me and I wanted more of him. Could this be right? In a dark parking garage on our first date? Or would we ruin the possibilities if we were to succumb to our nature?

I knew better, but my body told me that I was lying to myself. I wanted to be wise, but I needed to feel him right there, right then. His hand slipped under my shirt and he began to rub up and down my back. He put his finger on the hook of my bra.

"May I?"

I didn't want him to stop. Whatever was to be this night was destined. He struggled momentarily to unhook my bra, but finally it popped open. He lifted my shirt and looked delighted with my double Ds. He stared at me for a second.

"Your body is perfect."

A woman can never hear those words enough, especially when by most standards she's considered over-weight. I was five foot six and 185 pounds, and it wasn't every day that someone put my body and perfection in the same sentence. That aroused me more.

The armrest between us restricted our closeness. He kissed my breasts awkwardly before asking me to sit on top of him. I climbed over to his seat and he moved the driver's seat back. He lifted my shirt over my head and I wrapped my arms around his neck as he made oral love to my breasts.

"Can I have you?"

I nodded yes. From the bulge I felt through his jeans, I wanted to have him too.

"You sure?"

I nodded yes again. He put his hands under my skirt to feel me. "Ooh, you feel so good."

We kissed some more as I tried to come out of my panties in the confines of his car and he unbuckled his jeans and pulled them to his knees. He grabbed a box of condoms from the armrest storage compartment, taking one out before placing the box back. I was wet and he was rock-solid as we shared an inquisitive, passionate stare for a few seconds. Was this right? Was this lust just too strong for us to resist? He used his mouth to open the packet and quickly put the condom on. As he held on to my thighs and I slid down on him, we both exhaled. All our preoccupations and inhibitions dissipated as we united. We ground slowly and sighed deeply as if this was what we both needed. He kissed me passionately as if we were longtime lovers. He looked in my eyes with each stroke. The warm and humid air made our skin stick together, forcing us closer. It felt better and better the longer he was inside me. It felt like he belonged there. Finally he exploded and I felt brand-new.

We talked inside his car for several hours longer. Finally, at around two in the morning, he drove me to my car. I looked at him and I knew at that moment this hadn't been a mistake. His expression said he saw the same something in my eyes. We kissed. I knew that if I didn't take the first step we would stay longer.

"Cam, I had a wonderful night."

"I would ask you to come home with me, but..."

I didn't want to know what had caused the *but*, because I was certain it would taint the wonderful night. "Don't worry. We have to see those other condos tomorrow. I'll see you then."

"Ayana, you're cool," he said, still holding my left hand.

I reached for the handle and opened the door. "Tomorrow?"

"Definitely."

His grip was even tighter. I set one foot out of the car and slowly pried my hand away from his. Soon after, the second foot followed and I closed the door. I wanted to scream with excitement, disappointment, frustration, and anticipation all at once but I didn't. I took a deep breath and followed Cam out of the garage.

ayana

My state of ecstasy spilled over into the next day. Cam texted me bright and early in the morning: CAN'T WAIT TO SEE U THIS AFTERNOON.

I had planned to ask Quentin all about him since he was the one who had referred me to Cam. When I saw Quentin, I felt a little unsure of whether I should say anything. Cameron's energy was right. He was honest and sincere. I'm usually right about these things so I wasn't sure if I should solicit secondhand information. Then there was a side of me wondering if my analysis could have been wrong because I wanted it to be right. My intellect and my emotions battled as I tried to decide what to say to Quentin.

He interrupted my preoccupation. "How'd the home search go?"

"It was cool. We looked at two places and I'm looking at two today."

"See anything you like?"

I wanted to laugh. *Hell yeah, I saw something I liked.*

I only wished Quentin had forewarned me that his boy was so damn fine.

"Yeah, I saw one place that I really liked."

"Cool. Cam is a real good dude."

"He seems like it."

Quentin and I went over notes for the show and neither of us mentioned Cam any further. I decided to delve more into Cameron's background once we were off the air. I knew Quentin would know it, being that they'd been friends since high school.

When I started the show, it was the first time in twelve hours that I wasn't thinking about Cam, because I love my job more than anything. When I'm here, I feel most like myself. It's not exactly what I dreamed I'd be doing, but it comes so naturally.

While pursuing my PhD in psychology I started out on a journey to discover why all my good girlfriends and I were still single. We were all in our late twenties, attractive, and had good jobs or were pursuing professional degrees. Certainly the selection of good black men couldn't be that bad. There had to be something wrong with us. Were we too dominant? Were we too picky? Or did we just have bad luck? Assuming this would be the perfect dissertation subject, I began my research. Naturally, I decided to start with the women who were in seemingly healthy marriages.

After nearly ten interviews I was shocked to learn that many of these women in the socially imposed ideal situation were unhappy, and seven of them claimed they would not marry their husbands if they had it to do over again. While I had expected to get responses about how great it was to be committed to the *one*, I ended up disappointed with the reality that men are men.

Besides being single, my friends and I were happy. Most of all we were free. With freedom came options and we knew we weren't stuck. Maybe that was why we laughed, traveled, and absorbed life. Suddenly my research shifted to single women. Were they all as happy as we were? After interviewing a few single women, I found that a large percentage of them were unhappy too. They felt life had dealt them a bad hand. Could it be that being a woman is an unhappy existence in and of itself? Why did it seem that women were never satisfied? Finally it hit me. The one common denominator among the unhappy women was that none of them had really good girlfriends. The women, single or married, with thriving female friendships seemed to get the most out of life.

I went to my adviser to let him know that my dissertation would be called *Girlfriends: The Therapeutic Effect*. He found my topic laughable until I began to explain. Women forgo the chance for true commitment and intimacy with each other, assuming that it can be found only in a marriage. My adviser was still quite perplexed as I continued. Men are completely incapable of giving women the amount of emotional security they seek. Women in turn beg, plead, and worry men to be something that they can never be, leaving themselves eternally unfulfilled. Finally my adviser began to let down his guard and smile.

"Ayana, you're right. I think this will be quite interesting, actually."

"When women get in relationships, they feel like their girlfriends are disposable. 'Finally, now I can stop hanging out and just chill with my man.'"

He laughed. "This is very true."

"That's crazy. What is the shift in our brain that makes us believe that we can do without our girls now that we have a man?" I paused, hoping the concept would sink in. "Men don't want to go to the mall. They don't want to gossip. They don't want to watch romantic comedies. Men don't give up sports or beer when they get into relationships. So why do we give up our natural antidepressant? Real girlfriends?"

He chuckled. "Ms. Blue, I'd like you to keep me posted. If your research is strong, I'll approve the topic."

He approved it and offered to help me find a literary agent. I had never imagined myself as an author, but he encouraged me to turn my dissertation into a book. He found my research and recommendations profound. With the coaxing of my single-girl crew and my bestie/sister Aaliyah, I turned my research into a book titled *Where My Girls At?* I was offered a two-book deal from a major publishing house and had no clue what I could write as a second book. Then one of my good friends suggested that I write about how to be a good friend, because that was a skill not all women had.

My first book talked about the importance of friends but didn't give instructions. The sales for *Where My Girls*

At? were nominal at best. A year later *Girlfriend Confidential* hit the shelves. My friends vowed that this one would not go down like the first. We had learned our lesson: getting the book on the shelves means absolutely nothing if no one knows anything about it. We all put our skills together and I had my own in-house publicity team. We sent press kits to every media outlet, every female organization, and every sorority, and attended every chick conference we could find. *Girlfriend Confidential* became the topic of discussion at hair salons, book clubs, and girl groups everywhere. Women began to deem me the relationship expert. I started to get e-mails from people asking for my advice on every aspect of their lives. I'd only had my PhD for a little over a year; how was I supposed to help all these people? I wasn't ready for all this, but opportunity after opportunity came knocking at my door. The more speaking and workshop engagements I took on, the more popular I grew.

Within eighteen months I was approached with an offer to host my own satellite radio show. I was offered an afternoon slot, from one to two. The time slot already had a listener base, primarily African-American women. The show would be named after my book: *Girlfriend Confidential with Ayana Blue*. I accepted the job.

Before my first day on the air I was introduced to Quentin so we could map out the format of the show. He was a senior producer and had already designed a plan for success. On the first day he decided to have my girls in the studio with me. He felt that would give me an initial dose of confidence and he was right. Mandy, Cori, and my sister Aaliyah were there and it was just like a girls' night out. With each phone call I became more relaxed. With each day I was more certain that this was where I was destined to be. My listeners needed me, my voice, and my advice.

Now I listened to the caller on the line explaining why she was unhappy and why she felt neglected by her husband. Listening is the most important component of my job. Having compassion and understanding for people's feelings is the one thing I think comes naturally for me. I needed the caller to redirect her focus, because positivity is the first step to any happy relationship.

I said, "You really have to be thankful for the little things. Don't focus so much on what he doesn't do as opposed to what he does do. My dad's favorite saying is 'Accentuate the positives and eliminate the negatives.' If you try that for one week, I bet you'll feel differently about him and your relationship."

The caller didn't say anything. So I continued, "You see what I'm saying?"

"I guess it's just hard for me to understand why he can go play golf all day and not even think about how I feel."

"When he's out playing golf, he is thinking about you. He's releasing stress, possibly making business deals. Despite what time he comes home, he's happy. Right?"

"No, 'cause he acts like I'm not supposed to say anything to him."

"You mean he acts like you're not supposed to nag

him. Just imagine you're having a wonderful day and you come home to him asking you 'Where's dinner? Did you feed the kids? Did you wash the clothes?' Wouldn't that irritate you?"

"Probably."

"I'm sure it would. You don't want anybody blowing your high. It's really that simple."

She laughed. "I never looked at it like that."

"Before you start flipping out on the brother, put yourself in his shoes."

"Thanks, Ayana. I'll try that."

"You're very welcome, girlfriend. And thanks for your call."

Quentin gave me a thumbs-up as we neared the end of another successful show. He loved my insight into men, women, and relationships. As if it weren't enough that my words had the ability to talk a woman off the cliff or boost her self-esteem, Quentin's response was a daily reminder that I was called to do this.

I paused. "You've been listening to *Girlfriend Confidential*. I'm your host, Ayana Blue, and we have time for one more call."

Quentin signaled to me that there was a caller on the line. "*Girlfriend Confidential*. Tell me what you want to talk about."

The caller cleared her throat. "I wanna talk about you."

"OK," I said hesitantly, because I sensed agitation in her voice.

This type of call came in at least once every few days:

a woman who wanted to keep being a victim and disagreed with my trying to empower her. She huffed, "So you're everybody's good girlfriend, right?"

"I'd like to think I am."

"If that's the case, why did you fuck my husband last night? You fucking home-wrecker!"

The engineer quickly disconnected the call, but her point had come across loud and clear on air. Everyone thought it was a random angry woman, but I knew I had gotten myself into some shit. Quentin winced and it was clear he knew the caller's voice. The guilty look on my face probably didn't help either.

My heart pounded as I began to gather my belongings. The engineer joked about how crazy people were. I offered halfhearted chuckles, but all I could think about was calling Cam and getting to the bottom of this. The adrenaline in my body was on fast-forward as a million different thoughts stalked me. *Is he really in a marriage as opposed to near divorce as he claimed? How did she know we'd been together? What if this was really just a prank call?* No, it couldn't be. There was no way some prank caller would know that I had recently slept with a married man.

Quentin watched my frenzy in disbelief, sympathy in his eyes.

"You need help?"

"No, I'm good."

When the room cleared, I tried to avoid eye contact with Quentin. I could tell he wanted to ignore what he felt, but he couldn't. Finally he said, "I knew her voice when she first called. I should have never put her through."

"What do you mean?"

"That was Yasmin, Cam's wife. I mean his ex-wife."

I snapped. "Is she his wife or ex-wife?"

"She is his ex-wife. They have another hearing for the divorce in the next week or so. It's over."

I huffed. "This is ridiculous."

"She is ridiculous. I thought she had stopped stalking him."

Duh! Had he *not* thought that Cam and I might become interested in each other? Why hadn't he thought about that when he referred me? This wasn't good. I was writing Cam off as a one-night stand. There was no way I could risk my livelihood for a man with a crazy ex-wife.

"Wow," I said slowly. "So she's a stalker. Looks like I'm going to have to find another Realtor."

"Listen, once she realizes you're just a client, she'll chill."

"Yeah, sure. Tell me anything. Is he giving you a cut of his commission?"

Quentin laughed. "Not at all, Ayana. He's a good dude."

"Yeah, you said that once already."

yasmin

The three consecutive beeps that let you know the call has been disconnected came through the phone, but by that time I had made my point. All the women in the salon were laughing as I slapped high five with my girl Casey. She was shaking her head.

"What did she say?" Casey asked.

"She didn't have a chance to say anything. She really don't know who she's playing with."

"Yas, you are crazy."

"C'mon, Casey, that chick is bold. She's on here every day telling people how they need to act and she out here sleeping with somebody else's man. That's crazy."

Casey just looked at me. I knew what she was thinking, but until the divorce is final, he is my husband and he needs to respect me as such. Because I'm a hairstylist, nothing happens that I don't know about. I have eyes and ears in the strangest places. How bold of them? No, how trifling of them to have sex in a parking garage. I mean, we're not sixteen. I've told Cam a million times not to disrespect me and I wouldn't disrespect him.

I walked back to the chemical room. My client's color was ready to be rinsed. I loved to make Cam and his hussies uncomfortable. With Ms. Ayana being in the public eye, she was the ideal target. She had no clue what I was capable of and if she knew better she would just disappear like I'd forced all the rest to.

It was going to be fun to make her life miserable, because I would get instant gratification. As she signed off the show, the quivering in her voice gave me a feeling of victory.

My client looked at me and said, "You're happy."

"I should be."

"So do you know Ayana Blue or do you just listen to the show?"

I hadn't thought she was in on that whole discussion so I was caught off guard. My neck snapped back. She said, "You just called in. Right?"

"How'd you know?"

"Well, it doesn't take a genius to know you were calling in to the show. We were listening. Then you turned it down."

I laughed because I'd thought I was being discreet and clearly I wasn't but I didn't care. When I get angry, I can feel heat rising in my diaphragm. At that point I spit fire and I am completely unaware of my surroundings.

"Yeah, she slept with my husband in a car last night."

"Are you serious?"

"Yeah, they went to dinner and one of my clients waited the table. She recognized Cam and of course she recognized every girl's best friend. She didn't say anything to them because she wanted to spy. When she left work, she noticed they were still in the car. So she decided to watch them."

My client's eyes got big just as mine had when I heard the story for the first time. I continued, "These dummies decide to bump and grind in the car. I mean, damn."

"What?"

"And from what my informant says, they were clearly on a first date."

"What?"

She was as shocked as me. Not to mention that my clients didn't know it was over between Cam and me. We had been apart for about eighteen months, but I was still hopeful. See, the breakup was my fault and I figured it was my obligation to get the relationship back together. I don't understand why life doesn't come with a damn rewind button. It hurts my heart when I think about how I ruined my life.

When the new FedEx guy first walked into the shop, I knew it was trouble because of the thoughts running through my mind as I watched his sexy ass. He must have read my mind because he came back every day smelling good and looking good and I tried my best to look cute for him. That was my entire mission each day. Finally I said something to him and he was game. After I had Caron, I felt like Cam just stopped paying me any attention. He was so caught up in work and making money, I felt invisible. But this guy brought me back to life.

Six months later, I wanted to leave Cam. I wanted to be with Overnight Express, as I had dubbed him. Overnight Express made me feel young and special. Once I had my heart set on it, I did everything I could to make Cameron leave me. He would tell me things like, "Because of Caron, I'm going to ignore that." Or, "Yasmin, I want to work on this for his sake. He deserves two parents."

Overnight Express had me strung out on love and I couldn't hear a damn thing that Cam was saying. Every time I acted a fool, Cam would make an excuse for why we should stay together. *How stupid can you be, man? I'm trying to leave you.* It became clear that I couldn't just merely allude to wanting to break up. I had to be explicit. Even if I had walked in the door holding a huge poster that had our wedding picture on it with a big strike through it, he still wouldn't have gotten the message. Casey warned me not to leave a good man for good sex, but I just couldn't understand at that time. Cameron was an obstacle keeping me from my heart's desire. He became the enemy and I never thought about how hurt he would be. I only thought about how it hurt me not to see Overnight Express.

I got reckless and began to take Caron around my lover. We'd spend long days together. I hoped that he and Caron could get to know each other so that when we were a family, everyone would be familiar. Caron actually liked him too. I'd always say, "Don't tell Daddy about our special friend."

Little boys are so loyal, because he never even hinted

that we'd spent time with Overnight Express. One day I was at work and got a call from Cam. He started out slowly and calmly. "Yasmin, someone told me that they saw you and Caron with some nigga at the zoo."

"And?"

"Is there something you want to tell me?"

"If I had something to tell you, I would have told you."

"Yasmin, don't make me hurt you."

"Cam, you don't want that kind of trouble."

"Yasmin, who were you with?"

"My man," I said without remorse.

My words punched all the testosterone out of him. He was speechless, and the next thing I heard was the operator. I had to tell Cam what I was feeling now that it was out in the open. These emotions had been bottled up inside me for way too long. As I began to compose an e-mail to him, the words flowed effortlessly. I told him that I had been unhappy for a long time and had found someone else. I promised him that we'd split custody of Caron. I told him that I wouldn't fight for the house, assuming that battle would be too lengthy because the house was in his name: when we got married I was young and had racked up a bunch of bills from college, so my credit wasn't the best. The bad part about it was that I wrote the whole message on my BlackBerry. That's how pressed I was to just get the monkey off my back. I hit Send before I could proofread the message. I texted Overnight Express to let him know I had done it. He responded: WORD?

Word? I thought that was a strange response, but we

had talked about everything from running off to Vegas to even having more kids together. Maybe he was just shocked. Cam called moments later. I was hesitant to answer at first, but then I was like, "Hello?"

"Yasmin, I can't believe that you couldn't say all that bullshit to my face. You and I both know I realized that we weren't compatible a long time ago, but I was willing to work on it for the sake of Caron. So I'm going to ask you this one last time, is that really what you want?"

Didn't I tell you I was done? The more he questioned my feelings and the more he appeared to be fighting for our marriage, the more respect I lost. "Cam, I'm sure about this. I'm not happy anymore."

He chuckled. "And neither am I but I'm not selfish either. I know what my son deserves, but obviously you think about Yasmin before you think about Caron." He paused. "Have you been taking your meds?"

That angered me. I yelled, "That has nothing to do with me and you."

"Yas, calm down. So how soon do you want the separation to happen? You can stay in the house. I have a property that is vacant. I just showed it to potential tenants today. I can move in there until we work this out."

"I don't want the house. It's your house."

"Don't act crazy, Yasmin, that's Caron's house. He deserves to stay there."

I had plans to move in with my man and I didn't know if he'd want to live in Cam's house or if Cam wanted him living there. I said, "We can talk when I get off."

He asked one last time before we hung up if it was really what I wanted. I confirmed. I came home to a moving truck in my driveway that evening. Cam had spent the evening explaining to then-five-year-old Caron that Mommy and Daddy weren't going to be living together anymore. I was livid. No doubt I wanted it to be over, but he was moving out and my son was crying hysterically. It was too much for me to take. I started yelling and swinging on him. "Where are you going? Why are you leaving tonight? Why are you grandstanding? I told you we'd talk when I got home."

Caron cried louder. "Mommy, don't hit Daddy."

He was trying to make me look bad so I tried to reverse it. "You're just going to leave me and Caron so you can go do what you want, huh? Is that what you want to do?"

He just shook his head like he couldn't believe me. It was as if he was trying to belittle me and that enraged me. "You must have another woman," I shouted.

He laughed. "You one crazy-ass girl."

"I'm far from crazy."

"Yeah, I got another woman and yeah, I'm leaving tonight. I will pick Caron up tomorrow like I do normally and drop him off at the salon when you get off."

I started to scrape up his car, but instead I ushered Caron into the house. Cam hadn't taken much furniture, just two flat-screen TVs, his clothes, and the bedroom set we had in the guest room. My pressure was pumping and Caron was acting like a real brat. I sat on the couch and took deep breaths, trying to calm my nerves. I couldn't believe Cam had tried to play me like that. I was so irritated.

I turned on the TV and Caron climbed onto my lap. "Mommy, why did Daddy leave us?" he asked.

"Daddy's not nice."

"Are you sad?"

I said, "Yes, but we're going to be OK."

"Why doesn't Daddy love us anymore?"

"I don't know, baby."

After I put Caron to bed, I texted Overnight Express and told him that Cam had left. He responded, WHEN CAN I SEE U?

I let him come to my house that night. After I changed my sheets, he rocked my world in the bed I had shared with Cameron. He was so perfect inside me. I knew I had done the right thing. After we made love I lay there, staring at the ceiling in complete disbelief. Cam was gone and I had never been so happy. I was satisfied, single, and deeply in love with the man lying beside me. Caron's loud cry outside my bedroom door disturbed my bliss. I popped up and threw on a large T-shirt and rushed out of my room to escort him back into his room.

I said, "C'mon, baby. Let's go."

"I miss Daddy," he whined.

I huffed loudly. This had already gotten old. "Caron, Daddy is going to pick you up after school."

We walked into his room and he begged me to lie with him. I lay in his bed, singing nursery rhymes, trying to make him feel better. Seconds later he fell asleep and I tiptoed out of his room and back into mine. My man was lying there looking slightly impatient. After locking my bedroom door, I climbed on him and began to kiss his neck. "Now, back to what we were doing."

I giggled softly in his ear. His irritation seemed to be subsiding. Just as we were at ease and ready to get it on again, Caron knocked. "Mommy. Mommy."

My head fell into my hands. This had been much better when we crept out to a hotel. Caron never woke up at night and I had obviously underestimated the effect of Cameron leaving. This was certainly becoming an annoying obstacle. It was painfully obvious that though we'd gotten one monkey off our backs, we instantly had another. My man said, "Shorty will be a'ight."

Was he really suggesting that I leave my baby in the hall crying and begging for my attention? I wasn't going to do that and I was perplexed at his suggestion.

He kept kissing me and pulling me aggressively to him. "Shorty gotta man up."

Um, *shorty* was the key word. Why the hell was he suggesting that my five-year-old son get over me being hemmed up in the room with some man? I pulled away. "Baby, let me go."

He pulled me closer. "I thought you said you missed me?"

"I do, but I have to get my baby."

He huffed as I jumped out of bed and opened the bedroom door. I went out, closing it behind me as I walked into the hall. Stooping down to Caron's height, I looked him in the eyes. "Mommy wants you to go to sleep. You're tired."

"Can I sleep with you and Daddy?"

"Daddy's not here."

"But I just heard him."

I was growing agitated. Torn between my lover and my son. It didn't feel right. Overnight Express and I had spent months skipping out to hotels for lunch and happy hour. We loved to be in each other's company. We had talked for hours on end about how this day would be. The day when he could see me whenever and wherever he wanted. Our first evening was turning out to be a disaster.

I took a deep breath. Not wanting to scold him, but knowing that he should be in bed, I went against my better judgment. I pulled Caron's pajamas to his knees and spanked his little legs. "You have school tomorrow. Daddy is not here. Stop crying. You are not a baby. Stop it."

He cried loudly. I said, "Be quiet. Go to sleep."

He reached out to hug me and I grabbed his hand and guided him back into his room. He pleaded, "But Mommy—"

"Mommy nothing. Go to bed."

I left his room, closing the door behind me. After the entire crying episode, I was no longer in the mood. I just wanted to sleep. My lover was standing in the middle of my bedroom, his soldier standing at attention. *There is no way you're still turned on.* He seemed quite anxious as he tossed me on the bed, pushing my T-shirt up. He quickly slid inside me. My not-quite-ripe body tightened on him. He slowly pushed to loosen me up. When I was where he wanted me, he breathed heavily in my ear. "Uh...I been thinking about this pussy all day."

That was my cue to talk dirty back, but I was lying there preoccupied by Caron's crying. He pumped aggressively. I tried to return his energy, but I couldn't. Finally he released and I was so happy it was over.

I sat up on the bed and he lay beside me. *Should I ask him to leave or what?* He put his hand on my thigh. "You not tired?"

"No."

"What's wrong?"

I rolled my eyes. He had no children and he wasn't aware how quickly your child's cry could paralyze you. My baby was in the next room screaming for dear life and he was continuing with his plan.

"Nothing. I think you should leave tonight. I don't want Caron to try to come back in here. He already heard you."

"It's not like I haven't already been around him."

I put my hand on his face. "Yeah, I know, but I don't want him to accidentally see you first thing in the morning. That might be too much."

"I guess you right." He lifted his head and with a slight smile said, "Can I get another round before I go?"

I took a deep breath. I loved making love to him more than I had ever enjoyed sex with Cameron. He was nowhere near as fine as Cameron but he had sex appeal for days. He made my body do things I had never thought it could do. I thought about sex eighty times more than ever. My vagina pulsated all day waiting for the next time I could feel him. But at that moment, I just wanted him to leave so I could handle my emotional son.

"Not tonight, baby."

"A'ight, baby. There's always tomorrow."

"Yeah, I'll call you tomorrow and let you know if I have any breaks in appointments."

"OK. If not, same place, same time."

"Yeah," I said.

After I closed the front door behind him, Caron stopped crying instantly. I had to laugh. How crazy. Maybe he had unconsciously known my lover was there and wanted him to leave. I went upstairs into his room to check on him and he was knocked out. I shook my head.

The next day we tried again and it was a repeat. It was a week of more obstacles and finally my lover called to say that he didn't think it would be a good idea for him to keep coming to my house. He thought we should continue to go to hotels. He wanted it back the way it had been when I was married. Somehow it seemed we could see each other more when Cameron was there. I could always creep out whenever I wanted.

When Cameron dropped Caron off the next day at my job, I told Caron to go inside and stepped outside to talk to Cam. "You want to keep doing this?"

He looked at me angrily. "Doing what?"

"Pretending that we shouldn't get back together."

"Yas, you can't disrespect a man. Let my son hang out with another man and expect me to want this to work out."

"But you've always said that we could work it out for Caron. Remember, he deserves two parents. Right?"

"Yasmin, I've read your e-mail over and over again. You're mean, you're vindictive, and despite all the times I was committed to working it out in the past, I know I can't be with you anymore for any reason. It's one thing to speculate what you're doing but you said shit like this new dude made you do things that I never could," he said in a dismissive tone.

"Are you saying Caron is not important enough for us to work this out?"

"Yasmin, two weeks after I married you, I knew you had some real issues. I take commitment serious and you know that, so I was determined to work through it all with you, because you were my wife. Then you got pregnant. At that point he was worth staying there, fight for what was right. I never cheated on you. I never disrespected you and you tried to treat me like your bitch. I accepted that shit because of Caron. Now it's about being a man for my son. What the hell is he supposed to think of me when you got him hanging out with other dudes? I don't want him to think that's OK. So I'm completely done trying."

"But what if I'm done with that relationship?"

"You are careless. You didn't even think about what you were doing when you let that dude spend the day with my son. How the fuck y'all going to be out playing house and I'm financing everything in it? Let that nigga take care of you."

I touched his face and he quickly swiped my hand away. Caron came back out of the salon door. "Don't fight, Mommy."

Cameron's nose flared and his chest expanded. He hated the thought of Caron seeing him lose his temper. "Caron, go back in there and sit down."

"Cameron, I was wrong. You can forgive me if you try."

"Did I say I wanted to try?"

"Not exactly, but we've been through too much."

"You are crazy," he said, dismissing my plea.

He headed to his car and I followed. "Cam."

He ignored me. Before opening his car door, he said, "All we got to talk about is our goddamn separation agreement."

He slammed the door and I was still calling his name as he nearly ran over my toes. I screamed loudly in the driveway. "Cam!"

Tears welled in my eyes. I wasn't hurt because he didn't want us back together. I was angry. How could he treat me like that?

I was shaking badly and I just wanted to get back at him. I wanted him to feel what I felt. I couldn't believe he could treat me like that. It didn't help that my steamy love affair had simmered down to a chill. Overnight Express wasn't calling like before. I was suffering from rejection from both sides. I'd be damned if my *husband* would reject me. He was obligated to deal with me and I planned to make that painfully clear to him.

I sped through my clients because I had to confront Cam again. Caron and I left the salon shortly after six. I had the GPS service on Cameron's phone so if he was with a client and wasn't answering, I could always locate him. I pinged his phone and noted he was at his house and I quickly headed over.

When I got there, I banged on his door. "Open this door."

Caron was beside me, looking up at me like he didn't know what was going on. Cameron swung the door open. Caron hugged him. "Daddy."

"Don't ever drive off when I'm trying to talk to you."

"All we need to talk about is our divorce."

"We are not getting a divorce. I refuse. You need to come home. You need to come home now."

Cameron looked at Caron and shook his head. "C'mon, buddy. Come in the house. Your mommy is talking crazy."

Instead of going into the house, Caron stood closer to me as if we were a united front against Cameron. He pleaded, "Daddy, please come home."

Cameron looked into Caron's eyes. "Remember what we talked about? Remember?"

Caron nodded. "Daddy will always be there for you. Right?"

Caron nodded again, pissing me off.

"How the hell you plan to be there for him if you're living here?"

He shook his head and spoke under his breath. "You're a confused bitch."

"Cameron, I am your wife."

He chuckled. "And you was my wife when you and that dude took Caron to the zoo."

"I don't care. I'm still your wife."

"Unfortunately, you're the mother of my son. Aside from that, don't reference yourself as anything else to me." Raising his eyebrows, he said, "You hear me. And I need you to leave my house and take my son home. Or let him stay here. It's your choice, but I'm done talking to you."

I tried pushing my way in again. He slammed the door, and seconds later a police car pulled up. They asked me to leave and I headed home. Cam had me served with a separation agreement several days later. It was in my favor. He allowed me to have the house and he was providing a shitload of financial support. Only a fool wouldn't have signed it, but that didn't mean I wasn't fighting for my marriage. I was fighting with everything I had. I stopped telling my friends it was over. I would tell everyone stories about him spending the night or that we had kissed. My lies had prevented our divorce for nearly a year and I planned to keep it up as long as I could. It was amazing to me that if my friends and I declared that he and I were still intimate, the judge wouldn't support Cam's divorce request. At the last court date, I could have sworn Cam was crying. I felt no sympathy. He wasn't just going to get off that easy.

Cam should have known that he was never getting away from me, but he'd decided to do it big this time with Ayana Blue. When confronted I attack, and those two knuckleheads really taunted me.

"They didn't even have enough decency to take their indiscretions in somebody's house," I said, talking to Tayshawn, the stylist directly across from me, but my client chimed in.

"Well, I'm actually surprised. I used to see her for therapy. Relationship counseling."

"Whatever. She's a freak."

My client laughed. "She might be, but she seemed really cool."

"How long did you see her?"

"We still go to her when we need to."

"You shouldn't go to her anymore. She's a poor excuse for a therapist," I said, laughing.

Tayshawn shook his head. "Yasmin, you ain't no damn good."

"So what? Ms. Ayana is the one on the radio claiming to be a Miss Goody Two-Shoes. She shouldn't be frontin'. She's a ho. Keep it real, *Girlfriend Confidential*. That's a bunch of bullshit."

My client wasn't laughing anymore, so I stopped, but I was still irritated. *Women can, and should, have it all.* I'd heard her say that a million times. Maybe that was her way of saying that women can just take whatever they want. Not mine. She was not going to just come through and steal what belonged to me. Cam was mine and our divorce proceedings would continue to be a never-ending saga. I had more tricks than Cameron knew existed. He wasn't getting away from me and definitely not to go with her. *No chick, I am not the one.* My plan was to get rid of her and get rid of her for good.

Even if Cam and I didn't reconcile, damn if I wanted him to be with her. Hell, I didn't want him with anyone, but definitely not her. I vowed to make their lives miserable. *Party over.*

Cam wouldn't be able to move on with his life for a long time, at least not until he gave our marriage another chance. I messed up. I get it, but even rapists get second chances. As long as I'm still fighting for us to be together, he will not have peace with another woman. Divorce or no divorce. Nothing stands in the way of what I want. Not to mention that being one of the hottest hairstylists in the A gives me access to a bunch of loyal, pro bono private eyes. Cam has 24-7 surveillance and doesn't even know who's watching. As I directed my client seated at the washbowl to sit in my chair, I laughed out loud. I love scheming. It is my best asset.

Tayshawn shook his head. "Yaz, you go straight Lynn Whitfield on Cam's ass."

He was referencing the character she had played in the movie *A Thin Line Between Love and Hate*. "Tayshawn, please. He should have more tact."

"Poor Cam," he said, shaking his head.

"Poor Cam, my foot."

"Tell him that I'll take care of him."

I rolled my eyes. "Tayshawn, you think I wouldn't stalk you too? I will hound you until you gone like any other chick."

"Oh, honey, don't get it twisted. You may be looking at a chick, but I'm a man and I got man strength. I don't think you want trouble from me. I can pick you up with one hand."

He choked the air and simulated dropping me to the ground. He curled his lips. "Ploop."

The entire salon laughed hysterically. I didn't have a comeback, which was rare. I simply said, "Tayshawn, you're so crazy."

"Don't forget it, honey. You better be glad Cam don't go down two-way streets, 'cause you would have some trouble. He is one fine man."

We laughed again. That was the nature of the business at Bounce Hair Salon.

ayana

After leaving the station, I sat in my car, breathing deeply and wondering what to say to this man. We'd known each other less than twenty-four hours and drama had already come knocking at my door. My life was drama-free and I wanted to keep it that way. Before I could dial him, my phone vibrated in my hand. CAMERON SMALL popped up on the screen. I was slightly nervous and confused about whether or not I should answer, but I did.

"Ayana."

"Yes."

"Quentin just called me and told me about the phone call you got. I apologize. I shouldn't have dragged you into this. Things have been calm for a while..." He huffed. "Yeah, then again I haven't been out in a long time either. So I thought things were cool between me and her, but I guess not."

I breathed heavily because I didn't know how to communicate what I needed to say without sounding angry. He continued, "I think it's best if we keep it professional for now."

My eyes closed and I almost felt rejected, but I agreed so I tried to shake the adverse feelings. "Yes, Cam, that makes a lot of sense."

He said, "I had a good time last night, but she always finds a way."

A part of me wanted him to stop letting her rule his life, but the other side of me wanted to be sure they were through before I appeared as if I were coercing him to leave his wife. Too many things were unclear and I didn't think it was time for me to comment. The silence was uncomfortable and I could tell he wasn't sure what else to say. On a lighter note, he said, "Is it OK if I still help you find a condo?"

"I hope so."

"Cool. I'm going to text you the addresses. I'll meet you at the first one at three."

"So you'll meet me in fifteen minutes."

He laughed. "Yeah, something like that."

"Make sure no one is following you."

I thought it was funny, but it didn't go over well. He didn't laugh and he said, "OK. I'll meet you there."

As I headed to the complex, I felt nervous, confused, anxious, angry, upset, compassionate, and understanding all balled up into one. I pulled up and he was standing next to his car waiting for me. After several deep breaths, I got out. He was so handsome, patiently waiting as I walked toward him. He reached out for a hug. His sexy scent enveloped me as we embraced. A slide show of the night before shuffled through my head. It had felt so right and he had seemed so honest. What was the real story with his wife? Women are crazy, but usually for a reason, and I needed to know if Cam was the cause of this woman's insanity. I hated the thought that we couldn't further explore the passion and chemistry between us, but that's the way things go when you have sex before all the necessary research is done. I wanted to kick myself for succumbing to him. As he held me close in his arms, I sensed that he regretted things too.

He said, "A'ight, I think you will like this place. These are more or less town houses. One-car garages."

He opened the door and stood in the vestibule as I brushed past him to enter. There were a pair of stairs, one heading to the living room and the other leading to what I assumed to be the garage. I walked up to the living room and thought the layout was impressive. The living/dining space was open and the kitchen had granite countertops and stainless steel appliances. He said, "The cool thing about this place is that it's brand-new, but ready for you to move in. You know, sometimes financing falls through and you get to benefit from someone else's misfortune."

"How so?"

"Someone had a contract on it, but things didn't work out. Now the builder has to sell it."

"Oh, OK. I get it."

"So what do you think?"

"I like it. I actually like it a lot."

"I've got one more for you to see and then we can revisit the ones you've already seen."

We went to the other spot and I wasn't really impressed, so we headed back to see the penthouse condo that I loved. When I walked in, I felt the same way I had the day before. I was almost convinced that this was the place for me. I told Cam that I wanted to put a contract on the place and he suggested that I sleep on it for a night or two, then visit it again.

Before parting, Cam asked me for a hug. He held me close and tried to gain eye contact with me, but I looked away. He grabbed my chin and said, "Look at me."

We stood there eye to eye, neither of us saying a word, but the conversation was deep and filled with understanding. He knew how I felt and I knew he would love to change things if he could, but there was nothing that either of us could do. He shook his head. "Wow."

I thought that was an interesting word choice. He noticed the perplexed look on my face and smiled. "Sometimes good things come at the wrong time."

In a partially sarcastic tone, I said, "Or it's possible that we pursue good things at the wrong time. Perhaps we should do some housekeeping before inviting someone else in."

"Perhaps you're right, Dr. Blue, but unfortunately the average person isn't going to give it that much thought. They're going to go with what feels right."

"That's why you have to strive to be above average."

"The next time we go out, I will have my divorce papers in hand."

I rolled my eyes. "You think I'm open to being harassed by your wife? Not."

"Listen. I think it will be better when she's officially my ex-wife."

"Cam, court papers aren't going to change who a person is at their core."

He took a deep breath and let me go. "So I'm hopeless."

He took a few steps backward. I looked at him and there was something sincere about him. I felt sorry for him, but I couldn't jeopardize all I'd built for the possibility that my relationship with Cam could develop into something. It just wasn't worth it to me.

I shrugged but I felt bad offering him this death sentence. It was in my nature to give hope, but I wasn't sure that crazy, stalker-type women ever healed. He had made a bad choice and it was highly probable that she would continue to make his life a living hell for some time or at least until she found someone else or sought professional help. Unfortunately, the people who need the most help never voluntarily get it. Cam had a long road to travel and I didn't know him well enough to willingly go for the ride.

"So I'll give you a call tomorrow or Friday with my decision. I'm definitely leaning toward the penthouse."

I could tell he wanted to talk about his situation further, but I wanted to end it right there. He almost appeared lost for words and then he finally said, "Yeah, that'll be cool. I'll wait to hear from you."

"Have a good evening," I said, slowly heading to my car.

He watched me until I started the engine before finally heading to his car. He waved and I waved back. It almost felt like a breakup, except we didn't really know each other. As I pulled out of the parking lot with a sinking feeling in my stomach, I thought, *Ayana, get it together. It was a one-night stand and that's it.*

ayana

Two days later I sat in Cam's office signing the contract to place an offer on the penthouse. He was very gracious, but standoffish at the same time, as he explained each page of the document. He suggested we lowball the seller initially; if they didn't bite we could come back.

"You can gamble with condos. They don't go as quickly as some houses."

"Yeah, I know."

"And you realize that you'll be in that same situation whenever you want to sell. Are you comfortable with that?"

"I am and I'll definitely be there for a while. With traveling and all, I just need a place to lay my head."

"So what if you fall in love and..."

My eyes shot an invisible dart at him that landed right on his forehead. He wrinkled his brow and waved it off. "Never mind."

I hadn't really meant to respond that way, but something about his insinuating that I was looking for or that I needed love bothered me. Was it possible I had just wanted a one-night stand with him? I shrugged, hoping to decrease the tension in the room.

"No, go ahead. So if I fall in love..."

"It's possible you could be trying to get this off of your hands in a year or so."

"I would expect that I'd be dating someone longer than a year before I'd be willing to sign over my life to them for better or worse. You know?"

"You never know. Sometimes it takes years to make a decision about a life partner. Sometimes it takes minutes."

He paused and looked at me. *Does he think I'm that gullible?* I smiled and shook my head a little.

"I'm comfortable with lowballing the initial offer. I try not to be anxious for anything, so I'm up for negotiating. As long as I get what I want for the price I need."

"That's what's up," he said.

After the last of the documents was printed and signed, Cam took his time explaining and clarifying everything a second time. He seemed so patient and passionate about his job. I liked that about him. I found myself smiling at him for no reason and he returned a smile each time he caught mine. As time passed I found myself less and less angry, and more and more curious about this guy. My heart and my brain told me that he was who he'd told me he was. He'd backed off like he promised. He didn't bad-mouth his stalker ex-wife, like the average man would have been tempted to do. He simply admitted that he should get his business in order. He seemed noble in his words and actions. That was a rare combination and maybe that's why I'd felt so deeply connected to him that I wanted to rock his world on a first date.

Still, I yearned to know his complete story. The what, when, and why of this guy's being in any kind of domestic situation with that angry woman who had called my show. It would have been too hypocritical of me to pretend I was interested in hearing his side, so I suppressed the urge to ask.

After the paperwork was done, he suggested I wait for him to walk into the parking lot because it was dark out. He secured the building and we headed out to our cars. I noticed him staring at me as he held the door. I wished I could decipher what was behind his intense eyes: lust, lies, or a lonely man on a quest for love. I didn't know and I didn't slow my pace enough to figure it out.

I unlocked my car with the controller and he walked over and opened the driver's-side door. I smiled. "Thank you."

Ducking his head into the car he said, "I'll be in touch hopefully by tomorrow. The agent should have everything first thing in the morning. At least he'll be able to look at the offer and see if we're in the ballpark. I can usually gauge by their response what the seller is willing or not willing to do. I'll contact you as soon as I get a call from him. OK?"

I said, "OK. Hopefully we'll talk tomorrow."

"Definitely. You'll hear from me one way or the other."

"Sounds good." I paused. "Thanks, Cam."

"You're certainly welcome."

He reluctantly pushed my door closed and took two steps back. I felt awkward starting the car as he stood there, but I did. When I backed up, he raised his arm one more time in a wave. I beeped the horn, because I would have felt slightly stupid waving back. Finally he headed to his car.

I called my younger sister. "Aaliyah, what are you doing?"

"The same thing that I'm doing every night at eight."

"Right, tell my nieces that I said good night."

"Auntie said night-night."

They responded in their three- and four-year-old languages. God only knows what they said, but it sounded sweet and momentarily distracted me from what I really wanted to talk to Aaliyah about.

"So did you sign the contract?"

"Yeah."

"Did y'all discuss you-know-what?"

"No."

"Did he tell you why, you know, he acted like, you know?"

I knew she had to do that for the sake of little ears, but I was irritated and I wasn't in the mood to translate her cryptic phrases. Aaliyah knows me so well that when I paused before responding, she laughed and said, "Sister, let me call you when the girls go to sleep."

"Thank you."

"OK, Ayana. You can be such a jerk sometimes."

"Never that."

I headed to the grocery store to grab a roasted chicken for dinner. I rolled a cart into the store in something of a daze, simultaneously looking at messages on my phone. As I tried to prioritize whom I'd call back, I dropped a bag of grapes into the cart. My bottom lip nearly fell into the cart too when I noticed Cam staring back at me. Considering I was exhausted, momentarily I assumed I was hallucinating. Why was I imagining his smile? I rubbed my eyes to rid my mind of his image. Then I looked again. It was a real estate ad and it really was Cam. I was less than two miles away from my apartment and I frequented this grocery store. Never had I seen this ad.

As I strolled through the store with Cam's eyes staring into mine, I imagined what could have happened if he hadn't been married. With the type of attraction we shared, I was certain we would've been taking long strolls in the park, going out to dinner, making love any- and everywhere. He was probably the type that sent emotional text messages. Simultaneously, I snapped at myself. *What if isn't what is. Don't fantasize when the facts are staring you in your face.*

I was conflicted in my spirit. I was trained to analyze a person's character after speaking to him a few times. Cam had given me no reason to believe he was a shady person. Everything about him seemed sincere. So why did I feel this empty feeling in my stomach? Why did I feel as if I'd been betrayed? Maybe I was just disappointed in myself.

By the time I reached the register, I had explored every

possibility with Cam. He seemed little-boy sweet and as much as I knew it was never going to be, I wanted to know more about him. He seemed like an interesting and honest person. After interviewing one hundred men, I was convinced there weren't many Cams. But damn, why did his ex-wife have to be a crazy lady? Oh well, shit happens, and by the looks of things other shit doesn't happen.

When I reached my house, Aaliyah called back. There was no crying, yelling, or giggling in the background. I said, "Now that's better."

She laughed. "Leave my babies alone. It only sounds like that when we're in the bathroom."

"Geesh. You need to put them to sleep sooner."

"Why?"

"So you'll have time to talk to your big sister."

We laughed because Aaliyah was always the available one if you didn't mind the background noise.

She said, "Whatever, Sister."

"OK, so anyway, I told you how I slipped and fell on my Realtor's thing the other night. Right?"

"Yeah, freaky-freaky."

"Stop, you know he must have been extremely nice if I did that."

"Yeah, OK, you told me all of that after you did it. And then his wife called and we concluded that you kick his nice ass to the curb. Correct?"

When I didn't respond, she continued, "Ayana. You know better. We talk about chicks like you. Whether they are separated or not, they are still married. When he's done, go for it." She laughed. "I would say there are other fish in the sea, but I guess we all know that's not true."

We laughed really hard.

"So did he keep it professional when you saw him tonight?"

"Yeah, he did."

"Cool. Maybe he is a good guy."

"Duh, that's why I'm calling you. I feel like he's a really good guy and a part of me wonders if I should continue to talk to him until the divorce is done."

"What if it's never done? Would you be a mistress?"

"That's not what I want, but I do like this guy. He has a wonderful spirit."

"They all do in the first week."

I laughed. "True. You're not lying about that."

"If anyone trusts your opinion you know I do. So let's be honest, no one, not even Ayana Blue, can trust her own advice once the aura of romance is in the air."

"Ha ha. Really funny. That's my favorite saying, isn't it?"

She continued, "Once the love hormone starts circulating, you instantly become stupid. Is that correct, Dr. Blue?"

"You make me so sick."

"I'm just saying, this is shit you've told me. I'm only regurgitating it."

"Well, pick on somebody else. I just need a girlfriend to talk to right now."

She laughed. "A'ight, I'm listening. So you like this guy?"

"Yeah, I feel like he's a great guy."

"OK, give him thirty days."

Shocked by her words, I said, "You think?"

"No, I don't think, but that sounds like what you want me to say."

"I'm really not looking for you to say anything. I just want you to listen. You understand?"

"Yeah."

As I put my groceries away, I told Aaliyah about the many things Cam and I had in common. How we'd talked for hours when we went to Copeland's and how I connected with Cam in a way that I hadn't with other guys. I'd met many successful men on my journey but there was always something missing. People come in my office all the time wondering if connection is something superficial people are looking for in love. My response is that in any relationship, the initial interaction is one of the most important moments. There are many other things to factor in, but if your mind is right, you won't bond with the wrong people. I was caught in a war between my feelings and my ego. Could it be possible that my mind wasn't right if Cam was wrong?

Aaliyah listened and resisted offering advice. I appreciated it. After we got off the phone, I did a yoga DVD, hoping to calm my spirit. I reflected and prayed and forgave myself. After I showered, I hopped into bed and within minutes I drifted off to sleep.

As I prepared to go into the office, I got a call from Cam. I assumed my prayer had been answered because my heart beat at a normal pace when I answered. He said, "Good morning, Ms. Blue."

"Good morning, Cam."

"Got some good news. The listing agent got the contract and already spoke with the seller."

"OK, and..."

"Here's the bad news."

"What?"

"They want you to settle by the end of this month."

I looked at the calendar. The end the month was in ten short days. I huffed, "Is that even possible?"

"Yeah, if we finalize the contract this morning, I can speak with your loan officer. He's my man and I'm sure he can have an appraiser there tomorrow and an inspector out in a couple of days. I'll need to speak with the settlement company to see if they can fit you in, but I don't think it will be a problem. The condo association handles your property insurance."

"I don't have a problem settling by the end of the month but I'm not sure I can move in right away. I'm so not spontaneous like that."

"Is that right?"

His question seemed more like a statement and I wondered if he was thinking about my sexual spontaneity. It's hard to get past having sex on the first night with most men. They don't get the fact that they were just special. Instead, they think you must do this all the time. I see this often with couples: they have sex on the first night and the man always has a question in the back of his mind. I hoped Cameron didn't see me that way, but it was too late to fix it.

He continued, "Your first mortgage payment wouldn't be due until the first of the following month, so you have a little time."

"OK," I said hesitantly.

He asked, "Are you comfortable with settling this month? If not, we'll push it back. But if we do that, keep in mind that it's possible they may not accept the price then. You never know."

"I feel you. OK, the end of the month works."

"He's faxing me a copy with the amendment. I will fax it to you to get your John Hancock. The settlement date is April twenty-eighth. You're cool with that, right?"

"Yes."

I was really happy the seller had accepted the contract, but I felt pressured. After a few deep breaths, my spirit was calmer and Cam explained again what we needed to do. In order to get everything handled, I was forced to reschedule my morning appointments. I see patients Tuesday and Thursday mornings from eight to twelve and Monday and Wednesday evenings from five to nine. Since I'd cleared my schedule the night before, I was really putting myself into a bind, but I had no choice if I wanted to get the place at the right price. I would have to work both morning and evening to make up all the appointments I'd missed. Including the talk show, I was looking at a ten-hour day. Ugh! I was slightly irritated, but oh well. By noon everything was confirmed and I had a settlement appointment for April 28.

ayana

April showers pounded my car as I pulled into Roswell Oaks, the medical office complex where my practice is located. I'd leased this office space while I was finishing up my first book and studying for my board exam. There was never a question as to whether I would start my own practice. Although I'd done my internship under a very established psychologist, I wanted to build my practice from the ground up. I wasn't making a lot of money, so the fifteen hundred a month for my one thousand square feet of space was pretty steep, but I didn't regret it at all. The business started slow but progressed rapidly after the success of my second book. Most often, it's simply about being prepared when success comes knocking.

I was running five minutes late, because my body had naturally wanted to remain asleep on a Friday morning. Some of my patients depended on me to get through the week so I *had* to make up those hours. The goal of a psychologist is to help her patients change their way of thinking in response to stressful situations. Sometimes that happens in a few sessions. Often it takes up to ten sessions to notice a change. After six months to a year of seeing any patient, if the original behavior persists, I recommend a treatment program and/or a psychiatrist for medical intervention.

I noticed my first patient, Margo, standing in the rain in front of my office. She was one in particular I sometimes thought about referring to someone else, but then there were times when it seemed we were making strides.

I jumped out of the car quickly and pulled out my office keys. I felt so bad about her being outside that I forgot to grab my umbrella and I didn't even think about my fresh weave until I felt my bangs sticking to my fore-head. As I fumbled with my keys, my only goal was to get the door open so we both could be safe and warm.

The best way to describe Margo is *complex*. She hated everyone. She had known her father but he had married another woman, leaving her behind. Her mother had been abusive and later left her with her grandmother, who had a big heart and allowed any needy person to live in her house. Margo was sexually abused by various men, all of whom at some point lived in her grandmother's house. She didn't discuss her abuse with anyone until it was too late. She absorbed all the hurt and pain, making her heart stone. She had recently applied for disability, because she couldn't keep a job. I helped her get into a program that offered assistance, because applying for disability was a long process. I knew she was struggling to keep a place and had very little family support. I didn't want to see her out on the streets.

The program provided transportation to and from office visits for people with disabilities. I planned to give the office a call because the driver should've at least made sure the patient got into the office before pulling off. A part of me was irritated, but I guess I was to blame, because I was late.

"Whew," I said as we finally stepped into the office. I turned and smiled at Margo. "Good morning, how are you doing?"

She smiled wide and bright. "I'm doing great."

It was already turning out to be a good session. "Fantastic! I'm happy for you."

She covered her smile and nodded. "Thank you."

I said, "We're going to start in just a second. I have to set up the office. I haven't been in since Tuesday."

"I know," she said, almost as if she were offended.

I went in my office and lit the oil burners. I needed the aroma not only to calm the nerves of my patients, but also to calm my own nerves. When I opened the door, Margo was punching her fist into her hand. I thought that was slightly strange, considering she seemed to be in a great mood. I shook the concern and said, "C'mon in."

She walked into my plant sanctuary of an office where a nature soundscape CD was playing to calm the mood. As she sat, with as much compassion in my voice as I could muster, I said, "Tell me about last week. How was it?"

She leaned back in the chair and stared into the ceiling. "It was the best week I've had in a long time."

"So did you try a new activity like I told you?"

She nodded and smiled. I was glad she'd done the assignment. With good reason, Margo struggled with trusting people. It was hard for her to try new things because she thought people were out to get her. I was impressed with her obvious excitement.

"So what did you do?"

She took off her hat and exposed her platinum blond hair. I didn't like it on her, but I liked that she had stepped out of her box to do something that would possibly draw attention to her. I said, "Wow. I love it."

She continued, "After I got my hair dyed, I went skating."

"Really?"

"Yes, and I had so much fun."

"Did you go alone?" I asked.

"No, where I got my hair done, they go skating and I went with them."

"Had you been to the hair salon before this time?"

"Yes, once before."

"They all seemed welcoming?"

"They were so nice," she said in a perky tone.

That could be a positive or negative sign. Margo doesn't trust people easily. When she does, she tries to suffocate them with her presence. If someone slightly pulls away, she takes it as a rejection, which only thrusts her back into her shell so she swears she'll never deal with people again. I didn't want her to get hurt so I always warned her to take it slow.

I asked, "When are you getting your hair done again?"

"Tomorrow."

"So you're going every week?"

"I think I look pretty."

"You do, but I don't want you to become too attached to your hairstylist. OK?"

"You know I don't trust females anyway."

"It's OK to trust, but just don't get too involved too soon."

She smiled. "OK. I know what you're saying."

It felt like we were making progress. I continued to drill her about pacing herself in relationships and enjoying new things. Margo left feeling happy. She even gave me a hug and I watched her head out to the car waiting for her.

Though it was dreary outside, it felt bright and lively to me. My appointment with Margo had made everything worth it. She was developing beautifully and I wanted to keep her on that page. It had been three consecutive visits of progress. I was a little concerned about the possibility of her growing too attached to me and I didn't want to be yet another person to hurt her, but thus far there was no need to recommend her to a psychiatrist.

By ten thirty it appeared that my ten fifteen appointment was not going to make it, so I drove to Dunkin' Donuts to grab a bagel and coffee. I was famished.

yasmin

I woke up feeling happy that I had been given yet another day to convince a judge that Cameron was fully in love with me and that we belonged together. He didn't deserve to move on with his life without me. I'd been successful with this going on a year now. Cam wanted to divorce me so bad and I just didn't get it. Relationships are hard. Why would you want to go out there and find someone else? There's no guarantee that she'll be any better than me.

I glued on my false eyelashes and hoped that we'd get another male judge so that I could bat my eyes and explain that Cam and I had been intimate recently. They usually dismissed us and Cam didn't get what he wanted. It was for his own good and he didn't even realize that I was protecting him. I just didn't understand why he thought I was the enemy.

I put on a tight black pencil skirt and a white form-fitted, buttoned top. My push-up bra gave me enough breasts to entice the average stupid man. Even the most educated man, such as a judge, can't resist the lure of a sexy woman. It's how we make it in the cold, cold world. You either use sex appeal or settle for what these selfish men want to give you. And trust me, it's not a whole lot.

Tayshawn had been my witness each time we'd come to court, but the last time he'd really overdone it. His antics had almost caused us to lose, but this time I was bringing Casey. She'd been around both Cam and me and she was in my corner. She could see there was still chemistry. I glossed my lips and urged Casey to do the same.

Cam spoke as he, his attorney, and his mother passed us in the hall. I cringed because that was one of our major issues. Cam is such a damn mama's boy. What thirty-five-year-old man brings his mama to testify for his divorce? Her old ass rolled her eyes at me when she passed. She is close to eighty, damn near ninety years old and has the audacity to have a slicker tongue than mine. She called me all kinds of bitches through this process. I didn't even give a damn, I was trying to get my man back. I didn't care what she thought. It wasn't as if she'd be around much longer anyway.

They went into the courtroom and just as my attorney approached, I turned to see Ms. Mae, Cameron's mom, coming out. She hadn't spoken when she walked in and I wondered if she was coming back to speak. There was a suspicious smirk on her face as she approached. Her voice quivered. "Yasmin, can I speak to you for just a moment?"

Oh lord. This lady is going to make me curse her out in

the damn courthouse. I debated how to respond. Then I took the high road and smiled. "Sure, what's up?"

"How do you sleep at night?"

I knew where she was going. We'd had this conversation in the past. "In my bed and how's your sleeping?"

"I mean, how do you come in here time after time and just lie? Cameron has done nothing to hurt you. Why would you hurt him and keep hurting him? I just don't understand how a person could be so evil."

"I'm fighting for my family, Ms. Mae. Do you know anything about that?" I asked, knowing she'd dealt with infidelity in her own marriage and chosen to stay. She had told me that out of her own mouth many times.

"Honey, running the streets is one thing, but when you leave your home for the streets, you need to stay out there in the gutter with the smut and the trash."

"I never left home, Ms. Mae."

"You don't have to physically move out of your house to be gone. You left my son for another man. Now leave him alone."

"You're the problem. Why can't he speak for himself?"

She lifted her cane almost as if she were going to hit me. Instead she made a quick U-turn. "Hmph. You ol' selfish, lying whore. I hope this judge sees you for just who you are. A liar."

I said, "How are you so sure I'm lying? Do you sleep in the bed with him?"

She stopped at the courtroom door and looked at me. Her head shook almost as if she were vibrating. "I know my son. He's allergic to fleas. He wouldn't knowingly lie down with a dirty female dog."

My neck snapped back and before I could retaliate, she swung the door open and went back into the courtroom. *Old hag.*

My attorney was asking Casey a series of questions to be sure she knew how to respond. When I stepped back over to them, he turned to me with the same ol' bullshit. "You're certain that the two of you have been intimate in the last thirty days?"

"Yes. Multiple times."

Casey smiled at me inquisitively. I ignored her and my attorney continued, "And the two of you have talked about getting back together in the last thirty days? Am I right?"

"Absolutely."

"Good. Let's go in."

When we opened the door to the courtroom, Cam's entire row turned their heads. I decided it was the perfect time to blow Cam a nice, sexy kiss. *Muah.* He shook his head and smiled. He wanted me, I knew he did. Why did he try to act so shady?

When the judge finally called our case, Cam's attorney called him to the stand. He claimed he hadn't touched me in eighteen months. I begged to differ, but he continued. He claimed we hadn't lived under the same roof in eighteen months. Yada yada yada.

His mother was called to testify and confirm his claims. My attorney cross-examined both Cam and his mother.

I didn't feel like he really nailed it but I didn't stress it much, because I knew I had my story straight. It was now my turn to explain why I kept disputing the divorce. My attorney asked a series of questions and I explained that Cam and I had conversations about staying together for Caron and that Cam had stayed at my house and in my bed several times.

The female judge shifted uncomfortably in her chair as Cameron's attorney approached to cross-examine me.

"Mrs. Small, are you really telling the truth? Isn't this all made up?"

"No. It's my word against his. He sleeps at my house all the time and we sleep in the same bed together."

"You understand that by making this claim you prolong divorce proceedings. Right?"

"Yes, but that's not why I do it."

"What person in his right mind would continue to appeal and keep sleeping with you?"

"I don't know. I guess Mr. Small," I said, rolling my neck.

"Do you have all the dates in question that you're claiming you and Mr. Small were intimate?"

"Yes," I said, and began to run them down.

The attorney smiled. "Your Honor, Mr. Small installed a twenty-four-hour surveillance camera at his home, which proves he sleeps in his own bed every night."

My emotions got the best of me as I blurted out, "He didn't sleep in his own bed a week ago when he was grinding in the car with his mistress."

The judge frowned as she slammed her gavel. "Order."

Cam's attorney said, "No more questions."

The judge asked my attorney if he had a witness and he shook his head no. I wanted to pop him in his head. Casey had been quizzed on all the dates. Instead, he wimped out. I stomped off the stand to my attorney's table. As I sat, I angrily asked, "Why didn't you call Casey?"

"If you want to commit perjury and serve time for a goddamn divorce, you can do it on your own."

I looked at Casey and shrugged. She didn't know what was going on. Before I knew it, Cam had his dream come true. The judge granted him a divorce. She probably wanted him for herself. How could they really prove we weren't together? I broke down in tears as she explained the divorce was final.

Cameron looked at me with sympathy, but victory also sparkled in his deep-set dark eyes. They headed out of the courtroom first and we followed. Out in the hall, my attorney shook hands with Cam's attorney.

"You must be fucking her. Is that why you just quit in there?"

My attorney squeezed my triceps really tightly and pulled me farther away from where they were. "Listen, clearly I defended this case with all I had even though at times I knew you were lying. I still wanted you to keep your family. I'm not so sure anymore that you deserve it."

"Whatever. You're a wimp. Casey, let's go."

My attorney asked, "Do you want a copy of the divorce papers?"

"What difference does it make?"

"Today you feel that way, but when you fall in love and want to get married again, you're going to wish you had them."

"I'm not going to care because I'm not getting married again. This did it for me. I'm so over it. What's the purpose anyway?"

"Yasmin, you're taking a really immature approach."

"Who you calling immature?"

He mumbled something under his breath like "I see why he wanted a divorce." By this time Cam and his family had headed to the clerk's office to get the paperwork.

I looked at Casey and said, "Let's get out of here before I curse this bastard out."

When we walked into the salon, Tayshawn said to Casey, "So you did your thing, boo?"

"No, they never even called me to the stand."

He laughed. "Whew, I told you, girl, you should have taken the queen again."

"Drama queen," I said sadly.

His face quickly turned serious when he noticed I wasn't laughing. "Did you lose?"

My eyes filled up with tears and Tayshawn came over to hug me. The entire ride to the salon, Casey had been silent. She patted my back as Tayshawn said over and over, "Oh, honey child, I cannot believe this."

Casey added, "It's his loss."

I didn't want to hear any of this. I just wanted my family back together. I didn't know why I had wanted to cheat on Cam, but now that he was officially my ex-husband, my heart couldn't take it. I couldn't accept the thought of someone else being with my man.

ayana

Cam and I had talked on the phone a few times over the past week and had seen each other once for the inspection since the contract was accepted. He'd primarily kept it professional, but that didn't change the butterflies in my belly whenever I was within twenty feet of him. Shouldn't I be too old for these schoolgirl feelings?

We scheduled the final walk-through for the morning of the settlement. When I pulled up, my heart beat rapidly, as if it were fighting to escape my chest. I wanted to shake the uninvited emotions, but I couldn't. Cam pulled up seconds after I got out of the car. He beeped the horn as if I didn't see him. His big smile greeted me as he quickly stepped out of his car. He walked over to me and offered a friendly half-hug. Then he leaned over to kiss my forehead. My vagina quickly twitched. The slightest touch should not have the ability to turn me on like that. He was dressed more professionally than usual this morning. He had on jeans with a blue-and-white checkered dress shirt and a teal tie.

We got on the elevator and headed up to the twentieth floor to my penthouse condo. He opened the door. It was just the two of us in my lovely new condo and I wanted to kiss him. I liked this place, but I liked Cam even more.

"Isn't the seller's Realtor supposed to be here too?"

Cam shrugged. "Yeah, sometimes they'll come but a lot of times they don't."

We went into every room and Cam was diligent about checking that all the toilets flushed and the windows opened and closed as expected. He turned on the washer and dryer. I said, "Didn't the inspector check all of that? The place is only a year old, what could be wrong?"

"You'd be surprised. Early in my career, I had situations where the inspector came in and said everything was cool. We would go to settlement and six months later the water heater would break or the air wouldn't work. So I just figured it would be wise for me to get more knowledge on what they're checking for and how they determine everything is legit. This way my clients aren't faced with a big HVAC bill shortly after buying a house. Who has that kind of money?"

"Is everything good here?"

"Yeah, everything is good. I also tell my clients to be sure the energy in the place is right. What is it that you feel when you step through the door? I'm big on energy."

I was impressed with his advice. "Me too."

We paused and both were likely thinking about the

magnetic energy between us and what if anything we should do about it. To break the ice, he said, "Are you good with the energy of the place?"

"Yes, Cam. The energy is right."

He blushed and I shook my head. He asked, "You sure this is what you want to do?"

I thought that was something of an odd question. "Yes," I said slowly.

"I'm just saying people have doubts even on the day of a settlement. I always like to be absolutely sure. It's better to lose a deposit than to be the owner of a home you don't want."

"I guess if you put it like that it makes sense."

"I'm not a successful Realtor because I try to close every deal. I'm successful because I actually put my clients first. It's easy to be anxious for a commission check and manipulate clients to buy something they don't want. Realtors do it every day but that type is usually hustling for new clients all the time. I do minimal advertising. Ninety percent of my business comes from referrals. Why?" He didn't pause long enough for me to answer. He continued, "If I take good care of you and you feel like I really had your best interest at heart, whether you actually buy a house or not, you will tell your friends about me. Right?"

I nodded. As he held the front door open for me, he half-smiled. "When you live with integrity, you sleep so much better at night. Even if that means I don't earn as much, I'm going to do what's right."

"Very true."

"And I earn as much as, and most likely more than, the shady Realtors, and my soul is at peace too." He chuckled.

"That is a great way to look at it."

We headed out of the building. Cam asked, "Do you want to drive together?"

"No, we can drive separately."

"Yeah, that's cool. See you in a second."

"OK."

I drove to the title company and reflected on Cam's integrity. That was definitely a rare trait. I pulled into the parking lot right after he did, but he took a minute to get out of his car so I waited. When he finally stepped out, I followed. He put his arm around my shoulder. It felt natural walking with him this way. He asked, "Are you excited?"

"Yes, I'm very excited."

"Good. That's exactly what you should feel. A little nervousness is OK, but I'm always disturbed when people are too nervous. I feel like they're not sure or they can't handle it financially. You know?"

"Yeah, I can see that."

"And you hate to hear when anyone you've sold a house to has foreclosed. I don't like that feeling."

He opened the door to the title company and I walked in. Cam stepped up to the receptionist to let her know that we'd arrived. It was impressive for a man this successful to make decisions with his heart and not only thinking about his pockets. Cam and I were a few minutes early, so the seller and his Realtor had yet to arrive.

The receptionist ushered Cam and me into a small conference room. She told us that there were doughnuts and coffee in the kitchen. Cam seemed very popular at this title company, as every person we saw on the way to grab coffee greeted him as if he were the president. Men and women alike treated him with respect. He was personable and polite, confident and caring. I loved the way I felt walking beside him.

By the time we got back to the conference room, the seller and his agent were there. The representative for the title company wasted no time getting started. He put a stack of papers in front of the seller and me. He handed copies to our agents as well. He explained that he'd go through each page with me. We got started and as the representative talked, Cam followed up each of his statements with a layman's explanation of what I was signing.

I wondered if all of Cam's clients felt this protected or if I was special. I kept thinking, *I can't be wrong about this man*. I just wished he didn't have ex-wife drama because I would have hopped on it, literally. I missed most of the details that he explained to me as we flipped through the pages. His mouth moved, but I couldn't hear anything as I fantasized about his lips touching my skin. Cam nudged me and I jumped. He'd been calling my name, but I was trapped in a daydream and he was the main character. He said, "Sign here."

Kiss here. I was signing and smiling as Cam led the

way. I was partially happy that I didn't have to see Cam anymore after this, because this infatuation was definitely not healthy. Once everything was handled, the seller and his agent were told they could leave. They shook my hand and congratulated me. Cam, the title representative, and I were left so I could sign another long contract. Finally it was over and I was the owner of my new home. Cam and I walked out of the office.

He asked, "Have you decided when you're moving in?"

"I'm not sure yet. Probably in a few weeks."

"I like to bring all of my clients a housewarming gift, so let me know when you'll be there."

"My sister and my parents are going to meet me there now for lunch. Do you want to stop by?"

"Sure. I have a run to make but I'll meet you there in about an hour or so. Is that OK?"

"That's perfect."

I called Aaliyah and my parents to let them know that everything was final and that they could grab lunch and stop by. I had stopped at Target the night before for paper goods, cleaning supplies, and toilet paper. I asked my father to bring his card table and folding chairs, then headed straight there.

My parents were first to arrive. Daddy came in grinning from ear to ear. My mother gave me a hug. "Congratulations, sweetie."

"Thanks, Mom."

Daddy looked around the place, nodding with approval. "I like this place, Yana."

"Thanks, Daddy."

"It definitely suits you."

Daddy can fix anything, build anything, and he knows everything. He was my real-life superman. My mom always insinuated that he was the reason I was single. Daddy was the ideal man, and if I was going to be with someone he had better be like my daddy. He received his PhD from Morehouse College when I was a kid and worked as a school principal most of our lives. He and Mom met while they were in undergrad, he at Morehouse and she at Spelman. Dad went on to become the superintendent during my last year in high school. He had been retired almost five years now and had served on a consultant basis for a while. After my mother retired from teaching, he decided they would both relax and explore the world. Now they went wherever the wind blew them. He still did odd home improvement projects but nothing demanding.

My dad went upstairs to the loft while my mom helped me open the card table. The doorbell rang and it was Aaliyah and the crew. I love my nieces, but those little girls run through your house like a tornado. Whenever they would come to my apartment, I'd get complaints from the neighbors below. Being that it was midday I assumed no one was there so I didn't give them the no-running speech. My youngest niece, Troi, hopped right into my mother's lap, and my oldest niece, Tayme, met my father at the bottom of the stairs. "Pop-pop!"

It's amazing how history repeats itself. Without question, I am a daddy's girl and Aaliyah is a mommy's girl.

We didn't have any sibling rivalry about it either, probably because we weren't competing for attention from the same person.

Aaliyah had two big bags from Chipotle and I grabbed one from her. She said, "I love this place, Ayana. It is so you."

My mom said, "I agree."

"Well, I only see one problem," Dad said.

"What?"

"It's going to get really warm upstairs."

He pointed to a big vent on the wall in my dining room. "You see this."

"Yeah."

"That intakes the hot air."

My eyebrows wrinkled because he was confusing me.

"ACs don't just cool a place. This vent intakes the hot air, while these vent." He pointed to smaller vents. "They blow cold air out."

"OK."

"The largest intake should be at the highest level in your house. They have a small little intake up there, so that's going to be your hottest area."

"Daddy, you're literally over my head."

"Upstairs will absorb the heat from not only this level but from all the levels underneath you. And this big vent needs to be up there."

"So can you fix it?"

"Man, that would require ripping out a bunch of duct-work and you never know what you're getting into when you do that. At this point, you're going to have to leave it that way."

My lips curled with disappointment. He put one arm around me and said, "It'll be OK. What did you plan on putting up there anyway?"

"My office?"

"Yeah, I don't think you'll want to be there on hot days."

My mom interrupted, "Alan, don't get her all worked up right now."

"Well, it only makes sense that she knows what's going on. Knowing is half the battle."

Aaliyah proceeded to set everyone's food out and said, "C'mon, y'all, let's have lunch and celebrate Ayana's new place."

I sat down at the table and Daddy jokingly said, "And Lord, don't let my baby melt up in that loft."

We all burst out laughing. Aaliyah said, "Daddy, stop."

He finished grace and we started eating. We chatted about minor things and watched the girls run in circles. Daddy never failed to mention how much they were like Aaliyah and me. In the middle of lunch, the doorbell rang. Everyone looked shocked and their responses forced my heart to plummet into my lap. I smiled. "That's my Realtor."

Aaliyah raised one eyebrow at me and I shook my head. She was so obvious. When I opened the door, Cam smelled so enticing that I had to take a deep breath before saying anything. He had an edible arrangement in one hand and a bottle of champagne and a large envelope in the other. Passing the champagne and arrangement to me, he said, "Congratulations."

"Thank you so much."

He walked in and I introduced him to my parents. "You sold my baby this piece of crap?" Daddy said with a smile.

"I'm sorry, sir. That would be me," Cam responded, seeming like a good sport.

Dad stood and shook his hand. Laughing, he said, "Good job, son."

"Thank you. And I must tell the both of you good job, because Ayana was a pleasure to work with. Women like this can only come from great parents."

Dad chuckled. "Now you're going too far."

My mom looked at him out of the corner of her eye. She hated when he picked with people like that, but Daddy was the same whether he'd just met you or if he'd known you all his life. Aaliyah came over and shook Cam's hand.

"Aaliyah. I'm Ayana's little big sister."

Cam nodded. "OK, I get it."

My mother chimed in. "They are only fifteen months apart and when kids are that close, it's really easy for the younger one to take on the role as the oldest."

Aaliyah had always wanted to be someone's mother, which is why she had taken on that role, not because she was more mature than me. She was just bossier than I was. I rolled my eyes. By Cam's smile, I could tell he got the message.

My dad said, "Seriously, I think this condo is ideal for my butterfly. She's fluid."

Cam squinted. Dad raised his eyebrow, insinuating that Cam was slow. Cam said, "No, I get it. She goes with the flow."

"OK, I got a little concerned," Daddy said, laughing. "I've always told her that she didn't know where her career would take her, especially because it all happened so fast. One day she's a struggling doctoral student and the next she's a bestselling author, talk show host, and running her own practice. I advised her not to buy anything because she could get a call anytime to, say, move to New York or LA."

Cam said, "I hope not."

That comment got everyone's attention, except Dad. He continued, "And she's always enjoyed traveling. Even as a kid. She's been all over the world."

"Daddy, I have not been all over the world."

"I'll put it to you like this, she goes everywhere she wants to go."

"I do not. There are many places I'd love to go that I've never been."

Dad said, "Like where?"

"I've always wanted to cruise the Mediterranean."

"See what I mean, son, she's fluid. That's why I was always unsure if she should buy anything, but I think this place is perfect for her."

"I'm glad you think so, Daddy."

He nodded seriously. "I do."

My mother stood up. "Ayana, did you get any trash bags?"

"Yeah, I did."

I rummaged through the Target bags and pulled them out. "Here, Mom."

While she began to straighten up the place, Aaliyah took her chance to quiz Cameron. "So have you been a Realtor long?"

"Yup, almost fifteen years."

"That must be cool."

"Yeah, it has its ups and downs."

Aaliyah started cleaning the girls' mess. Cam asked, "How old are your girls?"

"Three and four."

"Yeah, that's a fun age."

Mom asked, "Do you have kids?"

"Yes, one son, he's eight."

My mother nodded. "OK."

Shortly after, Aaliyah and my parents left, leaving Cam and me alone. Cam opened the manila envelope he had been carrying when he entered and handed me some documents. Leaning his elbow on the ledge of my bar counter, he said, "Ayana, these are the court documents. My divorce is final."

I was at a loss for words. I wasn't sure how I should respond. Divorce papers wouldn't instantly change the personality of his ex-wife.

He said, "I'm putting myself out there. Say something. Don't just look at me like I'm crazy."

"I'm sorry, Cam. I don't know what you expect me to say."

"Say that maybe you'd be willing to go out with me again."

"And your ex-wife, how did she handle the decision?"

"My ex-wife is a very peculiar person. She doesn't want to be with me and I don't want to be with her. She treats people and relationships like objects. It's all about ownership with her. It has nothing to do with anything else."

"I understand, but I'm not sure I can risk everything I've built by dating a man with an impulsive, manipulative ex-wife—someone who will do anything to have her way."

He obviously sensed my confusion and saw through the words exiting my mouth as he leaned in to kiss me. I didn't resist. I wished I had the strength to push him away but I was breathless in his embrace. When he let me go, I wasn't sure what I wanted to do. He said, "Ayana, I dig you."

"I understand, but—"

"Don't let one little obstacle stop this."

His eyes were so sincere and I knew that I could make a mistake. I was conflicted. Should I take the risk? Should I ask him to leave? He swept my hair behind my ear and chills ran through my body. I said, "OK, Cam."

He lifted my chin and kissed me. "Thanks."

"I don't believe I just agreed to this."

"Are you fluid or what?"

I laughed. "That's what my dad said. I never told you that."

"But you did tell me that no one knows you like your dad."

"I did."

He walked over to open the bottle of champagne, so I backed up. The cork popped and bubbles spilled out. He poured some into my plastic cup and then some into his. We both sipped as he opened up the fruit arrangement. He pulled out a pineapple by the stick and put it up to my lips. I took a bite and juice squirted out and down the corner of my mouth. I went to wipe it off but Cam moved my hand and kissed it off. I turned my head in the direction of his mouth and kissed him, slowly. It felt warm and sensual. He laid the pineapple down on the counter and wrapped his arm around me as we continued to kiss. My legs were weak and if Cam hadn't been holding me I would have fallen.

When the kiss ended, he looked into my eyes. "It's been a long time since I've been ready to trust someone."

"Why do you trust me?"

"Partially because of what Quentin has told me about you and more because of what you've shown me plus the conversations we've had."

"Quentin?"

"Yeah," he said, smiling. "Quentin had this in the works long before we met."

My neck snapped back. "Really?"

"Yeah. When I was going through it and feeling like I

would never get into a serious relationship again, Quentin said, 'Man, when you get through with the bullshit, I want you to meet Ayana. She the one.'"

I had known Quentin respected me but I hadn't known he'd strategically set me up. How had he known we'd click the way we had? Then again, I believe the best relationships are when friends hook you up.

"What do *you* think?" I asked.

"I think Quentin was right. That's why I'm standing here in your empty new home, begging you to give this a chance."

I looked in his eyes and nodded. I was impressed with his determination. If a man wants to be with a woman, nothing can stop him. He'll do whatever is necessary to prove to her that he is sincere. I stood there, admiring his candor, and thought I'd be a fool not to give things a try.

"And I owed it to you to be legit when I approached you this time. I didn't expect us to hit it off like we did that night. When shit went down the next day, I was kicking myself, because even though I knew I was really close to the divorce, it still wasn't final. Now that it is, if I have to be at your doorstep every day, then I will. That's what it is, you feel me?"

Cam smiled and traced my face with his hand and leaned in for another kiss. I unbuttoned his shirt and pulled it out of his pants. I rubbed his chest through his wife beater. He pulled my blouse out of my skirt and began to unbutton it before taking it off and lifting my camisole. He unsnapped my bra and held my left breast like a bottle, stroking his tongue over my nipple, while twirling his finger over the other. My vagina was throbbing so hard, I thought it would tumble out of my panties. He lifted my skirt and yanked my stockings down. He lay his hand between my legs and stroked back and forth with his middle finger. It tingled and my eyelids fluttered. I brushed my lips back and forth across his chest while I unfastened his pants. His penis was hard and throbbing. Before his pants dropped, he pulled out his wallet and grabbed a condom. While he put the condom on, I took off the remainder of my clothes.

He carried me to the steps leading up to the loft, because they were carpeted. He placed me about four steps up and stood on the landing. He spread my legs far apart and licked my vagina quickly, then put himself inside me for a few strokes, then he licked again and stroked again. He did the lick-plunge action a few times, sparking fireworks throughout my body. I screamed his name and begged him to stay inside me. Finally he obliged. My body relaxed as we flowed together. Peace and ecstasy combined to bring me pleasure. This time was much more passionate and enjoyable than the first, which says a lot, because the first time was wonderful, but surrounded by doubt. This time I was sure that Cam was a good guy, so sure that I wanted to explore his heart and his mind. I had no doubts that this would last longer than one night.

yasmin

The day after Cam got what he wanted, he called me as if everything were going to go as planned. Caron meant the world to him and if I could stop him from spending time with Caron, I imagined he would feel compelled to come back home. When I answered, he said, "What's up, Yasmin?"

"You don't care. Cut the bullshit. What do you want?"

"I'm picking Caron up after school but I'm going to bring him to the shop because I have a showing."

I laughed. "I already have someone to pick him up. Don't bother."

"Who is the someone?"

"Don't worry. It's not you."

"Yasmin, don't play with me."

"Cam, I have to go."

I hung up the phone and I knew he'd be wondering where Caron was but I wasn't going to give him the pleasure. I wanted him to be stressed and worried the same way I was about the divorce. I'm tired of being mistreated. It is time for Cameron to get a taste of his own medicine.

Just as I expected, he showed up at Caron's school only to discover Caron wasn't there. He called me, yelling in my ear, "Where the fuck is my son?"

"Inquiring minds want to know."

"Yasmin, don't fuck with me."

His voice was filled with anger. Cameron's coolness was blown, so I knew I'd gotten under his skin. It felt good that he was hurting. I kept seeing the grin on his face as he walked out of the courtroom and I had no sympathy for him just as he had no sympathy for me. I didn't care if he or his family ever saw Caron again.

I hung up the phone and stared out the front window, waiting for him to come. Close to an hour passed and it became obvious he wasn't going to show up. I called my girlfriend and told her the coast was clear for her to bring Caron to the shop. Cameron didn't call later and he didn't call the next day either. It was his weekend to keep Caron and when I didn't hear from him, I figured I'd give him a call.

The phone rang and rang and I was furious. Although I had no plans to go anywhere, I was pissed that he was acting like he no longer cared for me or our son. My head started pounding and I felt betrayed. I hated Cameron for this. When I picked Caron up later that evening, his first question was, "Why didn't Daddy get me?"

"Daddy don't care about us anymore."

I thought Caron would ask more questions, but instead he hung his head low and water filled his eyes. I almost wanted to take back what I'd said, but I didn't. If his father didn't plan on being a part of his life, it was best for him to know the truth now.

Caron and I went to visit one of my girlfriends and her kids. When we pulled up, Caron said, "I hate coming here. My dad and I always do something fun."

"What would you like to do?"

"We go bowling or something."

I felt bad because I hadn't planned anything. I had hoped that Cam would fight a little harder to see his son. He obviously had better plans. As I sat in front of my girlfriend's house, I realized that all I was going in there to talk about was how men are no damn good. I was already angry and I didn't need any more ammunition to go knock down Cameron's door.

That's what he expected of me, but that's not what I was going to do. I wanted him to realize that he wanted to be with me. I was tired of chasing him. I told Caron to call him and leave a sweet message. Caron called and said, "Hey, Dad, I thought we were chilling this weekend. Call me back."

Seconds later my phone rang and it was Cameron. Well, he was skilled in ignoring me, but it was really hard for him to ignore Caron. He had such a big heart for his son. Where was his compassion for me? I wanted to cry. When I picked up, I said, "Hi, Cameron."

"Hey, Yasmin. How are you?"

"I'm good. So I take it you're not picking up Caron this weekend."

"Well, if you knew how to communicate like you were older than a teenager, maybe we could have discussed what my plans were for the weekend."

Whenever he doubted my ability to communicate, that took me to the next level, where I wanted to slash tires, bust windows, and do harm to him and anyone else who cared about him. I took ten deep breaths before responding.

"What are your plans?"

"We need to swap weekends. I want to get him next weekend instead of this weekend. I have a few meetings."

"Where are you? It doesn't sound like you're at a meeting."

"Yasmin, I'm not at a meeting right now, but I do have some things to do. I was trying to tell you this when you pulled that stunt the other day."

"What stunt?"

"Yasmin, I'm at a very crucial point in my life right now. I have a lot of things I'm working on and my schedule may switch up some and I need to be able to communicate with you."

"You don't have to communicate with me. You need to make arrangements. If it's your weekend, then you need to find a babysitter."

I wasn't going to sit around and adjust my schedule for his busy weekends. Prior to the divorce, he got Caron faithfully. Now he thought he had a get-out-of-jail-free card. No, I wanted to make dating as much of a challenge for him as it was for me.

He huffed. "OK, do you want me to come get him this evening? I will take him to my mom's house."

"What makes you think he wants to sit around with that old hag while you're out frolicking with God only knows who?"

He said, "What do you want to do? You want me to get him, 'cause I will."

"I want you to get him and spend some time with him."

"That's not going to happen tonight."

"Why?" I shouted.

The nice approach wasn't going in my favor and I was angry with him. I wanted to know where he was, whom he was with, and what was more important than Caron. He said, "Yasmin, I have an important meeting tonight and tomorrow and I would prefer to get him next weekend."

"So some bitch means more to you than your son?"

"I'm not going to do this with you."

"You have a court order to get your son every weekend. You are in violation."

"Where are you? I'll come get him now."

"No, keep doing what you're doing."

I hung up the phone. He needed to think about the effect this was going to have on Caron. All of a sudden, after the divorce, he wanted to switch up his weekends. I couldn't wait to go back to court and tell them he didn't deserve weekend visits. Cam could afford a nanny if he wanted to. He obviously was chasing some trick around town.

I asked Caron, "Baby, do you still know Daddy's garage code?"

He nodded. "Yes, Mommy."

"OK, I have to get something out of his house. He said it's OK for you to give it to me."

I pulled out of my parking space and sped over to Cam's house. I knew he wasn't home but I needed to know what he was up to, whom he was seeing, and when he was seeing her. In addition to his electronic calendar, Cam wrote everything down, and he organized receipts every day. I could track his whereabouts just by those. It sounded as if it would be a while before he came back.

I pulled into the short driveway in the back of his house and Caron gave me the code. I told him to stay in the car and of course he had a million questions. I tried to open the door with the code that Caron had given me. The door wouldn't open and the lights on the keypad kept blinking as if they were saying, "*Nope. Try again, bitch!*"

I closed the keypad cover and banged frantically on the pad. It was my enemy at that moment, because it was the obstacle standing between Cam and me. Caron opened his door and asked, "That didn't work, Mommy?"

"Get back in the car, Caron."

I walked up onto the deck and tried the glass door. It was locked, so I tried the window over the kitchen sink. *Bingo.* I pushed the window up and prayed that Caron had been right about the security alarm code; otherwise

I'd have to run out quickly. I climbed through the little window and felt like I broke my arm when I fell into the sink. I jumped up and ran downstairs to turn off the alarm, but quickly realized it hadn't been set. Cam had obviously left in a rush.

I went into his office looking for his receipt folder but I couldn't find it anywhere. I didn't find anything. I looked at the calendar on his desk and he had written DIVORCED in big red letters with an exclamation point on our court date. Was it really that bad to be married to me?

Momentarily I felt nauseous and forgot why I had come. I rummaged through his desk drawers, then headed upstairs to see if I could find any female residue. A bra, an earring, a bobby pin. I found nothing.

I went back into the office to get on his desktop computer. Although he carried a laptop, I figured it wouldn't hurt to see what he was doing on there. I touched the mouse so the screen would appear. Ayana Blue's picture was on his desktop. I wanted to throw up. Why did he have her head shot as the backdrop? They couldn't have been seeing each other for longer than two weeks. What a goddamn pussy. My hands trembled as I looked at his Internet browser. His Facebook account was up and I looked at his in-box. I saw a message exchange with one of his friends and the subject was "Ayana." Cam told the friend thanks for the hookup, that Ayana was cool now that she knew the divorce was final, and that they were meeting for dinner. His friend, Quentin, told him to seal the deal.

I felt like wrecking his house. I felt like crying hysterically. I felt like running them both over with my car. I felt like someone had just shot straight through my heart. *Seal the deal?* What the fuck did that mean?

I left the house through the sliding glass door on the deck. I didn't give a damn if it was unlocked. I didn't care if someone broke in and stole everything he owned. I just didn't care anymore.

When I got in the car, I called Tayshawn. I was literally shaking and screaming at the top of my lungs. Caron looked at me, confused, as I ranted on the phone.

"He's out with her. They went to dinner! I can't stand her. I wish she was dead."

Tayshawn said, "Sweetie, even if she was dead, it don't mean that you and Cam are going to get back together."

"You never know, Tayshawn. You never know."

My hands were trembling and tears were streaming down my face. I considered popping up on them at dinner. Tayshawn said, "Yasmin, you need to take your anxiety medicine. Don't you go popping up on those people! You will be in jail. Why don't you come back to the shop?"

Caron was the only reason I didn't meet them for dinner. Instead I drove back to the shop as Tayshawn had suggested. He and Casey still had several clients left. I noticed Casey was working with one of my new clients. I said, "Excuse me, you didn't like how I did your hair?"

Casey spoke for her. "No, she just dropped in and I told her I could do it since you left early."

I felt some kind of way about that. Tayshawn cut his eyes at me because he knew I didn't like it. The client said, "Yeah, I was looking for you."

"I'm sorry, honey, I'll have to give you my cell number for last-minute appointments."

I quickly went to the next subject at hand, Cam and Ayana. I wasn't sure I could handle Cam being on the scene with this chick. As I ranted in the hair salon, all the clients were all ears and I wanted them to be. I wanted everyone to know that Ayana had stolen my husband. Tayshawn laughed with me but kept trying to force me to take my anxiety medicine. My doctor had started prescribing it to me after I explained my mood swings. Since then I'd been cured. I didn't need that poison anymore. All I needed was my family back together and everything would be OK.

ayana

After Cam and I had each other for lunch, he suggested we hook up for dinner somewhere close. He had a few showings and I needed to rest. I had to turn in the first draft of my book and currently it seemed scatterbrained and rushed. I really felt that my first couple of books had been easy and simple to research. The book I was currently working on was about marriage. While my sister and my parents seemed to have relatively healthy marriages, I didn't have a lot of hands-on knowledge. I had been somewhat reluctant to write this new book, but I was under contract and had to write something.

I hadn't imagined that buying a house would take so much of the emotional wind out of me. I wasn't sure if I should go home and rest or if I should try hashing out a couple of chapters. I felt so uninspired.

When Cam and I parted, he had looked so happy, as if he'd been touched by an angel. Not to say that I am one, but he just seemed at peace, as if nothing in this world could bother him. I went back to my apartment, showered, and curled up in my bed.

Almost immediately after I began to doze off, "Hey sista, soul sista, hey sista, soul sista" blasted from my phone. I grabbed it. "What's up, Aaliyah?"

"OK, Sister. You have my consent to date Realtor boy."

I laughed. "Thanks, but..."

"You already hooked up with him again?"

"No," I lied.

"Well, he looks finger-licking good."

"Ill, Aaliyah, that sounds nasty."

"I mean it in a respectful kind of way. I like him for you. Now what's the story again with his wife?"

"He showed me the divorce papers."

"Oh well, you better get to work."

"You ought to know me better than that."

"Yeah, I know you all right. I know you are good at talking yourself out of a relationship."

"Chick, you're the one that talked me out of dating him."

"I did, but that was before I saw him. He is so adorable. And plus I loved that he interacted with the girls. That's a plus. What can I say? I like him."

"Well, thanks for your approval, but I have to go to sleep."

"No, don't go to sleep. Stay up and talk to me."

"I wish I was a housewife and could sleep when I wanted but I have to get it in where I can."

"Don't play me like that, Ayana. You know my job takes serious skills." She laughed.

Nothing takes more skills than being great at three different careers. I was exhausted. She said something else but I had dozed off. Jumping awake, I realized she had already hung up the phone. I turned my ringer off before going back to sleep because I didn't want anything or anyone to interrupt me.

When I woke up, it was close to seven o'clock. Cam and I had agreed to meet at the Cheesecake Factory at six. I checked my phone. He had called three times and left one text message. WHERE R U?

I leaped up and called him. "Cam, I'm so sorry. I fell asleep and I'm just getting up."

"Well, lucky for you, I didn't get here until six thirty and it's like a two-hour wait. I figured you'd be here sooner or later."

He didn't seem to have questioned whether I'd really show. Rather confident, but I loved it. My one concern with Cam was the possibility that he'd been so scarred by his ex-wife that he would have a hard time trusting. He didn't seem anxious because I hadn't arrived and that was appealing. I quickly put on my clothes and rushed to the Cheesecake Factory.

I valet-parked and ran in to find Cam sitting at the bar. He smiled. "We lost our table."

"I'm sorry."

"It's cool. We're going to have fun anyway," he said with a smile.

"Thanks for being a good sport."

"Always."

"What did you think happened?" I asked.

"I wasn't sure, but I didn't think you wouldn't show

without calling. I thought maybe you got caught up at work. I lose track of time all the time, so I understand how it is."

"I'm glad you understand. After wearing all these different hats, sometimes I don't know my head from my ass."

"Yeah, I can see that. Well, I'm glad you're getting out to have some fun."

"Yea," I said, laughing.

"Working like that, how do you plan to take your trip to the Mediterranean?"

"I don't know."

"Are you flexible? I mean, can you take off if you need to?"

"I can always take a break from my practice, but your boy would have a conniption if I have to take off from the show. There's another female psychologist that stands in for me when I'm on vacation, but she and Quentin butt heads."

He laughed. "Yeah, I know. He can't stand her."

We had dinner, shared a piece of cheesecake, and talked for a while longer. Neither of us asked where the other was going next. We just seemed to walk out of the restaurant with the intent that we were going somewhere together. In the parking lot, I handed a valet my ticket, as did Cameron. Cam's guy swiftly ran off into the parking lot. My guy was still rummaging through the cabinet. He came back and asked, "Ma'am, are you sure that was your number?"

"I'm positive. Why?"

He didn't answer and went back to search through the

keys. By this time, Cam's car had arrived. My eyes shifted back and forth and my breathing got heavier the longer I waited. Finally the guy returned. With a distraught look, he said, "I can't seem to find your key."

"So where do you think it could be?"

He shrugged.

"Is there a manager here?"

Cameron stepped in and said, "There is obviously some confusion. Can she look through the keys you have to see if her key is there? Maybe there was a mix-up with the tickets."

The guy said, "Sure."

Cam rested his hand on the small of my back as I frantically looked through the keys.

"Mine aren't there and I assume one of the employees must be off on a joyride."

The valet said, "I'll get my manager."

Cam's jawline throbbed as if it were revving with anger. I reached out for his hand because I wanted to let him know that I was calm and there was no need to get confrontational yet. The young valet whom I'd given the car to originally looked nervous and frightened. Obviously someone had messed up, but I wasn't going to take it out on him. Not yet, anyway. Cam on the other hand looked as if he could take the poor kid's head off. When the manager arrived, Cam spoke first. "Listen, man. My lady parked her car here around seven forty-five, we had dinner, and now her keys are gone."

"What kind of car do you drive?" he asked.

"White Toyota Prius."

With a troubled expression, he said, "Hmmm. We've never had this issue before."

"Well, you have it now and what are you planning to do about it?" Cam asked irritably.

The manager looked at the guys. "Did you see the car parked?"

They both shrugged and one said, "I don't even remember you coming in and I was here at seven thirty."

I looked at the other guy and said, "He's the one that parked my car."

He said, "I don't remember."

The manager covered his face. "Today's his first day."

Everyone turned to the valet and he looked as if he wanted to crawl into a hole. I felt bad for him, but still wanted to know where my car had gone. The manager asked, "Where's the ticket?"

I handed it to him and he quickly said, "This ticket is blue. We are using yellow today."

The guy who had parked my car raised his hands defenselessly and said, "I don't know what happened."

The manager attempted to explain. "We change ticket colors every day and it's primarily for this reason. So there is no confusion. I don't understand how you'd get a blue ticket. Look right here. There are only yellow tickets available today. I don't even put a different color close to the tickets."

"So you're saying there is no way a blue ticket could have gotten in this stack?"

"Exactly."

"Listen, I don't know how it got there. I wasn't here yesterday. I came today and parked my car and the new guy gave me blue."

Noticing the situation was getting out of control, Cam dialed the police. I continued to debate the situation with the manager and the kid. Still my car didn't appear, and my blood was beginning to boil.

It took the officer nearly fifteen minutes to arrive at the scene. Cam and I stood there discussing what might have happened. I suggested his ex-wife or someone else. We ruled it out merely because of the ticket-color issue. The perpetrator had to be an employee. There was no question about it. When the officer flashed his light on my ticket and the tickets in the cabinet, he said, "This ticket is blue and the ones in here are yellow." Looking at the manager, he asked, "Is there any reason for that?"

The manager said, "The reason is to avoid situations like this. I was just telling her there is no way she could have gotten this ticket from here. Not today. We change colors every day."

"It doesn't take a rocket scientist to park cars, so certainly one of the goofs can screw up," Cam said impatiently.

It vexed me that the valets were running back and forth fetching other cars and mine was missing. I just covered my face. Cam massaged my shoulder as he debated with the manager.

"There is no way you could have gotten *this* ticket today."

"She wasn't here yesterday so there's no way she could have gotten *this* ticket yesterday."

The officer then turned to me. "Are you absolutely certain that you parked your car here?"

"Yes, I'm very certain."

The officer took notes while asking questions. I got irritated after a while. "I am the victim. Why are you speaking to me as if I did something wrong?"

"Just trying to get the facts."

"Listen, man. Obviously her car is missing. We need you to write a report so she can call her insurance company," Cam demanded.

"Have you been drinking or doing drugs?"

"I had one drink this evening and I am completely aware of what I did when I pulled into this lot. I gave my car to him, tipped him two dollars, took the ticket, and walked into the restaurant. That's all you need in your report."

The officer looked at the manager. "Can I see your tapes?"

The manager huffed. "We've been waiting all week for someone to come to fix the cameras."

"What do you mean?" the officer asked.

"Our surveillance is broken."

Cam stepped in. "OK, so there is no surveillance. No one has seen her car that she parked right here. Wow. You all will be hearing from my attorney in the morning."

The manager said, "There is no need for all of that, sir. We will get to the bottom of this. Trust me."

Cam laughed. "She trusted you with her car. I think that's enough." He turned to the officer. "So are you going to report it stolen or what?"

My heart sank. *Stolen.* Despite the entire fiasco, I hadn't been considering my car stolen. When he said it, it sounded so finite, as if the car was gone forever. Cam noticed the air leaving my body and put his arms around me, holding me tightly. I felt safe despite all that was going on around me. I leaned my head against his chest and he stroked my back.

The officer called the car in as a stolen vehicle and handed us a report. He got all our contact information, and then explained, "When you call your insurance company you'll need to give them this report number. If your car ends up in the pound we'll give you a call."

"The pound?"

"Yeah, usually that happens, and unfortunately you'll need to pay to get it out. I just want to give you a heads-up."

"Gee, thanks. So the victim is victimized twice. I love America," I said, shaking my head.

"Sorry, but that's the policy. It's possible we'll find it before it's towed. You never know."

"So is the Cheesecake Factory in any way liable?" Cam asked.

"Yes, if you can prove that you really parked the car here, but that's something you'll have to speak to your attorney about, like you said earlier."

Cam shook the officer's hand and got the names of all the employees standing around. Finally we headed to his car. With everything going on, I had failed to notice that Cam's car was different. He opened the passenger door of a Bentley Continental GT coupé. It was black and shiny with a flashy dashboard. It felt luxurious. The leather bucket seats hugged my hips snugly. I'm so not a car person and I didn't want to be impressed, but I was. Cam was even finer in this car. He looked so expensive in it. I felt as if I were dreaming. Where had this guy come from and why was he so interested in me? He was handsome and rich, but most important he was respectful and smart. His character was much richer than he could ever be and that's what I liked the most.

He grabbed my hand and looked at me. "I'm sorry, Ayana," he said.

My lips pouted. "It's not your fault."

"I know, but I'm sorry this happened while you were with me."

"I had a good time though."

"Your house or mine?" he asked with confidence.

I didn't want to leave him any more than he wanted to leave me. "Actually, I don't have my house keys. They are with my car, unfortunately."

I gasped at the thought that whoever had my car keys also had my house keys. Cam said, "It's going to be OK. We'll get your locks all switched tomorrow."

"This is just so random."

"Yeah, I know. We may as well just go to my house tonight and relax and deal with the rest in the morning."

"Are you sure you're allowed to have company?"

"I'm a single man. Why wouldn't I be able to have company?"

"Well, your ex-wife thinks you guys are still together, so . . ."

He laughed. "She's delusional."

"I just don't want any drama."

He reached for my hand and I gave it to him. "No drama. I promise."

"Pinky swear," I said jokingly.

"Pinky swear," he said with a wink.

When Cam jumped on Route 400 heading to Alpharetta, I said, "I thought you lived in Buckhead?"

"Yeah, I have a house there too, but . . ."

"Are you taking me to the incognito spot?"

"Nah, I'm taking you to my home. My Buckhead spot is just somewhere to rest my head and keep my son."

"Your son doesn't come to your home?"

"His mom is obviously psycho and I don't want her to know where I really live. I have to keep as much as possible away from her."

I nodded, appreciating that he put effort into keeping her at bay. "How do you pull off living in two places?"

"Right now it's really easy. Most of my belongings are in Buckhead. I haven't really moved into the house yet."

"What you waiting on?"

"I bought it because I got predevelopment pricing, but

I didn't want it to come out during the divorce that I owned it. So I kept it on the low."

"How did you manage that? If you don't mind me asking."

He chuckled and looked at me. "I don't mind at all. This may sound shady but I assure you, I'm not a shady person. I started a business in my mother's name and purchased the home with that business. Now that the divorce is final, I can transfer the title to my own business."

I laughed. "Whoa, that *is* shady, Cam."

"Like I told you when I met you, I want to remarry and I want to have at least two more kids. I got a deal I couldn't resist and I hopped on it. Even though I wasn't in a domestic situation, I looked at it like I was buying this house for my family. It would just be there, waiting for the right woman to walk through the door."

Maybe it was in my mind, but it seemed that he gave me a look as if to say that she was me. I wondered if I was the first woman to enter the house since he'd bought it or if there had been others. I momentarily felt uncomfortable, because my mind was going places that I was too mentally disciplined to permit, so I changed the subject to halt the thought that Cam and I were meant to be together from flooding my mind.

I said, "Oh, I forgot to mention I like your car."

He blushed. "Do you really?"

"Yeah, I like the *B* with wings everywhere."

He laughed really hard, obviously catching on that I was insinuating that the *B* stood for my last name.

"Yeah, I'm glad you like that. I usually drive this car when I'm trying to sell million-dollar homes."

"I can see why."

"Yeah, money likes to see money."

"That's so crazy."

"It's the nature of the business. When I mentor agents that are new to the game, I try to tell them they have to look the part to seal the deal."

"Really?"

"Yeah, sometimes you have to take the risk of buying a two-hundred-thousand-dollar car in order to sell that five-million-dollar house."

"What happens if you don't sell the house?"

He laughed. "You'll be broke."

"That's a shame. I don't believe in buying things to impress people."

"You don't have to in your field. In sales, you have to look the part. It's unfortunate but that's the way it is. People don't take chances on someone that looks like they need money. When you look like you have money, the trust is almost immediate."

"I guess I see your point."

As we drove, we passed several communities with sprawling estates. Cam pointed out the homes he had sold. It was obvious that he was doing well. Finally we pulled up to a golf course community and Cam entered. The houses were mini-mansions and I was excited to see what Cam had selected for the family he anticipated. I didn't want to seem as if I'd never seen nice houses, but these places were fabulous. "How long has this community been here?" I asked.

"Last house went up this past August."

"I love this community."

As we pulled into his driveway, I took a quick glance at the quintessential Colonial with an exterior of stone and beige stucco. When he pulled into the side-loading three-car garage, he stopped and smiled at me. Looking into my eyes he said, "Good. I'm glad you like it."

When we got out, we headed into the kitchen. There was a card table with four folding chairs, similar to the table in my empty condo. The kitchen was large, with antique white cabinetry and multicolored brown granite countertops. His appliances were all stainless steel, but the massive home looked lonely and unloved. I took a few steps to see the rest of the place and my footsteps made an echo.

Cam noticed my confused look and said, "I figured I'd wait for you to decorate."

I laughed. "Wait for me?"

"Yeah, I settled on the house last July and since I had to keep it on the low, I really haven't settled in yet. You know?"

"She really doesn't know you live here?"

"Nah, she would act a fool."

"Is this the one place you feel like she's not watching?"

"Exactly."

"Do you think she's a stalker?"

"She's a harmless stalker but yeah. Her whole mode of

op is to tell women I date that we're still married. She can't do that anymore. And most of the time, I was going on dates for the hell of it. I wasn't really into those women. So when they would question me about me and her, I usually wouldn't fight to get them to understand."

"Kind of like you did with me?"

"Nah, I knew for sure I was going to fight for you. I just had to come correct."

"Why were you so sure that you wanted to come back for me?"

He laughed. "Having an older mother gives you a certain kind of wisdom that the average dumb dude doesn't get. My mother taught me what I should be looking for in a woman, so I'm only attracted to a certain type of chick."

"What kind of woman is your ex, if you don't mind me asking, because obviously you have a character requirement when it comes to women. It just seems like she's not that certain type. I mean, based on what you've told me."

"It takes a certain level of maturity to really get the lessons you're taught as a young man. When I met Yasmin, I had just graduated from college and I knew I wanted to be a businessman. And all the successful businessmen I knew had a wife at home taking care of the day-to-day while they provided for the fam. I wanted that. She was cool and fun. She didn't have a close family, so she just fell into line. We got married and she was cool until after we had Caron. I sometimes think she went through postpartum depression and never recovered. The woman I took to the hospital ain't the same one that came home," he said, chuckling nervously.

"What initially attracted you to her?"

"To be honest, Yasmin is very pretty and she can pretend to be normal."

"I'm sure there were signs."

"Yeah, there were some signs, and even after we got married her personality changed."

"Do you think she had bipolar disorder or something?" Before he could answer, I said, "Does anyone in her family suffer from mental disorder?"

"Well, not that I know of. She's never been diagnosed, but she does take medicine for anxiety."

"Really? You know that anxiety disorder is a mental illness."

"Word? I didn't know that."

"Anxiety can be caused by chemical imbalances, other changes in the brain, or environmental stress. Treatment for anxiety isn't always effective, especially if her therapists haven't fully identified her triggers."

He said, "I wish someone would have explained that to me a long time ago."

He looked slightly saddened that he was just discovering this information. I wondered how he would have handled their relationship if he had known.

"Do you think you two would still be together if you would have known?"

He shrugged. "Doubt it very seriously, but I probably could have handled her differently."

"Yeah. It's never too late."

His neck snapped back. "Oh, it's definitely too late for me and her."

"I'm saying it's not too late to help her."

"In that case, you're right."

I could tell it was still emotional for him. From all the body language, I knew he was ready to scrap that topic and move on. I hugged him.

"I'm sorry I brought her up."

"Nah, you're good. Sometimes you got to put the car in reverse to get to where you're going. Right?"

"You're right."

"I come across a lot of women, especially in my profession because I network so much, but most of them aren't even sure of what they want in a relationship. If I just want to get laid, I can do that every day, four and five times a day if I want."

"Spare me."

"Nah, I'm just saying. But that's not what I want. I like having a relationship, but it has to be with the right woman."

I was puzzled. Either he was speaking generally or he was saying I was the right one. Or was he saying he was still looking? I didn't know so I just nodded. "Understood."

"When a man gets ready he's ready. But I guess you already know that, Dr. Blue."

"Yes, I do."

He invited me up to his bedroom. It was the only place

in the house that looked lived in. He pulled his shirt over his head and I stood in the middle of his large bedroom, feeling awkward. He walked over and kissed me.

"I like being with you."

I was so wrapped up in the unveiling of the real Cameron Small that I had forgotten about my car, so my response to his compliment was an irritated huff. "This is so crazy."

He backed up. "What? Me and you?"

I laughed. "Nah, my car."

"We're going to handle it tomorrow. Don't worry. You need something to sleep in?"

"Yeah."

He went into his walk-in closet and tossed a T-shirt to me. "Here you go, baby."

His voice felt so good to me. Everything about him turned me on. He stood there in his boxer briefs with a towel over his forearm. "You want to take a shower with me?"

I shrugged, because I did but I didn't. I wasn't sure if we were doing too much too soon. As I contemplated, he went in the bathroom and turned the water on. I walked to the bathroom door and said, "I need a towel too."

I didn't want to get my hair wet. Despite having a weave with Remy wet and wavy hair, I wasn't totally comfortable being this free with him. He said, "Yeah, go in my closet and the towels are in there."

I stood in his closet and looked around at all the clothes he had. It was like a miniature men's store. He had a wall of drawers and cubbies to store his things. His cologne took up two shelves. I'm not certain how long I was there, but it must have been a while because it stunned me when he walked up from behind and said, "You don't see the towels."

I jumped and he pointed. "Right over there."

"Oh. I didn't see them. I was admiring all of your nice clothes," I said. "I guess you figured you could fill up the closet since you're the only one living here."

He shook his head and gestured for me to follow him. He opened the door catty-corner to his closet and there was an even bigger walk-in closet. It was completely empty. He said, "This would be hers."

I said, "Hers or mine?"

"I told you that I want you to be her."

I sucked my teeth. "Cam, you did not tell me that."

"I've been trying to tell you that since we met."

I shrugged. "We'll see."

We headed to the bathroom and the glass doors to the shower were steamy and inviting. I took off my dress and Cam stepped out of his boxer shorts. He opened the shower door. "After you?"

When he got in, he wrapped his arms around me from behind. He pushed my hair to the side and kissed my neck. Chills rushed through my body as the steamy hot water splashed on my skin. He turned me around and put his tongue in my mouth. Water ran down our faces and through my hair and it didn't even matter. Cameron's muscular body was beautiful and he was close to me.

I was falling in love with this man and now I wondered why I'd just purchased a condo when he had prepared this palace for us.

I tingled all over and as Cameron washed my body gently I rubbed every inch of his torso in amazement. How could one person feel so perfect? How could he have every outrageous quality I'd dreamed of? How could he be saying everything I needed him to say? He sat down on the shower seat and invited me to sit on top of him. I sat down, and he stroked his tongue up and down my spine. My back arched as he held me in his arms, pulling me closer. His penis pressed against my lower back. I squirmed, and his hand traveled up and rubbed my breasts. Then he slid one hand down between my legs. He cupped my vagina and stuck his middle finger inside, sliding it in and out.

"You want it this way or you want me to turn around?" I asked.

"Turn around, baby."

I stood up and turned around to straddle him. I lowered myself down and he positioned himself to slide into me. As soon as we connected, I kissed him. I wanted to be closer than we already were. I twirled on him and he rubbed my back. He made sounds like he was trying to hold back. I wanted to bring it out of him. I said, "It feels good to you."

"Yeah."

"You want it all the time?"

"Every day."

"What are you going to do to get it every day?"

"Everything."

I liked that answer so I figured I'd stop talking and enjoy him. He put his arms under my legs so he could take control. He aggressively shoved himself into me over and over again. I moaned and thanked him for making my body feel so good. I worked harder, and finally he released inside me. It wasn't until that moment that it hit me: we hadn't used protection. *What the fuck was I thinking? Shit, I wasn't thinking. Oh my, I like Cameron but I don't know enough about him for this.* My post-sex exhilaration was immediately overpowered by frustration. *How the hell could I have been so caught up in the moment?*

I hopped off him and opened the shower door. I covered my face with my towel, partially because I was embarrassed, but the other part I couldn't quite figure out. From whom was I hiding? Cameron quickly noticed that I was acting strange.

"What happened?"

"We had sex with no protection. I should be more responsible, Cam," I said, frowning.

"Is there something you want to tell me?"

"Yeah, I feel stupid and irresponsible."

"Well, I can tell you now, I just took out a large life insurance policy and they do a full screening. I'm straight."

"Have you been screened for everything?" I asked with doubt.

"Yeah, baby, you're good, right?"

I nodded.

"It definitely ain't cool to be sleeping around with no protection but we made a mistake. I think we can forgive ourselves. What do you think?"

He hugged me and I nodded on his chest. I wanted to see that life insurance policy, but I figured I might as well have a good night's sleep and not worry about it. I'd already interrupted our enjoyment.

We lay in his king-size bed and he held me close. "It's OK, Ayana. I'm good."

Seconds passed and Cameron was snoring in my ear. *Ugh! I guess he's not perfect, but he is damn sure close*, I thought with a smile on my face.

The sun had barely peeked through the window when Cameron hopped up. He told me that he had several listings to show and that he was trying to make a move on some land. Basically, it was time for me to go. I thought that was a pleasant way to explain it, but I understood. It's good to have someone as busy as I am. Most men can't understand my schedule or give me space so this was a breath of fresh air. I smiled. "Cool. I'm going to need you to take me to my sister's house. She has my extra house key and I can get her single-chick car."

He laughed. "Single-chick car, huh?"

"Yeah, she and her husband said they weren't having kids for five years after they got married. Baby number one came nine months later. Her BMW coupé sits in the garage because she won't let it go."

"That's funny."

"It's going to come in handy today."

"Just let me know. You can borrow the Audi if you need to."

"It's no problem. My sister's car is in the garage dying to be driven."

Cameron put on a pair of khaki dress pants and a white tailored dress shirt. He left the top buttons open. His cologne smelled edible. I looked at him proudly as we walked out of his bedroom and down the right side of the double stairway that led to the empty foyer. I joked, "If I didn't know any better, I'd think this was just a house you were showing and you decided to sneak me in."

"That's a good idea, but luckily, I'm not that guy."

"OK, I trust you."

"I'm glad you do."

We headed back to town. Close to eight in the morning, I received a call from the detective telling me that my car had been taken to the pound and I could pick it up on Monday morning. Cam asked, "Where did they find it?"

The detective said, "In Sage Hill Shopping Center on Briarcliff Road."

Cam squinted and looked at me strangely. "Really?"

I shrugged. "That's what he said."

I asked the detective a few other questions, and based on what he had been told it didn't sound as if the car had been damaged. The keys were in the armrest. There hadn't been any crimes committed in it. Everything was one big mystery, but I was happy the police had found it.

It appeared that someone had swiped the keys from the valet cabinet and gone joyriding for the evening.

"Your keys are with the car. I really apologize for any inconvenience."

"Thanks for calling."

When I hung up, I said, "This just makes no sense."

Cameron agreed. He just kept saying, "Wow."

After a while I said, "Cam, say something else."

He laughed. "A'ight, baby, when we hanging out again?"

"You know I have a book due that I haven't really started writing."

"So you're working later?"

"It depends on what my options are."

He pulled up to my sister's house and I stepped out of his car.

"I'll call you later, a'ight?"

I waved goodbye as I headed to the door and he was still there. He said, "Have a productive day."

"OK."

"Hopefully I'll see you later."

"Maybe."

I had no intention of seeing him later. That was too much face time in a little over twenty-four hours. It was time to reel it back in on Mr. Small. I waved one last time and finally he drove off.

yasmin

Everyone in the salon gasped in shock as the grille of Cameron's Bentley nearly came through the window of the salon when he sped into the handicapped spot directly in front. He hopped out of the car dressed like a *GQ* model. He yanked the door of the salon open. "Yasmin!"

My neck snapped back. He was obviously angry, but I didn't know why. I hadn't left any evidence that I had been in his house. *Shit.* It just dawned on me that he had mentioned twenty-four-hour surveillance. Maybe he saw me rummaging through his things. I got a little nervous, but I planned to defend myself. I headed to the door, because I wanted to take this outside.

"What's up, Cam? Why are you here acting like a lunatic?"

"When are you going to just let this go?"

I shouted, "It's not easy letting someone go that you love."

"Cut the bullshit, Yasmin. I'm tired of this crazy-chick shit."

"I haven't done anything. What the fuck are you talking about?"

"You stole Ayana's car? What type of shit is that? What the fuck? Do you have a goddamn LoJack on me?"

I laughed. "That's a good idea, but no. You know how I can get one?"

"Yasmin!"

He screamed my name so loud that it felt as if the earth shook.

"I'm not fucking playing with you. I'm telling you now, I'm in a relationship and I dare you to keep fucking with us. I will have custody of Caron so fast your fucking head will spin. I will have your ass psycho-evaluated because I'm convinced you're crazy."

"So you're in a relationship? You come here to yell and scream at me because you're in a relationship? You want to take my son from me. Fuck you, Cam. No other bitch is raising my son!"

"Keep acting like you're crazy and see what happens. I've done nothing but respect you and this is my payback? It's over, Yasmin. Leave me the fuck alone."

I started crying. "After everything we've been through, you meet this bitch and in two weeks you're telling me you're in a relationship and you want me to leave you alone."

"Damn right."

"What about your son?"

"I'm going to keep doing what I been doing, but get me and you being together out of your twisted mind."

I looked him in the eyes. He didn't mean what he was saying. Cam came across strong but he hated to upset the people he loves. I said, "Cam, it's too hard. It hurts that we are divorced."

His anger subsided. "Look, Yasmin, I know it doesn't feel good, but we have to move on so we both can be happy."

"The only way I'm going to be happy is if we get back together."

"You need professional help. I'm serious."

He turned around and I grabbed his arm. He yanked it away. I hated that he pretended not to love me anymore. I had no intention of letting him go and allowing him to move on without me. Everything that Cam had was because of my hard work. I'd be damned if he was going to take that and give it to some already-privileged bitch. I hadn't taken her car, but I had some other shit up my sleeve, especially now that he wanted to grandstand and come to my shop to proclaim his love for this freak.

I tried to shake the anger raging inside me when I walked back into the shop, but I couldn't. The client sitting at my station just looked at me. I'm sure she, like everyone else in the salon, had witnessed the shouting match, even if they hadn't been able to hear exactly what he was saying to me. Tayshawn looked at me with his lips curled. "Girl, that Cam is fine."

"Tayshawn, stop. I'm not in the mood."

I had a lump stuck in my throat. I wanted to cry. I wanted to tell Tayshawn and Casey what he'd just said, but I couldn't. Since I met Cameron, he has never claimed another woman. A little part of me believed that he wanted to be with that chick, but the other side of me knew that he didn't know her and that their relationship was only temporary. *Why would he come here and claim her like that?* I was so confused and hurt that I couldn't find the words to share the event with my friends. I wanted to make Cameron's life miserable. I didn't deserve this type of treatment, especially not over a chick he'd just met.

After I rushed through several of my clients, Tayshawn looked at me and said, "Lunch, mama?"

I nodded, and we headed to the break area. "What's Cam mad at you about now?"

"He said something about me taking Ayana's car. Tayshawn, I didn't do anything to her car, but I wish I had. I actually broke into his house yesterday, but I swear I didn't do anything to her car. I swear."

He laughed. "Yasmin, stop."

"No, I'm serious. Cam just told me they are in a relationship. I hate him."

"Yasmin, are you serious?"

I nodded.

"I've been telling you to whip it on him before someone else did."

"Tay, he hasn't touched me with a ten-foot pole since he walked out of that house."

"Boo-boo, I hate to say, you really fucked up. A man always want some nookie."

I took a deep breath. "You think I need to give up?"

"Hell no!"

He pulled out his iPhone and connected it to the Bose system. Beyoncé's "Ring the Alarm" blasted through the speakers. He swung his arms in a psychotic fashion and shouted, "I been through this too long but I'll be damned if I see another chick on your arm."

The look in Cam's eyes when he said he was in a relationship almost made me want to throw in the towel, but Tayshawn had me fired up as he ad-libbed lyrics. "Hell no, Ayana Blue, you ain't gon' be rockin' chinchilla coats. 'Cause Yasmin ain't letting go."

I gave him a high five. Damn right. I wasn't just letting him go. I was a part of Cameron's success. Why should I let her reap all the benefits?

I sent him a text: CAM SORRY ABT WHAT U THINK I DID TO AYANA'S CAR. PLEASE BELIEVE ME.

He responded, LEAVE ME THE FUCK ALONE.

I sent back, WHY DON'T YOU BELIEVE ME?

He replied, HER CAR WAS IN THE SALON'S PARKING LOT. WHO ELSE PUT IT THERE?

I stood up, slightly baffled. Who else could have put it there? I questioned myself for those brief moments. Had I put the car there? I was letting his accusations make me crazy. How would I know how to find her car? And why would I park it in front of my salon? My head was spinning, and Tayshawn was still shouting out reasons why I should fight for my man.

I said, "Tayshawn, did you take Ayana's car?"

"OK, Yazzy, I'm all down for you fighting for your man, but I'm not trying to go to jail for you."

I laughed. "I hate you, Tayshawn."

"Don't hate me, baby. I'm too much to hate."

ayana

Although I'd thought that I wouldn't see Cameron if he called, I couldn't resist. When I answered the phone, he said, "You got a nice cocktail dress you can put on?"

"I do, but I'm sitting here typing up some notes for my book and—"

"You'll have all day tomorrow. I promise I won't bother you. I have a real important meeting this evening and I'd like to have you with me."

He seemed so transparent, but I just didn't understand. A man with so much to lose is usually a little more reserved when it comes to courting someone. I just didn't understand his motives.

Around seven thirty, Cameron called to let me know that he was outside. I wore a plain strapless black dress that fit my size-ten hourglass figure perfectly. I'd pulled my hair into a bun on the side. I walked down the stairs and toward the car. As I got closer, Cameron stumbled out of the driver's side and came around to open the door. I said, "Did you trip?"

"Nah, I was just caught up in how beautiful you look tonight that I almost forgot to open the door."

I sat in the car and he walked back around to hop in. He smiled at me before pulling off. "You look so good."

"So do you."

He had on a black European-cut suit with a black button-down shirt. As always, he smelled even better than he did when I left him that morning.

"Where are we going?"

"I'm meeting with a group of investors about a property that I'm trying to buy in midtown. It was going to be just the guys, but they decided to bring their spouses. And I figured I'd ask if you wanted to come along."

"So they bring their wives and you bring one of your clients."

He laughed really hard. "That was cute, Ayana."

"No, I'm serious."

He reached over and touched the top of my hand. "I bring a beautiful woman that I'm attracted to. Doctor of psychology. Author. Radio talk show host. I'm batting one thousand. I mean, do I need to continue?"

"I understand where you're coming from."

"I'm glad you do."

When we arrived at the Ritz-Carlton restaurant, we were ushered into a private room and seated at a long table. Cameron introduced me to two older white men with German accents. He proudly ran down my list of accomplishments, making me feel slightly self-conscious. I smiled. He said, "I stole her from the computer tonight. She's working on her next book."

Everyone seemed impressed. "Wow, how did you get started?"

I didn't mind answering questions about my career, but I'd thought I was just supposed to be the arm piece, not the center of attention. Finally another couple arrived and the attention was shifted from me to the business at hand.

Cameron pulled ten small black spiral-bound books out of his Prada backpack. He passed one to each person at the table, including me. Then he put his Apple MacBook Pro on the table while everyone flipped through the investment plan. It was titled *Blake's Overlook*. I scanned the detailed plan of how Cam intended to use his realty connections to purchase a piece of land in midtown Atlanta and erect a condominium high-rise. The community would have a resort look and feel. The target buyer would be young, successful, business-minded, and possibly living and doing business in other cities as well. The condominium association would also provide property management services for owners needing to lease. His prospectus was detailed and he made comparisons to other midtown projects that had had astronomical returns.

After we all flipped through the pages, Cam started a movie on his laptop. It was a simulation showing the land as it existed. Construction began and a lovely building appeared. We saw a lavish lobby. Cam clicked on six different floor plans; for each he could click to add or remove options. It was so easy to visualize the project after

looking at the presentation. I could see in the other investors' eyes that they wanted to throw millions of dollars
into the project. Based on what I'd seen, I would have
given him all the money he needed, if I could have. He
was so well organized that it made me horny. I stared at
him in absolute amazement, as did the others—so much
so that when he finished they clapped.

Cam and I both were sure he'd nailed it. He reached
under the table and held my hand after he put his laptop
away. I could feel the moistness, so I took the napkin on
my lap and wiped his palm. He looked at me and smiled.
There was that extra-special something in his eyes. It
might have been relief, but it made me smile too. He was
swiftly sweeping me off my feet, and I was actually enjoying it.

When we left the restaurant, we sat in the parking lot
quietly for a second. He took a deep breath. "Thanks for
coming, Ayana."

"No problem."

"Those guys are realty tycoons. If they're in on this
project, that means I'm really onto something. And if it
goes as planned, I will be able to fly around the world
and invest in other people's dreams."

"I'm happy for you."

He looked at me. "I'm glad you were able to come
tonight. They like to see stability. You know?"

"I see where you're coming from."

"My place tonight?" he asked, almost as if there were
really no question that we were going to be together.

I had him stop at my place so I could grab some clothes. While I was there I got two flute glasses and a bottle of champagne. We headed back to his empty six-bedroom house. During the ride, he asked, "What's going on in your mind?"

I smiled. "It's funny. I'm usually the one asking that question."

"I'm sure, but honestly though. Be straight up with me. What do you think about what's going on?"

"I think it seems like a lot in a little bit of time. It feels like we've been together every day for a week, yet it's only been two days. I'm not sure where it's going, but I'm enjoying the time we've been together."

"You think we're moving too fast?"

"Yeah, kinda."

"I agree."

My heart skipped a beat. I wondered if this was where he was going to say maybe we should slow down. Instead he said, "You have no idea what it's like to be a man like me, looking for a woman like you out here."

"Make me understand."

"I've known Quentin practically all of my life and we've had a lot of conversations about the next woman I would settle down with and he'd always say, 'When you get ready, I'm going to introduce you to Ayana.' When I met you that day, I wasn't planning on saying anything, but the attraction was there for both of us."

"Yeah, I think so. Quentin never said anything to me about you until I said something about the house."

"He wanted the divorce drama to settle down some and ideally I would have liked that too. But I just want you to know that right now, I'm not seeing anyone but you."

"Thank you."

I wanted to retract my words because they sounded silly, but I guess in reality I was thankful that he had been straight up with me. I was thankful that he was capable of expressing himself and that we were getting the opportunity to know each other. There was an awkward silence. Finally, Cam said, "You seeing anyone else?"

"No, but I do have some dates lined up," I said, wanting to see what his reaction would be.

His eyes quickly shifted. Then he noticed that I was smiling and he said, "Well, you need to cancel."

"Already taken care of," I said with a chuckle.

I liked that he didn't try to play cool and pretend that I should do what I felt. I loved the transparency. This was probably the first time in thirty years that a man had come straight out and asked me to mark yes or no. The windows were half down and the night air blew through the car. The music played, and I felt as if I and this man I'd known for only a few weeks were Bonnie and Clyde.

I asked him to stop at the grocery store because he had nothing but beer in the refrigerator. He'd told me Sunday was his day to relax and I didn't want to chance waking up to beer. I grabbed a few necessities, and we headed to his house. We sat down at the card table and opened the champagne. He poured, and I said, "So we're exclusive?"

The side of his mouth curled. "Ayana, we had that long talk and you still got questions?"

"Just confirmation, Cameron, that's all."

"That's cool."

We sat and chatted about how well the meeting had gone as we polished off the entire bottle. We went upstairs to his bedroom and lay across the bed in our clothes. He said, "Let's do our devotions."

I agreed. I'd never had a man suggest this before we romp in the hay. He pulled out a large book of Christian devotions. He began to read and my eyes got heavy. Before I knew it his words had faded and I was asleep.

When his alarm clock went off at seven in the morning, he quickly started looking for his phone. I looked at myself, still in my dress, and him in his slacks. We must have been tired, and I wasn't ready to wake up. I said, "Do you have somewhere to go this morning?"

"Nah, I usually go to church. I try not to schedule anything on Sunday unless I have to."

I took a breath. "Can we go back to sleep?"

"Yeah. You may want to get a little more comfortable."

I peeled off my dress and put on a T-shirt he'd given me and tried to drift off to sleep. Cam lay beside me and rubbed my back. We started talking and before I knew it, it was after nine in the morning. I sat up. "Cam, I have to go home and start working on this book."

"OK. I promised I wouldn't bother you. I may as well go to church now."

"It's interesting. You didn't strike me as a faithful churchgoer."

"Look. There was a time, when I first started in realty, when I didn't know how I was going to pay my rent, and God has blessed me with all this. I have to go thank him as often as I can. Plus church is me and Mom Dukes's quality time. Then I take her to the grocery store."

"You're a good son."

"Yeah, you'll have to meet my moms. She's the bomb."

That made me blush. Men who have healthy relationships with their mothers are typically good guys. Then there were the mom-son relationships that could be detrimental. From what I could tell Cameron and his mother didn't have that type.

"You know my mother is eighty. Right?"

My mind was calculating as I said, "Yeah, you told me."

"My sister is fifteen years older than me and my mother didn't think she could have any more kids. She was forty-five when she had me and I came out perfect."

"Now I wouldn't go that far," I kidded.

"Seriously though, she was pretty old and back then there wasn't all this technology."

"That's true. I guess you were meant to be."

"Don't get Moms on that. She says I'm her golden child."

"That's sweet."

"Yeah, at the risk of my sister's self-esteem. She's fifty and still carries baggage from when we were kids. She thinks my mother loves me more."

"What do you think?"

He shrugged. "I think she loved the miracle and I just happened to be a product of that miracle."

"Yeah, but parents really scar their kids when they favor one child over the other. And those issues don't disappear with age. They actually worsen."

"Yeah, my sister is still pretty bitter. She loves my son though. We manage. You know?"

"Yeah, it's still sad."

By the time I got home it was a little after eleven, and instead of sitting down at my computer, I started straightening up and talking on the phone with my friends. It had been a few days and no one had been brought up to date on my weekend love affair. I had several friends linked in on the call as I gave them the 411 on Cameron Small. They all agreed that he seemed well worth the risks. Cori said, "Everybody has a past, and at our age they all have crazy baby mamas. I'm almost afraid to date a man with no kids and never married. I think they have a whole different issue."

"You're right. My gaydar goes crazy when I see that. No kids. No ex-wife. No serious old girl. No Mandy," said Mandy.

"Yeah, that's true. I guess in theory everyone has drama, but when it comes knocking at your door, you're like, I can't deal with that," I said.

"But when I look around at all my girls with good men, they all had a cross to bear. Whether it was finances, stepkids, ex-wives, ex-girlfriends. In the beginning it's always something," Cori said.

I needed their encouragement, because as much as I believed Cameron was a good guy, that phone call from his ex-wife kept playing in my head. I got off the phone with my friends and reminded them to be at the station on time. I had a segment called Martini Mondays, where my friends stopped by to talk about weekend relationship highlights—either our own or those we'd heard about. Cori laughed. "Can we discuss whirlwind love affairs tomorrow?"

I said, "We certainly can."

I hung up with my girls and went to the computer. The Internet was distracting so I tried to keep my browser window down when I worked, but as soon as I opened it, a bunch of pornographic videos popped up. Every time I closed one, another one would pop up in its place. I was sure that I hadn't gone to any porno sites. Why was this happening? My computer was moving like a snail and these pictures and videos were invading it.

I spent half of the day trying to clean up my computer. I ended up having to take it to Best Buy to see if they could fix it. It was yet another day that I'd gotten distracted from writing. I was so irritated. Maybe I should have gone to church with Cam, because every evil force in the world was coming at me. I called him just to touch base and blame him for losing an entire weekend of writing.

Sometimes I think it's better not to date when you have things to accomplish. If I hadn't been smiling in his face, I could have gotten a lot of work done. He probably could hear the frustration in my voice. He said, "OK, I'm not going to bother you. Let me know if you need me to take you to get your car in the morning."

"OK."

I knew that I was blaming him for my own irresponsibility and he picked up on it. He immediately got off the phone. I wanted to call back and apologize but I figured I would just let it go and began reading up on the first phases of love and/or lust. This way, in addition to what I was feeling, I'd have some fresh information to share with my listeners. That was the least I could do.

I was in the bed with my reading glasses and sweatpants on, with no makeup, when the doorbell rang. I jumped. Who could that be?

I tiptoed to the door and peeped out but no one was there. I wasn't about to open the door, so I walked back to my bedroom. My cell phone rang and it was Cam. I picked up and said, "Are you at my door?"

"No, I left something for you. I'm headed back home."

"So you're not going to stay for dinner?" I asked as I returned to the door.

"Nah, I want you to get some work done."

"Well, I can't do a whole lot without a—" My mouth fell open and I was at a loss for words when I opened my front door. There was a large Apple shopping bag, and inside was a MacBook Pro laptop box. I screamed in his ear.

He said, "I'm glad you like it. I felt really bad for distracting you this weekend for my own selfish reasons. That was the least I could do."

"Cam, that was too sweet of you. Are you sure about this? This is a really expensive gift."

"Ayana, you're worth it."

"Wait, are you going to come in?"

"I'm halfway down the road now."

"But I want to see you," I said, taking my glasses off and letting my hair down. "You can't be too far. You may as well come halfway back up the road."

"If you insist."

"I do."

Cam was at my door in a matter of seconds. He'd probably just wanted me to beg to see him, since he'd been the initiator all weekend. We ended up chilling on my couch watching an NBA playoff game and ordering pizza.

yasmin

It seemed like the whole situation was slipping from my grip. I took Caron to my god-sister's house and went over to Cam's house so we could talk. I sat there from five in the evening until close to ten at night. I didn't want to go inside, because I didn't know what time he'd appear. I just wanted to have a civilized conversation with him.

If I could get him to sit down and talk without all the yelling, maybe we could get somewhere. When it appeared that he wasn't coming back, I decided I would walk back on the deck to see if he'd even noticed that the sliding glass door was unlocked. It was still open. When I entered, the same cereal bowl was in the sink. Everything was in the exact same position as two days ago.

Out of nowhere it hit me, Cam was living with that bitch. How could he be so deep so fast? I had to find out where she lived. I just wanted to watch their interactions. I needed to know why her and not me. He wasn't even interested in getting Caron. What did this bitch have on him?

I browsed through Cam's photo albums and it was as if he had completely erased me from his life. There were pictures of Caron but I was cropped out of every one of them. I didn't like feeling invisible. I didn't like that it was so easy for him to forget about me. I needed to find one thing that still connected us, something that would remind him that we had been happy at one time.

I lay across his bed and I could smell him. I could feel how alone he must have felt when I told him I wanted to be with Overnight Express. I bunched his quilt up and wrapped my arms around it, imagining that I was holding him. Tears streamed down my face. It was so hard to accept this. No one understood how I felt. I wasn't crazy. I just wanted to erase it all. I wanted to make it right. Maybe it was just a bad dream. I wanted to go to sleep and wake up to Cam and Caron. I didn't want to do this alone anymore. I didn't want to keep shuffling Caron from house to house.

I lay there and didn't realize that not only had I been crying hysterically, I was sweating. The house was hot and I was curious about just how many days Cam had been with his new girlfriend. As I got up to turn on the air, I wondered how long he'd continue to pay my mortgage now that he was moving on. I didn't know how I'd imagined this whole story playing out, but I'd never dreamed I wouldn't get just one more try.

I took all my clothes off and lay in his bed. I hoped he'd smell my scent when he returned and be compelled to feel me. I wished that he would walk in and find me there. As the time ticked away, I knew Cam was spending another night out. I felt confused and hurt. People suggested that I should be over him, but I just didn't know how to get over a man who had never done anything to hurt me. He had never cheated on me to my knowledge. He had never done anything but love me. I hated myself.

I headed to his medicine cabinet and looked at what he had. There was a bottle of prescription drugs. The label indicated it was oxycodone with an expiration date that had passed. I wanted the pain to end. I was tired of the embarrassment. I was tired of hating myself. When I opened the bottle, I discovered there were only six pills left. From what I'd been told, this medication was potent, and I thought it could take me away. I turned on the faucet and threw the pills to the back of my throat. Cupping my hands under the water, I washed them down. I looked in the mirror. I was ready for the dumb chick in front of me to disappear. As I came to peace with my choice, my cell phone rang and I jumped nervously. Who could be calling me right now? I felt as if someone was spying on me until I realized it was Caron calling from my god-sister's phone. He said, "Mommy, I have to go to school tomorrow. It's really late."

Suddenly I wanted yet another replay. I stuck my finger down my throat. My whole mission turned into me getting this medicine out of my system and picking up my son. I forced myself to throw up and put my clothes back on. Rushing from the house, I didn't think about straightening up after myself. I had to get Caron and I hoped that puking had really worked. I didn't feel strange as I rushed to my god-sister's house. It was only five minutes away, so I was there quickly. Just as I called to tell Caron to come out, I started feeling strange. I was slightly dizzy, but I felt I could make it home. I was nauseous. When Caron got in the car I thought I saw four of him.

Cam stood over me, shaking me, yelling my name. "Yasmin! Yasmin! Yasmin!"

I didn't know where I was. I must have been in Cam's house since he was calling me. I looked up at him and Caron standing beside him. I was out of it. He said, "Yasmin."

I slowly rose and asked, "Where am I?"

"You've been drinking again?"

"No," I said, rubbing my eyes.

"Well, what's wrong with you then?"

"I don't know."

"It's one o'clock in the afternoon and Caron called me saying you were dead."

I couldn't believe that I had done something so stupid. Caron stood beside him looking as if he had been crying all day. The thought of him trying to wake me up and thinking I was dead made me feel horrible. Why had I put him in that predicament? He didn't deserve this.

When I tried to sit up, my head was pounding and my heart racing. I wondered if I should admit to Cam what I'd done. Instead, I said, "I was having trouble sleeping and I took two sleeping pills last night."

Caron said, "Mommy, you musta took them before you

picked me up because you was sleeping while we was driving home."

Cam said, "I'm going to make you some coffee. Just lie down."

He came back upstairs with water and coffee. He sat on the side of the bed and asked, "Yasmin, why did you take the sleeping pills?"

"'Cause I really wanted to go to sleep."

"Did you take them before or after you picked Caron up?"

"Why does it matter to you? You didn't care enough to have him with you this weekend."

"Not today, Yasmin. This is serious. You could have killed him."

"I was sleepy when I picked him up and I've been waking up in the middle of the night. I really needed to sleep."

"Where did you get the pills?"

"They were over-the-counter sleeping pills."

He put his hand on my shoulder and said, "Maybe you were just tired, Yas."

It was as if he cared about me again. I looked at him and said, "Thanks for coming here to check up on me. You treat me like you hate me."

"Yasmin, I don't hate you. I hate a lot of the things you do."

"I'm sorry for all the things I put you through."

"We cool. It's no need for all of that."

I said, "I know, but I just wanted you to know."

He hung around the house for a while longer to make

sure I was OK. He and Caron ran out to buy me lunch. I wanted to let go of the possibility that we'd get back together, but today had only reignited the spark. He was a good man and I wanted him to be mine again.

Before he left, he talked to me about seeing a psychiatrist about my anxiety. He told me that he'd support me and be sure that I got the right one. I really didn't think I needed help, but if that would bring him back to me, I would consider it.

ayana

Cam and I had been together nearly every day from the moment I'd gone to settlement a month ago. I had yet to move into my condominium. I had scaled my office hours back to a minimum, primarily so I could finish my book, but also because with my new relationship, it was apparent I had left no time in my life for myself.

Cam had been staying at my apartment after his ex-wife picked up Caron on weekdays, and we'd stay at his home over the weekends. We were doing something fun every day and time just escaped me.

I woke up five days before I was finally scheduled to move and shook Cameron. "Honey, we have to start moving stuff to the condo today."

"Yeah, let's just hire movers."

"That's fine, but I'll need you to help me pack."

"I'll call the movers and they will have this entire place packed and labeled and unloaded in about four hours."

"You sure?"

Cameron called the movers and they said they would put me on the schedule for the next day. That gave me another day to procrastinate. My plate was so full that I didn't have much time for all the extra stuff, so I was happy Cam had offered to hire movers. By the time they arrived, I'd gotten enough organized that their jobs wouldn't be too hard.

Cam had some business to take care of so I stuck around while they packed. Once the truck was loaded, I told them I'd meet them at the condo. I hopped into my car and headed over to the condo. I opened the door and the place had been vandalized. There was spray paint all over the walls: HOME-WRECKER.

My heart pounded. Who would do this to me? Why would anyone do this to anyone? It had to be Cam's ex-wife, and I was angry that I'd let him so deep into my spirit. I was in love with him now, but I should have just let it go in the beginning. Fuck a good man: a man is only as good as the women in his past. If he's been with crazy whores, then he wasn't worth being with. In the midst of my rant, I forgot to call the movers. I told them to wait. I called Cam screaming and yelling.

"Your ex-wife ruined my house!"

"What are you talking about?"

"There is bleach all over the wood floor and carpet. Spray paint all over the walls. The house is ruined thanks to you."

"I'm on my way."

I sat there in the middle of my first home bawling. I couldn't believe that this woman would do this. I wanted to fight her. I wanted to strangle her. I hated that she was so committed to this fight. If this was the way she rolled, she could have Cam back for all I cared. I didn't have the heart to call my sister or any of my friends. They would have wanted to kill her and it wasn't worth it. I knew what I had to do. I had to let it go.

Cam pushed the front door open and looked around as if pained by the vision. I shook my head and tears streamed down my face, because I knew I had to break up with him. I simply said, "She wins."

He tried to hug me and I pulled back. "Don't let her win. We'll file a restraining order on her. It's that simple."

"It's not that simple. Look at this place."

"I will pay for everything. Don't worry."

"I have to be out of my apartment in four days. What am I going to do?"

"I had the movers take your things to my house."

"Why, Cam, why? It's over! I don't want to be a part of this fatal attraction anymore."

"I want to be with you and I'm going to fix this. Come stay with me for a little while and we can work it out."

"Work what out? We cannot fix her."

"We can focus on us and if we're strong, she can't penetrate us. You can't fall apart now."

"I should have gone with my first instinct."

He got in my face. "And what was that? Tell me what your first instinct was when you met me."

"I'm talking about when she called my job."

"And I'm talking about us, not her. What did you think when you first met me?"

Tears welled in my eyes, because I couldn't say what I'd felt when I first met him. I'd felt that he was a great guy. I'd felt that any woman would be lucky to have him. I'd felt an overwhelming desire to get to know him. My mind was a seesaw. I wanted to let him go, but I wanted to agree to temporarily move in with him.

He stood there in front of me, fighting for our relationship, and I was lost, confused, and upset. "What have you felt over the last thirty days? Not about her but about us? You said yourself that you dreamed about a relationship like this. Don't punish yourself because of her ignorance."

I ran my hand down my face to wipe away the tears. I looked at him pleading and begging, and wondered how any woman could turn her back on a man like this.

"Cam, I will move in with you on two conditions. One, we file a restraining order today. Two, you request police intervention during pickup and drop-off of Caron. She is crazy and I just can't imagine how she got into this place."

"I have something to tell you." He looked at me.

His eyes scared me and I wasn't sure what he was about to say. "What?"

"Your car was found in the salon parking lot and—"

"Why are you just telling me this?"

"I wasn't sure if it could have been a coincidence or what. Were all of your house keys on there?"

I nodded. I had never even thought to change the locks on the condo. I started to rethink my decision. She was worse than I'd originally imagined.

"Cam, what else do you think she's capable of?"

He shrugged. I really didn't feel comfortable with his response. I let out an angry sigh. "Why me?"

"I never imagined that she would do the things she's done. So I don't know what else she'd do. But I promise to protect you."

"How can you protect me and she is so random? How can you be sure of her next step?"

"We'll get a restraining order and I will request a psychological evaluation in our custody battle."

I took a deep breath and he wrapped me in his arms. "We need to head out to the house to meet the movers. They're probably waiting on us."

yasmin

B ounce Salon. Yasmin speaking."

"Yas, it's Cam."

He was calm but I knew him well enough to know he was angry. "What's up?"

We had been getting along much better since he'd come to the house when I nearly overdosed. We were talking with a lot less fighting. Reluctantly, I was sitting back watching him and Ayana get closer. I hoped to be more of a friend, and when the rocks came tumbling down, I would be there to console him. My new strategy seemed to have improved our relationship.

"You need help."

I wasn't sure if that was a question or a comment. So I said, "What do you mean?"

"You need to start seeing someone again about your anxiety."

"I didn't need to go when you made me go."

"If you didn't need to go then, you definitely need to go now."

"Where is this shit coming from? Your girlfriend?"

"Yas, I'm real concerned about your mental stability."

"Cam, go somewhere with that!"

Little did he know I had already made an appointment. I had known I had to do it when I almost killed Caron and myself. I didn't like hearing it come from him though.

"Honestly." He continued speaking to me like he was talking to a crazy person. "The shit you pulled with the car and the condo, it's just unacceptable. From now on, we need to meet at the police station when I drop Caron off."

I couldn't believe my ears. I excused myself from my client and went into the break room. "That bitch got you hemmed up like that? Now you scared to be around me? What kind of shit is that?"

"These stunts you been pulling are beyond reason anymore and to prevent me from doing something I have no business doing to you, let's meet in front of witnesses."

"You're so caught up with this chick that she got you convinced that I'm doing something to her?"

"I've seen it for myself. Yasmin, only you know what's going on in your head. Only you know why you're doing this stuff."

"Cam, I will admit that I've blasted her on blogs. I'll admit that I had people call in to the show to challenge her, but this car and condo shit is not me."

I continued to dispute and he kept accusing. It was confusing me why he'd think I would do this, after we'd been getting along so well. This was frustrating for me.

Maybe this crazy chick was making up shit to draw Cam closer to her.

Nearly two weeks later, a sheriff walked into the salon and said, "I'm looking for a Ms. Yasmin Small?"

Even though I wanted to pretend I wasn't there, everyone turned their heads in my direction. I said, "Yes, that's me."

"Can I speak to you outside?"

"Sure," I said as I walked to the front.

He explained to me that both Cameron and Ayana had filed restraining orders against me and I was expected in court the next week. I was stressed out and I didn't understand why Cam would do this to me.

I flipped through the case and there were a bunch of lies in there. They accused me of stealing her car and vandalizing her home, but there was no proof. All he had was a bunch of accusations. Anyone could be doing this to her. Cam might not have been the only man she'd stolen. How could they be so sure it was me? I wasn't going out like that. When I got back to my chair, Casey said, "Was that about Cam?"

I nodded.

"Custody?"

I shook my head no.

She kept prying. "Child support? Damn, Yas. What was it for?"

"He and Ayana have both filed restraining orders against me."

Tayshawn yelled from across the room, "OMG. When fighting for your man goes too far."

"Everything I've done is harmless."

"Well, obviously Ms. Thing doesn't think so," Tayshawn said.

"They are both wack. I can't believe Cam is so weak that he's letting her do this."

"She must have that ill na-na."

Casey laughed. "Or that good-good."

"Stop laughing!" I yelled at the top of my lungs. I was so angry I was shaking and I felt as if I could explode.

I had to get out of there. I couldn't think about my appointments. I just wanted to run away. I rushed to Caron's school and picked him up and just started driving. I didn't know where we were going but all I wanted to do was get away. There were only two school days left. If Cam wanted me out of his life I was gone. I was leaving forever. I wasn't going to sit in Atlanta and let him and his new woman parade around like the goddamn golden couple and treat me as if I were nonexistent. If he wanted me gone, then his son was leaving too. I was over this. I was over him and I was definitely over them.

Caron gave me a frightened look. "Mommy, are you OK?"

"Yes, I'm OK."

"Why are we driving so fast?"

"Because we have somewhere to go."

"Like where? It looks like we are driving in circles."

"Be quiet, little boy," I demanded.

"Am I going to Daddy's house today?"

"Daddy doesn't want to see you anymore. He has a new life. He doesn't want to see me or you."

I felt bad when he sniffled, but it was the truth. It was better he know it then than later.

"Can we at least say goodbye?"

"Caron, stop asking me a million questions."

I was watching my life from the outside in and I wasn't in control. I wanted something or someone to save me from myself but I was too mad.

"How could he? How could he?" I cried, banging on the steering wheel.

Caron just watched me. Finally he said, "Mommy, I love you."

He sounded so sincere and I wanted to take him away from all the drama. We went to my house and packed up our things and headed to North Carolina. I didn't know exactly why I'd chosen North Carolina but I had and I wasn't going to let anyone know where I was. I called Tayshawn and told him to let my clients know that I was gone indefinitely.

"Look, Yasmin, whatever is going on is not worth giving everything up. If Cam is in love with somebody else, just let it go. Stop ringing the goddamn alarm. We heard you, mama."

"It's not just Cam. I have to get my head straight. I need a break. Some peace and quiet! I want to be away from everyone."

And just like that, I was gone. My therapist had told

me that maybe getting out of town for a while would help me come to terms with my life as it had come to be. When he'd told me that, I'd said I couldn't leave everything, but now I wanted everything and everyone to disappear. Caron and I deserved peace. We deserved to be away from the stupidity of it all.

ayana

After I'd moved into Cam's house, it seemed like the right thing to do. With my furniture, it didn't seem as empty. I'd never imagined I would move in with a man after just a month of dating, but fate can't be questioned.

When I left the station and headed to the office, I really didn't have the energy to talk to patients, but duty called. Last time I'd checked, I had a really light schedule for the evening.

My first patient arrived a little late. He was a father of three with major anger issues. His wife had died of breast cancer a year ago and he was referred to me by the employee assistance program at his job. His coworkers recognized his anger and he was required to get help in order to keep his job. He was always down in the dumps. Though he loved his kids, he resented having to raise them alone. Sometimes I saw a glimmer of hope, but other times I thought I'd never break through. Thankfully, he was having an upbeat day. I'd encouraged him to join a single-parent support group. He was excited to tell me that over the weekend, at one of the group's social events, he'd met a woman around his age with two kids.

When we were done, I felt pretty good, thinking how wonderful it was to watch people grow. I was typing on my laptop when Margo arrived.

"How are you today?" I asked.

She didn't respond and I figured it was one of those days for her. Instead she questioned me. "Why did you cancel our last two appointments?"

"I'm sorry, Margo. I had other things I needed to work on." I smiled nervously. "I'm just one person."

"And I'm one person too. One person that needed you and you·haven't been here," she snapped.

Intentionally not feeding into her rant, I said, "So what's going on?"

"I guess you got someone else to spend time with now, huh?"

I didn't respond. She had been doing so well. I had never imagined that two missed visits would put her in the space she was in. I asked again, "So how are you?"

She didn't answer. Instead she kept shaking her head as if there was something heavy on her mind. Sweat beads formed on her nose. It looked as if she had jogged to my office. My eyes moved from her face to the damp-ness on her shirt.

"Did the car service drop you off today?"

"Yeah, why?" she asked in a curt fashion.

"It looks like you've been running or something."

She took a deep breath and I knew this was about to

be one of those sessions. I opened my notepad and wrote the date down. She readjusted in her chair and dropped her head in her hands.

"I've gone over and over this plan in my mind for the last ten years."

"What plan?"

"What I want to do to my father in front of his other kids."

"What do you want to do to him?"

Her chest puffed up and she shook her head. The look in her eyes warned me that whatever she'd been planning was serious. It surely wasn't about approaching him and saying, "Hi, I'm Margo. I'm your daughter."

I said, "Before you go any further, let me remind you that I am mandated by law to protect you, me, and anyone else from harm."

I wasn't sure what she was about to say, but I wanted to be clear that if she had plans to hurt this man, I was obligated to let someone know. In my experience, when people are bluffing they stop when I make that statement, but when the anger is raging high, they can't stop themselves. I knew there was cause for concern. Her head ticked a little, as if she was cracking her neck. Then she said, "Yeah, I know."

I interrupted her. "Can I ask where this is coming from and why it seems so urgent now?"

"Every year, when they start showing Father's Day commercials, I get this sense of urgency, like I need to get rid of him."

"Your biological father, that is?"

She snapped at me, "I don't have another father!"

"Correct."

"I just want him, his wife, and his other kids to feel all the pain I felt growing up. I want him to feel all the nights that I was hungry when we couldn't afford food or when my mother would leave me for days."

"You want to hurt your father?"

"No, I'm going to kill him." She looked dead in my eyes. There was no remorse just absolute hate.

"You understand that killing him won't take your pain away. Right?"

She ignored me and continued, "I can smell his corpse."

"You smell that now?"

"Yes." She chuckled. "I'm going to do this on Father's Day."

"This Sunday? Why is it so important to kill him then?"

"Why not?" She looked at me as if daring me to say something. Then she continued, "I'm going to go to his house."

"You know where he lives?"

"Yes. I know exactly where he lives. I sit outside his house a lot. I watch him and his wife come in and out. His kids and everyone come over for Father's Day, like he's this great fucking man."

"I thought you didn't have a car?"

She let out an irritated, quick huff. "I know how to catch the bus."

"I understand. Do you want to hurt his kids and wife too?"

"No, I just want them to witness me blowing my father's brains out."

"Do you feel like it's their fault you didn't have a relationship with your father?"

"Sometimes, but I mostly blame him. I can see the blood splatter on them. All over them. They're going to cry." She imitated her siblings. "'Daddy! Daddy!'"

Before I could speak she leaned forward in her seat. "I hate to hear someone say, 'Daddy.' I hate it. I think it's selfish and mean and inconsiderate," she said as she cringed.

"Why do you think that?"

Her eyes narrowed. "Everyone doesn't have a daddy."

The inflection in her voice gave me frightening chills as if she were attacking me personally. I was afraid for this man and his family, but I had to keep talking to get as much information as possible to turn over to authorities. This woman needed intensive inpatient treatment.

"What's your father's name?"

"Asshole."

"OK, so do you think it would be better if you gave me Asshole's number and I call him and ask if he'd be willing to talk to you? That way, you can express some of the things you felt growing up and he can tell his side of the story."

"Fuck his side of the story, Ayana. He left me to die and I want him to die too."

"Do you think he knew everything you were going through?"

She huffed like I was irritating her. "Don't you get it? He didn't care. He knew that my grandma ain't have no money. He knew it was a bunch of people in and out of my grandma's house. He knew my mama ain't care about nobody but herself. He just didn't care. All he cared about was that nobody knew I was his child."

"I'm sure that really hurt."

"Say something else. You say that all the time."

My neck snapped back. Margo was definitely experiencing a manic rage. I had to contact the authorities fast, before she really harmed someone.

She continued as if she hadn't insulted me. "After I shoot him, I'm going to walk over to him and make sure he's gone. Then I'll go out and sit on the steps with my arms up and wait for the police."

"Seeing your father dead is worth more than your freedom."

"No such thing as freedom when you've been through what I've been through."

I said, "I understand."

We talked to the end of the session and nothing I said could change her mind. I knew that I would have to call 911 once she was gone, because I also had to protect myself. Because I had no way of contacting this man, I started to go against my better judgment and call while she was still in the office. When we were done, I walked her out to the car picking her up. I took down the tag number and called the service, making them aware that I needed to have her restrained by authorities. Then I called 911 and explained to them exactly what she had told me and my professional opinion. It would be best if they picked her up and took her to an inpatient program.

I called the car service and had them confirm the location at which she would be dropped off. The cops headed directly there. They called to let me know they had taken her to the hospital for psychological evaluation. It all happened in the space of an hour. I was so ready to go home.

Instead of waiting for the psychiatrist on call to contact me, I called the hospital as I headed home. I was told that she hadn't been evaluated yet but that they would keep me in the loop. I advised them to admit her into an extensive care program. Margo needed more help than I could give her.

With all that had gone down, I hadn't spoken to Cam all evening. When he answered, I asked, "What did you eat for dinner?"

"Chick-fil-A."

"Aw, honey. You eat Chick-fil-A every night."

"Yup."

"Is that what you fed Caron?"

He cleared his throat. "Nah, I didn't pick up Caron today."

"Why?"

"I'm not completely sure but we'll talk when you get home."

I was a little confused, but I could have sworn I heard a bit of sadness in his voice. I didn't pry too much. I knew that whatever it was, he'd rather have the conversation in person. I said, "OK, baby. I'll see you soon."

When I pulled up to the house, I noticed the exterior lights were off. Cameron always left the lights on. They showed the house's beauty. That was strange. I pulled into the garage and sat in the car for a minute. I had to meditate because I wasn't sure what was going on and I wanted to be free and open to hear him. My work drama was likely to overpower anything he had to say, so I told myself I wasn't going to discuss Margo's situation.

When I walked into the house, I called out for him. Since I'd moved my living room furniture into his family room, he was often in there watching TV when I got home. But then he said, "I'm in the room."

I took off my shoes and headed upstairs. My heart sank deeper and deeper as I reached the top. Walking into the bedroom I said, "Honey..."

He was lying on the bed in the dark.

"Are you OK?"

"Yasmin got the court order today."

"OK..." I said hesitantly.

"No one has seen or heard from her or Caron since."

"Do you think she would hurt him?"

"To be perfectly honest, I don't know what she would do right now. She's not in a good place. I really don't think she'd leave her clients and all, but I just don't know. At this point, we will have to wait and see."

I sat on the bed beside him and gave him a half-hug. "I'm sorry. I'm so sorry all this is happening. You don't deserve this."

"Yeah. I know, but that still doesn't change things."

"Are you regretting the restraining order?"

He shrugged.

"Do you feel like I made you do something you didn't want to do?"

"No, because the stunt she pulled at your place was unacceptable. I'm finally on the path I've been trying to get to my entire career. I've got a partner that I've been searching for and now she wants to act plumb crazy. The only thing I regret right now is ever meeting her. Caron deserves a better mother."

"You can't change who his mother is. Right now we just need to make sure he's OK. Where is most of her family?"

"They're in Atlanta. I checked with her god-sister and she hadn't heard from her. Her friends at the shop described it like she snapped. I'm just worried about Caron."

"I don't think she would hurt him. Do you?"

"Right now I'm starting to think that she would do anything to hurt me. And she knows he's the only way she can hurt me."

I lay down beside him and rubbed his back. There was no point in talking. We needed to sit in silence and reflect on all that was occurring. Would this be happening if I weren't in the picture? I don't believe either of us slept that night. I tossed and turned, thinking about Margo and

Yasmin. I could hear Cameron breathing heavily, but we remained silent.

We woke up to his phone ringing. He quickly picked up and hopped out of bed. "Yasmin," he said.

My heart dropped because I wasn't sure what she was saying and I didn't want to be all up in his face. I felt that I should fall back and let him handle it. I walked out of the bedroom and paced back and forth in the upstairs hallway.

"Yasmin, I didn't get a restraining order because I hate you. But you've been making my life miserable. I don't like things like this either, but you're unreasonable."

She was more than unreasonable, I thought.

"Where are you? Where is Caron?"

I could tell that she wasn't revealing any of that, but I was confused about why she'd called. If she didn't want him to know anything, why contact him at all? I think she wanted to hear his voice and needed to see if there was a chance her disappearance made him vulnerable. Suddenly, Cam's voice got louder and he shouted, "Yasmin! Yasmin! Bring my son home now!"

After she hung up, he stormed out of the room with the phone at his side. I assumed he had hung up and I just watched him. "Cam, sit down, baby. She's not going to hurt him. Just give her a little space right now while she figures this all out. I'll be moving into the condo soon and things will get better."

He leaned over and kissed me. "Everything is going to be OK," I said. "It will all be back to normal shortly."

He laughed. "You trying to break up with me?"

"No, but I think things will get better once I move into my place."

"Ayana, I'm not in a rush for you to move. I like you being here. Moving to the condo ain't going to change Yasmin."

"It might. She just wants to know there is hope for you and her. She feels hopeless."

"And she can't handle that the person I'm with is you. She'd prefer it to be some knucklehead woman that's going to stoop down to her level. You're above catfights and she knows it. You're respected by every woman in the A. It's just hard for her to get over that."

"I'm starting to get a short fuse."

He laughed. "Don't get a short fuse now."

He was so handsome even in the morning. I asked, "Why?"

Ignoring my question, he said, "I've been thinking."

"What?"

"Never mind. Just forget it."

ayana

It had been nearly a month since Cameron had seen Yasmin or Caron. I felt like he was slipping into a slight depression, but he pretended to be upbeat. He'd hired a new lawyer to handle his custody battle and was hoping to get custody of Caron. Yasmin called a few times a week to let him talk to his son, but no one knew where she was and she always called from different numbers.

My condo was finally finished and ready for me to move in. Cameron and I had gotten so comfortable living together. A part of me felt that I should move to the condo, but then there was the part that wanted to see Cameron every day. I rationalized that every good relationship needed a break.

We were headed out to dinner one night and I spent a really long time in the shower, thinking about how much I loved Cam's house and how much I was going to miss coming home to him.

When I stepped out of the shower Cam was sitting on the side of the soaking tub. He had all his clothes on and was staring at me as if it were the first time he'd ever seen me. I looked back at him, confused. He said, "Ayana, I had planned to tell you something while we were out to dinner, but the longer you stayed in the shower, the more anxious I got."

Hesitantly, I said, "What?"

"This has been the best three months of my life. Even with all the other background noise. You're so level-headed and beautiful and understanding. I just don't know how I could live the rest of my life without you."

I said, "Awwww."

He pulled a jewelry box out of his pocket, and I couldn't believe my eyes. Still, I was thinking maybe earrings or a necklace. He opened the box and a big diamond ring shone my way.

"Will you marry me?"

I stood there in shock, unable to speak for several seconds, and finally I nodded. "Of course I will marry you, Cameron Small."

I truly believed that it took longer than ninety days to really get to know someone, but Cameron proved my belief to be wrong because I felt that I knew the real Cameron Small and not just his representative. I had all these rules of thumb when it came to relationships. But this one had taught me that sometimes you just had to go with it. I really couldn't imagine there was anyone more compatible with me in Atlanta.

He hugged me and my towel dropped to the floor. He whispered in my ear, "You still wanna go out to celebrate or do you want to celebrate here?"

"I want to do both."

He unbuckled his pants while I unbuttoned his shirt. We kissed passionately and I was glad that he was a man who knew what he wanted and wasn't about games. He was all that I thought a man should be. Provider. Leader. Lover. And he was mine. I pulled his shirt off as he stepped out of his pants. He carried me over to the bed and slowly entered me. Gently he thrust himself in and out while holding my legs up, giving me long, wet kisses while he loved me. "Ooh." I sighed.

It was slow and passionate as he whispered words of commitment in my ear. He wanted to feel me forever. He never wanted to lose me. He wanted me to be the mother of his children. He belonged to me. Tears rolled from the corners of my eyes, because this was real and I knew it.

Cam and I had a small ceremony at our house four weeks after the engagement. It was something we felt compelled to do. I was no spring chicken and we both wanted to start a family. We had concluded that we could spend a year planning a fabulous wedding for everybody else or we could just have Cam's pastor come over and have an intimate ceremony with my parents, his mother, our sisters, and our close friends. It was exactly what it needed to be. The energy in the room was perfect. There was no question that everyone in the room was cheering for us and wanted us to win. I think it's so important to make that step with people you know are in your corner. The wrong energy can destroy the right connection any day of the week.

I knew it bothered Cam that Caron wasn't there. When we exchanged vows I added a section about committing to his son and tears came to his eyes. There had been many nights when he'd go into himself and I knew those were the times he thought he'd never see Caron again. As time flew by Yasmin seemed to have left without a trace. We often prayed together that God would touch her evil heart and make her come back to Atlanta. In the meantime, we had no choice but to go on with our lives.

After the ceremony, a caterer came in to serve brunch, and my nieces ran through the house like it was a playground. I was so happy and Cameron appeared happy too. Quentin had his chest stuck out, telling the story of how he'd known we were compatible. He'd known that we would have an instant connection—he'd been so sure, he claimed he hadn't told me just to see if it would come naturally.

Everyone stayed around for a few hours afterward. It wasn't exactly how I'd imagined my wedding to be but I was content. After my parents and the minister left, we had sunset cocktails on our brick patio. We gave all our friends a chance to make a toast. I think that when two people fall in love and get married really fast, their close friends often feel left out of the process and are reluctant to accept everything. My friends are very important to me and I wanted to give them all a chance to say how this union made them feel. The general consensus was that everyone thought we had great chemistry and there was no way we could have ignored what was between us! It felt good to have that support. Aaliyah brought everyone to tears when she spoke.

"Anyone that knows me knows that my sister and I are inseparable and I love her so much. I know her so well and when I met Cam, I knew he was special. I felt like he would take care of my sister. She is my life partner and when you share that closeness with someone you want to be sure the person they dedicate their life to will love and protect them." She turned to Cam. "I trust you. I respect you and I think you've made an awesome woman your wife."

We clapped and sipped champagne. We talked into the night and cooked on the grill. It appeared as if we were going to have an adult slumber party, but close to eleven everyone began packing up and rolling out.

The caterers stayed and cleaned up. Cam and I sat in the family room reflecting on our day. It would have been easy to make it an all-out star-studded event, but this had been more personal. We planned to do an African safari vacation for our first anniversary. He didn't want to leave the country until we found Caron.

yasmin

I was reading one of the Atlanta celebrity gossip blogs and I thought I would drop dead when I saw "Atlanta Real Estate Mogul and *Girlfriend Confidential* Host Wed over the Weekend." All the resentment in me wanted to spill out and strangle them. What made him think she was the one? I sabotaged the blog with a bunch of negative comments about her. I logged in with different names to comment on my comments. I wanted everyone to know that he was still married when they'd started seeing each other. I made false accusations about his being on the verge of bankruptcy and marrying her for the money.

It fueled my frenzy when other people began to comment and give their opinions about the short courtship. Women hate women who steal husbands and I wanted to destroy her. I wanted to destroy them. They were treating me like a null factor. I continued to make more shit up. Real love doesn't just happen overnight. He should have been worried about his son's whereabouts. Instead he was marrying someone else. I didn't know who they thought they were.

Moving to North Carolina had been a bad idea, but my purpose had been to have Cam run after me. Instead he'd fucking gone off and jumped the damn broom. What type of shit was that? I wasn't going to take this lying down and I needed Cam to know it.

I called him and there was no answer. He usually picked up on the first ring. How could he just pretend that his life was fine? How could he just go on and forget that he had a son?

I called Casey and Tayshawn. I expected them to unload all the drama on me. Instead they seemed really concerned, wondering if I was OK after hearing the news. I told them that I was fine but that it was time to return to the A with a vengeance. I'd been lying down way too long. I wasn't sure I'd ever win Cam back but I was certainly going to fight for more child support. If I couldn't have his heart, I would settle for his pockets.

Tayshawn asked, "When you coming back?"

"Maybe today."

"Do you have any clients up there?"

"No, I just came here to get my mind right. Caron is in day camp but I may just come back for a few days. You know, whichever way the wind blows."

"You be careful, I was concerned about you," Tayshawn said.

Casey added, "There have been several summonses that have come here for you."

"Fuck those summonses."

"Yeah, but they come like every week."

"That's cool because I want to go to court now."

"Really?" Casey asked.

"Yeah, I want more money. How about that?"

"Oh and yeah, I heard they have a mansion in Alpharetta."

That struck me right in the jaw and left me speechless. Cam and I had always said that when things really turned over we were going to purchase a home there. It's as if we broke up one month and the next month he was nearly a millionaire. He had several major deals come through, after all those years. And I'd been sitting back being the cheerleader. All of a sudden, when I got tired, he blew up. He got labeled Celebrity Realtor. What about me? I didn't get it. How could my luck be so bad? His success was partially because of me.

I was running around the little extended-stay place we were living in, packing up our belongings. When I was done, I picked Caron up from camp.

"Guess what, baby? We're going back to Atlanta."

He nodded but didn't respond. "Aren't you happy?" I asked.

"I'm good."

I was surprised that he didn't ask if he could see his father. He'd asked about him nearly every day for the first two weeks we were gone. I was so glad that had ended.

We stopped to have a bite to eat before getting on the road and Caron almost seemed depressed. I'd thought going back to Atlanta would be fun for him.

"Are you OK?"

"I didn't say goodbye to my friends."

"I'm sorry, honey. It's going to be OK."

His head hung. "That's what you said the last time."

I had to ignore his overemotional response, because I had a lot going on in my head. My ex-husband had just upgraded. Everything I'd done to get his attention had backfired on me. I was hurt and angry. I felt like an outsider looking in on my own life. I felt as if one mistake had spun my life out of control and the loser I'd left Cameron for hadn't even been worth it. Now I lay down each night and tried to force time to rewind, but it didn't. How does one mistake mess up everything?

My heart was on fire and my body was trembling. I didn't know if I should stay or go back. I was confused and stressed. I felt like a fool going back to Atlanta after disappearing. As I drove down the highway, I looked over at Caron and he was crying.

Was I transferring my emotions to him? I felt bad that he was caught in the middle, but I didn't know how to fix it. I wanted to make things right but wasn't sure how. The first thing I planned to do was visit my therapist. There was no way I could handle this all alone.

When I pulled up to my house, there were certified letter notifications stuffed in my mailbox and a bunch of summonses. We walked into the house through the garage and the heat smothered us. Caron said, "It's like an oven in here."

"Yeah, baby, we haven't been home in forever. The air hasn't been on."

When he came into the house, he smiled for the first time all that day. He was happy to be back in his house and I felt bad that I had taken him away. I wasn't sure if I should call Cam and tell him we were home or wait until the morning. I was sure he'd be happy to see Caron. I turned on the AC and sat in the kitchen. I didn't know when it would be appropriate to start calling my clients and letting them know that I had returned.

I told Caron to come snuggle with me and watch TV. He grabbed a blanket from the ottoman and lay beside me. He looked into my eyes and said, "Mommy, it's going to be OK."

"Thank you, baby."

We had gotten really close over the last month. I was glad that we'd had the opportunity. Without any distraction from Cameron, we were able to really build a bond that we'd never had before. He was a daddy's boy from the second he was born. I'd gotten readmitted to the hospital because I kept having a fever. They discovered that some of the afterbirth had been left inside me. I was in the hospital for nearly two weeks after Cam and Caron went home. Caron connected with Cam as if he were the mother and that closeness stayed. I was always fighting for that closeness, hoping that one day he'd cry for me the same way he always cried for his father.

When Cam had said he wanted to move on, I didn't know what else to do but take the one thing I owned from that relationship and run. There were nights that I regretted it but mainly I was happy with my decision, because this was the end result—a son who loved me unconditionally. A son who could tap into my feelings and know just what to say to make me feel better. I wouldn't have traded that for anything in the world.

I began going through the stack in my mailbox. I paid all my bills online so I was up to date and pretty much tossed those to the side. I was most interested in the court papers. *Small v. Small.* I quickly scanned the document. Cameron had filed for full custody. The thought angered me. What made him think that he was a better parent than me? Caron hadn't even met his new wife, so how the hell did he think he was going to steal my baby and give him a new mother? I was the only mother he needed. If Cam didn't want to be with me, he didn't deserve to be with Caron, plain and simple.

I sat up on the couch and Caron looked at me. He said, "What's wrong, Mommy?"

I paced the floor. I wanted the morning to hurry up, because there was so much business I needed to handle. The deadline to counter-file had passed. We were scheduled for court in two weeks. I was so unprepared. I wondered if I should return to work or lie low for the next two weeks.

ayana

Despite not having spoken to Yasmin, we showed up to court ready to fight for Caron. When we arrived, I was shocked to see her. She looked gorgeous with a pretty smile and long flowing hair. She was caramel brown and looked almost angelic, which was nothing like the terror I'd imagined all these months. I actually couldn't believe my eyes. She could easily find another man. Why was she so committed to getting Cam back?

She tried to explain her disappearance, saying that she was the best parent in the situation, but Cam's attorney tore her out of the frame. And just like that I became a wife and a stepmom in less than thirty days. I knew how important getting his son was for Cameron, but I was really excited and nervous at the same time. While I counseled people about blended families, I really wasn't sure that I was totally prepared for this. Not to mention that Caron and I had never met. I was scared, but I was open to the challenge. Cam seemed like a really good father and I wanted to support him. The judge granted Cam full custody and visitation for Yasmin every other weekend. He also appointed psychiatric help for her. Yasmin claimed she was already seeing someone, but the judge told her the therapist had to be someone he referred. She looked pissed, but I was happy he'd done that. Every therapist is not equipped to help everyone.

She would have to turn Caron over within two weeks. Cam cried at the verdict and I was so happy for him. After listening to Yasmin speak, our attorney said, "You should have never been with her."

"I know," Cam replied.

For some reason, he didn't say it with enough confidence to make me believe he believed it. We had to wait for the clerk to print out our court documents and Yasmin followed us to the clerk's office.

She called his name in an argumentative fashion. "Cam. Cam."

Our attorney advised him not to answer, so he didn't. She walked behind him and pushed him. "Cam, I know you hear me."

He turned around and shouted, "What?"

She looked like she was burning with pain when she said, "What kind of man takes a child from his mother? I never thought you'd be such a sorry motherfucker!" She turned to me. "And you! Your day will come. You fucking take my husband away from his family and now you want my child too? Bitch, you can't have your own kids?"

I sympathized with her, but I knew she wasn't in her right mind and I wouldn't be able to reason with her. She had a broken heart, but I hadn't caused it. I wished she knew how to let go, but letting go is so much harder when you carry guilt. Our attorney pulled Cam to the side. "Don't get into a shouting match with her. Let's go."

We turned around and kept walking. Then we heard a screech, almost as if someone had stabbed her. "Please," she cried. "Don't turn your back on me, Cam."

I could see that ignoring her was upsetting Cam. Speaking to the attorney, I said, "He may need to go back and talk to her."

"I don't think it's a good idea."

Just as we were debating what should be done next, security guards surrounded and restrained her. My heart went out to this woman. She noticed me staring at her and cried, "Girl power. Girl power. You're a fucking hypocrite, Ayana Blue. You steal my man and my baby!"

I hated that she blamed me for all her problems. I knew I couldn't fix an imaginary gripe, but I wanted to sit her down and let her know that I hadn't stolen her husband or her child. It was a sad scenario, and so many nights I wondered how I'd gotten involved in this complex relationship. God could have let me fall in love with any man in the world, but it had been Cam and all his drama. Maybe I had a purpose here. I didn't know.

Yasmin was restrained until we got on the elevator. Cam was the type of man who hated to hurt people and I could see the pain in his face. I told him to let me know when he was ready to talk, then stayed silent until he did so. He asked if I wanted to go to breakfast and I agreed.

He didn't mention Yasmin or the verdict until we sat at the table. When he spoke, I already knew what he was thinking. "I'm happy but it's hard to see her like that."

"I know. It was hard for me too. It really upset me when she said I'm a hypocrite because I do believe in girl power, but I don't believe women should use their power to be manipulative."

He reached across the table and held my hands. "That's why I had to make you mine. You don't think like most women. You have your own philosophy. I think every woman in the world needs to hear what you have to say."

"Yeah, but sometimes it's discouraging because it's only the women who want better that will read my books. All the others think that what they're doing works. It actually hurts when I see women in the way of their own happiness. Staying stuck in a situation or absorbed in regret. It will tear you apart and you'll spend months and years angry, instead of just letting go."

"Right, and I would have never tried to get custody of Caron if she hadn't tried that disappearing shit. I can't have my son in an unstable situation."

"Honestly, none of it is healthy. You know you don't want to strip a child from his mother, but you don't want a bunch of inconsistency either. It's just so hard."

He nodded. I knew this was hard for him. It had to be challenging to see someone you had once loved and thought you'd spend the rest of your life with acting like a crazy person.

After breakfast we went furniture shopping. We'd been

slowly decorating the house. We'd had an interior designer come in and we were pretty much done with the first level. A lot of the pieces and art had yet to come but when it did, the house was going to be fabulous. We were moving my living room furniture from the family room into the study. The sixty-five-inch flat-screen TV was going into the man cave in the basement, so Cameron wanted to find another one. He was so obsessed with electronics it drove me crazy.

We went to a kids' furniture store to buy Caron's bedroom set. When we got there, I started to feel like this would be too much change and I said, "Cam, maybe we should just move his furniture from your town house?"

"Nah, I plan to keep that place for times that I may want to crash there."

"That's cool, but if Caron will be in school out there, you'll have no reason to stick around in Atlanta until late."

"Yeah, maybe, but I still want to get him something new."

"This is my professional opinion, not something I'm pulling out of a hat. I think that would be too much change for him. A new house. A new woman in his life. A new bedroom set."

Cam looked at me like I was a lunatic for saying these things. "Are you fucking kidding me?" he asked.

Up until this point, Cam had never spoken a harsh word to me. I was shocked and didn't know how to respond. I wasn't sure I *should* respond, because clearly he was tripping.

My bottom lip sat paralyzed for a second waiting for an apology, but he just shook his head. I turned around and walked to the car. I sat there waiting for him to come out. I understood that he was also dealing with the pressure associated with the change and wondered how all this would work. I was sure he had a bunch of worries and concerns that he wasn't capable of expressing, but there was no need to take it out on me. Still, when he came out of the store, he didn't have an apologetic expression. He said, "Let's go."

I sat in the car with folded arms. I didn't want to be bothered. Here I was taking the only morning I had in the office to be there for him and he snapped at my professional opinion. *Cool. Don't ask me shit else!* My mind was racing and regretting and reconciling. Then I told myself there was no need for all this. The first altercation or harsh words in a relationship were probably the hardest to deal with. I worked with couples every day and knew they all fussed and fought, but it didn't feel good coming from my Prince Charming.

I stared out the window, hoping to soak up some wisdom from the sun. The longer we were silent, the more questions swirled through my brain. Finally he reached over and put his hand on my thigh. "I'm sorry. I shouldn't have taken my frustration out on you. I'm really excited about getting Caron and I just want him to have a fresh start. Everything new."

I nodded. That is where most parents make their mistake. When kids have a major transition, the last thing you want them to do is have everything new. They need to have something familiar.

"I know how you feel. I was just offering my professional opinion."

"But I didn't ask for your professional opinion. I want to buy something nice for my son. I can afford it. What's the problem?"

"No problem," I said absolutely.

I was done with it. He wasn't paying me for my professional opinion so I was going to keep my mouth shut.

We didn't talk for the rest of the ride to the radio station. When he pulled up, he said, "I'll be back to pick you up. I have to go settle everything with that land auction and I'll be back."

"If you're not done in time, Aaliyah can pick me up."

"I've already won the auction. I just have to hook up with my investors to pay it off. No longer than a few hours."

I still had an attitude, so I shrugged. *Whatever.* I'd rather ride in the car with my sister than deal with his nasty disposition. I set one foot out of the car and he grabbed my arm. "Love you, hear?"

I smirked. "Yeah, love you too."

"Give me a kiss," he said, leaning toward me.

I gave him a peck and got out of the car. All my wisdom was telling me not to be upset, but I couldn't resist it. I walked into the station and saw Quentin and he could tell something was wrong. From the day I'd met Cameron I had been beaming, and today there was a dark

cloud over me. I questioned everything. I'd initially believed Cam's ex-wife was the primary issue, but here his
son hadn't even moved in yet and I was being confronted
with the biological parent overprotection issue.

In most blended families, the biological parent over-
protects the child, forcing the stepparent to feel like an
outsider. I had thought Cam was too rational for that, and
I prayed for this to be a one-time occurrence, but a large
part of me knew it wasn't. I knew I was in for a wild ride.

Quentin said, "Are you OK?"

I nodded. "Yeah, what's up?"

"What happened today?"

"Why?"

"We're getting a bunch of messages about you guys
getting custody of Caron."

I took a deep breath. "What do you mean, messages?"

"A bunch of listeners want you to discuss how you can
be a girl's girl and take this woman's child away."

"Quentin, please tell me you're lying."

He looked me dead in the eyes and said, "Ayana, I'm
not. I don't know what else to do. I think you're going to
have to address it."

"Why?"

"Your followers want to know and you have to address it."

If Cam and I had been in good spirits, I would have felt
better, but instead I wanted to throw my hands up and
say, "Fuck it." I had no idea how I was going to broach
the subject.

When I opened up, I said, "Good afternoon. I promised not to discuss my relationship on air, but today I think it's important for me to clear things up. I met my husband, Cameron Small, nearly four months ago. And we've been married now for three weeks. He and his ex-wife were in a custody battle before I met him. I am merely supporting him. I have no intention of taking anyone's child. I believe that children should have a healthy relationship with both parents. If at all possible, I think parents should try to make it work for the children. And if that isn't possible, I feel that both parents need to work hard at making the breakup as seamless as they can."

Phone calls began to come through, and I wanted to be sure I answered each question with absolute compassion and as politically correctly as possible. This girl was crazy and she was out to ruin me. I was thinking I'd made a big mistake.

Some women called with complete support and others defamed my character. It was a pleasure to hear my best friend Mandy's voice. She said, "Ayana . . . honey."

The second I heard her voice, I could feel her arms telepathically surrounding me and my emotions welled up. "Is that you, Mandy?"

"Yes, Ayana. I'm just calling to say I don't know who started these rumors, but I'm calling to tell all your listeners that you are the most committed person I know and even if it's to your own detriment you are going to do what's right. I will go to my grave defending you because you are girl power. You are truly every woman's best friend and that is not a role. That is real. I love you. Keep your head up."

I said, "Thank you, Mandy. For all of you wondering, that is my best friend Mandy from Martini Mondays."

The power of a best friend can't be compared with anything. I would have broken down if I hadn't had my sister and my friends. At the end of the day, whether this marriage was a bad decision or not, they were going to be there. Several of my friends had sent text messages inviting me for drinks. My girls were slowly cheering me up. My real listeners were down for me too. I gave it to God. He knew one way or the other what was best for me.

As soon as I got off the air, I walked into the lobby and Aaliyah was there. She said, "You OK, Sister?"

"Yeah, you didn't tell Ma, did you?"

"Nah. I didn't tell anyone. As soon as I heard your intro, I dropped the girls off to Mom and headed right down here. I knew you were hurt; I could hear it in your voice."

I hugged her. "Thanks, Sister."

"You know I'm here for you."

"Yeah, I know. I just had a really rough morning, and to come in here and deal with this . . . it just threw me."

She laughed. "Yeah, but you're strong. This too shall pass."

"Yeah, after I get a divorce."

Her neck snapped back. "Ayana, nooooooo."

I gave her the no-bullshit look. She said, "Wait, Cameron is a good guy and you know it. I'm certainly convinced."

"Why are you so convinced?"

"When you first started seeing him, I asked anybody who was somebody about him and all I heard were good things. This is just an obstacle."

I told her about how he'd snapped about the furniture. She said, "Honey, all men snap when they're under pressure. You just have to gauge when you should or shouldn't challenge them." I laughed and she shook her head. "I think a wise psychologist told me that."

"Theory is one thing. Reality is completely different."

"Yeah, but the advantage that you have is that you know all of this. You just have to put it into play. Imagine all the women out here like me who have to figure it out for themselves. Some people learn a day late and a dollar short of a good guy."

As we walked out of the station, I noticed Cam parked outside waiting for me. Aaliyah said, "Go talk to your man, girl. I just came here to have your back."

"Thanks, Sister."

Aaliyah walked to the car with me to speak to Cam. He jumped out of the car smiling. He hugged Aaliyah. Cam joked, "Y'all are definitely a package deal. You upset one then you gotta deal with the other, huh?"

Aaliyah laughed. "Yeah, ask Stan. He'll tell you. When I'm mad, she is too, and vice versa. So don't play with us, Cam."

He ran his hand down my face. He was speaking to

Aaliyah, but didn't take his eyes off me. "I'm not. I know your sister is a blessing and I respect that."

"And get that wild animal in check before I have to put her in the zoo."

"You got it."

He pulled me to him and hugged me tight. He whispered in my ear, "I will never hurt you. OK?"

"Yeah, I know."

Aaliyah said, "A'ight, y'all. Ayana, call me if you need me."

Cam gave Aaliyah a handshake. "I love it," he said, smiling.

I gave Aaliyah a hug and she got in her car and drove off, leaving Cam and me in the parking lot alone.

He said, "Let's go home and have a quiet evening alone."

When we got there, away from all the noise and negativity, I didn't question why I was with him. In fact, I couldn't imagine being without him. He held me until it was all better and I was more than prepared to battle the haters.

yasmin

In a million years, I would never have imagined that Cam would turn out to be this much of an asshole. I felt like he wasn't the man I'd known. I refused to pack any of Caron's clothes. I didn't give a damn whether Cam had bought them. Since I wasn't voluntarily giving him up, I didn't think it was fair. If they wanted him, let them restock his wardrobe and everything else. I let him put a few toys in his backpack only because he pleaded. I tried to assure him that he was only going for the summer.

"Now that Dad is married again, does that mean I have a new mommy?" he asked.

I pressed hard on the brakes and looked at him. "Hell no! I'm your only mother. You hear me?"

He nodded his head and I repeated, "You hear me?"

"Yes, Mommy."

The thought that he would be living with another woman brought tears to my eyes. "You OK?" he asked.

"Listen, Caron. I am your mommy and I love you. Nobody can replace me. Nobody."

"Yes, Mommy."

"And you call her Ms. Ayana. Don't ever call her Mommy and nothing like Mommy. OK?"

"You think she's nice?"

I ignored him because I didn't think it was healthy for me to tell him what I thought of her. I figured I should let him make his own determination. One thing I knew for sure was that Cam loved Caron without limit and wouldn't let anyone harm him. So I wasn't necessarily worried about that.

What bothered me most about the situation was that in thirty days my child support would cease. Plus, Caron was my primary hold on Cam and if he took my baby and swept him up into his own little world with his new wife, I would just be background noise. A part of me wanted Ayana to be good to my baby, but another part of me wanted Caron to hate her. I was torn about whether I should plant seeds to make him hate her or not.

I pulled into the police station. Cam and Ayana were already sitting in the lot. My heart sank and I suddenly hit the brakes before turning into a parking space. Anxiety smothered me and my heart started beating faster. I began taking deep breaths to calm myself. Then anger crept in. I wanted to jump out of the car and start swinging a bat at both Cam and Ayana. They were out to hurt me. It wasn't fair. I didn't understand. The sheriff told them to stay back as he approached me.

I finally stepped out of the car. "So what, you're just going to pull him out of the car and give him to these thieves?"

"We're hoping to do this in a peaceful fashion, miss," the sheriff said.

Caron opened his car door, excited to see Cam because it had been months. My eyes shot to Caron. "Didn't I tell you to stay in the car?"

"But I thought you said—"

"Caron, close that door."

He sat back and the sheriff touched my shoulder nicely. "I know this is hard. It's hard for any mother. But look at it like this: it's America, you can always appeal a decision and change things. But today, we are going to hand him over to Mr. and Mrs. Small."

He spoke very gently and kindly to me. He looked in my eyes and made me feel respected, as if he understood, not like everyone else in the situation who had treated me like the dirty gum on the ground.

"You think it's a possibility I can get my son back?"

He touched my shoulder again. "It's a long process but you have to keep fighting. You ready?"

I nodded.

"Does he have any luggage or other personal belongings?"

"No, sir, just what he has on and a backpack."

He didn't question why that was and I wondered if it was typical with parents forced to hand over their children. I walked to the passenger-side back door and opened it. Caron peeped his head out with a big cheesy grin. My eyes filled up. He said, "Mommy, it's OK. I'm coming back."

I nodded. I had made him think this was temporary but to be perfectly honest, I wasn't sure. Cam had married his quack psychologist and I was certain she could find a bunch of her colleagues to prove that I wasn't mentally stable. This whole situation had me feeling dizzy and helpless, like I wasn't protected by the court system.

The sheriff said, "Say bye."

Caron sprinted to Cam. "Daddy!"

Cam picked him up and swung him around and Caron laughed loudly. I stood there staring at Ayana, who was smiling at Caron and Cam. I thought about yanking her weave out but I knew I'd be locked up and I wasn't down for that. The sheriff went over to them and said something and they got back into the car and pulled out of the parking lot, leaving me standing there with tears streaming down my face.

The sheriff noticed that I was paralyzed and walked back in my direction. "That's your only?" I nodded as my lips trembled. "It'll be OK. You submitted your appeal yet?" I shook my head. "Make sure you do that ASAP."

As he headed back into the building, I said, "Hey, can I ask you a question?"

He turned. "Yes, you need my phone number."

I laughed at his flirtation. "Nah, actually I wanted to know if you think I should change attorneys for the appeal."

He shrugged. "I'm not sure. It all depends on what judge you get on a particular day. It's a gamble, but one worth taking."

"Thanks."

He handed me his card and said, "If you have any questions, just let me know."

We both started laughing because he was clearly coming on to me. I looked at the card while I sat in my car. He was rather attractive and I had been so caught up in handing Caron over that I'd pretty much ignored his advances, but as I played the tape back in my mind, it was obvious that he was interested.

I went to work afterward and when I walked in, there were flowers at my station. Momentarily I imagined it was the sheriff but that would have been too fast. I quickly yanked the card out and they were from Tayshawn.

I looked over at him and smiled. "You love me, don't you?"

"Of course I do."

"I love you too, boo," I said as I hugged him.

"Yeah," he said, "I'm just glad you're back in the A. I sure missed your crazy ass."

"I missed you too."

Tayshawn didn't even mention my having to give up Caron. He knew this was the day, but he also knew that it would hurt too bad to talk about it. You can't buy a friend like that.

ayana

Caron was a charming little boy and seemed to adjust almost instantly. I knew it was a temporary adaptation. He would shortly begin to wonder if this arrangement was permanent and why his normal routine was being interrupted. While the common saying that kids are resilient is true, they also fail to interpret situations on an adult level, which often leads to the wrong interpretation. Then they get older and their childhood interpretations result in negative behavior. I tried to tell Cam that it was important that we explain everything to Caron.

Cam immediately disputed my thoughts. He told me that I might be a psychology expert but he was the expert in Caron. It was clear that was his opinion and it wasn't going to change. It was unfortunate that he refused to listen to someone with all the knowledge in the situation. I wondered if he'd ever listen to me when it came to Caron. I wasn't sure, but what I was positive about was that I wouldn't lose any sleep over it. I didn't plan on arguing with him daily about what I knew to be right.

After we picked Caron up, we headed to Cam's house

in Buckhead to pack up some of his things. When we got out of the car, Caron asked, "Do you live here now too?"

I looked at Cam to see if he was going to tell Caron now that we had a new home. Cam just smiled.

"We'll all be living together, but not in this house," I said uncomfortably.

"In the house my mommy lives in?"

Cam finally rescued me and said, "No, remember I told you we were going to get a new house with a basketball court?"

Caron squinted and pretended to be thinking hard. "Yeah, I think so."

"Well, that's where we'll all be living."

"Cool," Caron said excitedly.

It concerned me that Cam didn't want to tackle real issues with Caron. He just wanted Caron to be ecstatic about moving in with him, because the first thing he mentioned about the new house was the basketball court. His approach made me uncomfortable.

We all walked into the house. You could almost tell that Cam hadn't been there since the last time he'd had Caron, which was nearly three months ago. He told Caron to pack up his games. Caron had a Wii, an Xbox, and a DS. He gathered up everything and began throwing items into a duffel bag. "Does he have clothes here?" I asked.

"A few, but I think we're going to have to go to the mall."

"Are you going to pack up what he has?"

"Yeah, I got it."

The way he responded left me feeling like he didn't want to include me in this. As if *he* was getting his son, not *we*. I felt a little betrayed, but I decided to let him soak up the joy of reuniting with Caron. I didn't want to rain on that. My lips were sealed and I wasn't going to comment about anything unless he asked. I went into Cam's office and downloaded the book that I had been working on since we met. I figured that instead of giving Cam advice, I would type my thoughts for people who cared about what I had to say. It had been weeks since I'd opened the document. After Cam proposed, I'd gotten a sixty-day extension from my publisher. It seemed like that time had flown by and I was under the gun again. As I scanned the pages and realized there were so many other topics to cover, I felt overwhelmed. I knew I would need to request another extension.

Finally they were all ready to leave with a duffel bag filled with game systems and a backpack carrying Caron's MacBook and DVDs. I only observed and wondered if Cam and Yasmin ever forced him to do anything besides what he wanted to do.

I wanted to stop by my condo to pick up mail that had been transferred. Because I had rerouted my mail to two separate addresses in the same week, a lot of my stuff was being misdirected to the condo. No one had rented the place yet and we'd subsequently dropped the price. I didn't have to pay any bills with Cameron so it wasn't killing me to pay the mortgage, but I preferred not to pay for an empty place if I didn't have to. Cam pulled up in front of the building to let me out.

I stopped in the mail room before heading up. There was nothing in the unit, but since the vandalism, I always checked to be sure nothing was wrong. When I got to the front door there was a letter taped to the door. It was from the same law firm that had left a certified slip in my mailbox. Suddenly I was confused and anxious to see what this was about. I opened the door and quickly ripped open the envelope and began to read.

It stated that I owed a property management company eighteen thousand dollars. The company was claiming that I had signed a one-year lease, stayed for two months, and never paid any rent. I assumed this was a mistake having to do with my apartment until I noticed the property was located in Charlotte, North Carolina. What the hell? I quickly dialed the attorney.

When the receptionist picked up, I immediately began explaining that there must have been a mix-up. She transferred me to an attorney. He was adamant that I had signed a lease in May and ditched the place as soon as an eviction was about to occur. I was disputing him when it dawned on me that the dates mentioned coincided with Yasmin's disappearance and return.

"I've obviously been a victim of identity theft. I have never lived or worked in North Carolina. I have no reason to sign a lease. I'm not exactly sure what this leasing company did to confirm the tenant's identification, but it obviously wasn't enough. I have no intention of paying this."

"Ms. Blue, I understand, but I hear the same thing every day. At this time, with the information we have, you have not given me any reason to believe this debt doesn't belong to you. We have every intention of continuing with the debt collection process."

I gasped. Cam was calling repeatedly on the other line. Every time he hung up he'd call right back. My head was spinning. "First of all, I need a copy of the lease and the rental application. Is it possible for you to fax it to me?"

He agreed, and I hung up the phone pissed off and wanting to strangle Yasmin. I felt like I was in a twilight zone. I stood there in my empty condo and wondered why this was all happening to me. Cam as a single entity was everything I'd ever dreamed of, but his past baggage was getting too heavy. I wanted to just drop it in hopes that all this drama would disappear if I gave him back to her. I held my phone in my hand wondering if I should call Aaliyah or Mandy. I certainly didn't want to bring all this energy into the car with Caron and Cameron, but I did want to talk about it. I'd have to censor my conversation when I got in the car with Cam. And I wasn't sure what kind of roads my mind would take if I called one of my friends. I paced back and forth, breathing deeply, meditating. My phone startled me.

"Hey, babe," I said nervously.

"Whatchu doing in there?"

"I got this letter from an attorney claiming I signed a lease to a property and didn't pay the rent. Now they are trying to sue me for an entire year's rent."

"That by itself is illegal. For them to get an entire year they would have to prove they weren't able to lease it after you left."

"The point is that I never signed this lease, Cam," I snapped.

"Yeah, baby. I got it. Don't worry. Just c'mon down. We'll call my attorney when you get here."

My heart was beating rapidly. I wanted to cry. I knew that I could prove the renter wasn't me, but why was I dealing with this? What was the purpose? I couldn't find the answers. I was agitated. I'd gone from mistress to vandalism victim to car-theft victim to child thief, and now to property squatter, in a little over three months. I wanted out. I wanted to pack up my shit and move from our sprawling estate into my fourteen-hundred-square-foot condo.

I walked out of the building. Steam was probably rising from my ears as Cam unlocked the doors. Caron smiled at me and said, "I thought you got lost."

I smiled. "Let me read the letter," Cameron said. He looked it over. "The address is in North Carolina."

"Me and Mommy went to North Carolina for a break," Caron said.

A sudden silence swept through the car. Cam had just figured out what I already knew. Yasmin had somehow stolen my identity. Cam's jaw muscle began to pop. "We'll talk when we get home."

I wanted so badly to shout, "I'm leaving!" Instead I said, "I'm pressing charges."

"You should," he said hesitantly.

"I need you to stop by my office. I have to get the fax from the attorney."

He agreed and didn't ask any questions. We drove there in silence and I imagined that Caron figured he'd said something wrong, because he played with his DS in the back of the car silently. I was preoccupied with one of his mother's crazy stunts. I wanted to be kind to him but every time I looked in the backseat, I saw her. I saw her anger. I saw her jealousy and I hated it. How was I supposed to love a child who came from a woman like that? I'd counseled many people and told them love was a choice, but as I sat there in this adverse predicament, my emotions were overpowering my intellect.

Cam pulled up in front of my office and when I opened the door, he touched my arm. "We'll get through this, I promise."

I walked into the office and there seemed to be an extra-strong eucalyptus scent. I turned on the lights and walked into my therapy room. The lights were already on. That was strange. I hadn't left the lights on and I knew for sure that the receptionist hadn't. I wondered who had been there. Then I thought maybe I *had* left the lights on. Everything was moving so rapidly, I wasn't sure of anything these days. I walked over to the fax machine and picked up the papers. The entire application had been completed in handwriting that certainly wasn't mine. My Social Security number was on there and I felt sick. I felt nauseous. Just before heading to the front door, I turned the alarm on and headed out.

A flashlight was pointed in my eyes as I lay on a gurney. Cam was standing over me. The paramedic was saying, "Ayana, can you hear me?" He kept repeating it and I was confused as to where I was and how I'd gotten here. "What's your name?"

"Ayana, Ayana Blue."

"How many fingers am I holding up?"

"Two." I looked at Cam and asked, "What's going on?"

"You fainted as you were leaving the office."

I felt overwhelmed and confused. "Wait."

One of the paramedics said, "Just relax, ma'am. We need to take your vitals."

"Cam?"

"Just calm down, Ayana."

This thing was overwhelming me and I couldn't rationalize the situation any longer. They took my pressure and checked my pulse. Everything was fine but they decided to take me into the hospital just to be safe. They claimed my heartbeat had been really faint while I was out. Good relationships don't include all this drama. Cam was a good person, but the relationship was not healthy.

Cam dropped Caron off at his older sister's house and came to the hospital with me. By the time he got there, they had done my blood work and we were waiting for the results.

He could probably see the finality in my eyes when he walked through the door. Before I could say anything, he said, "I know you didn't sign up for this and I was probably selfish to think I could have a peaceful, happy relationship."

"I don't think you're selfish to want that, but obviously you have an irrational person on your hands and I'm not sure I can do this anymore."

He stepped closer to my bedside and grabbed my hand. "I don't think it should end this way. We don't have problems. All of our problems are external to me and you."

"But they are an extension of you. She's done all of this because of you. What do you think she's going to do now that Caron is with us? She's lost you and him. Why would it end? It's only going to get worse. I don't want to wait around to see what else she's capable of."

"You're just going to throw our vows away?"

"For peace . . . yes, I am."

He leaned over and hugged me tightly. "Ayana, I really want to be with you. I want this to work, but I understand how you feel. I understand that being harassed isn't what you deserve. Let's think about our options. Maybe we can hire a private detective or file charges against her. We can't quit so fast."

"That's easy for you to say."

"No, it's not easy. It's what I feel. I don't want to lose you, especially not for an insane person."

The nurse came in to give us the results of the blood

work. She asked if I would mind Cam staying while she discussed the results and I told her I didn't.

"Well, Ms. Small, we know why you fainted."

"You do?"

"Yes, congrats are in order."

My eyebrow rose, as I was lost. Cam began to smile. I said, "Huh?"

"You're pregnant."

I could have fainted again. Instead I lay there with a baffled look on my face, wondering who was playing all these tricks on me. Why now? Why, when I'd finally made up my mind this was over? Why? I visualized banging my head against the wall. What the hell had I been thinking of? How the hell had I gotten caught up in this situation? I wanted to hide under a rock and never come back out.

The nurse said the doctor had prescribed some pre-natal vitamins. My iron and vitamin D levels were low. She suggested I get plenty of rest. I'm certain she felt polar opposite energies coming from Cam and me. He looked like God had given him an opportunity to redeem this relationship and I looked like, *You've got to be fucking kidding me*.

When she walked out, Cam's smile turned into an all-out grin. I looked at him, questions looming in my heart and mind. I was connected to this man forever, which in turn made me somehow connected to Yasmin. I lay there wondering if I would be able to sleep if I made the decision to terminate. I wasn't sure I was willing to do that. What I knew was that I wanted this lady out of my life and there was no way I could have that and have Cam's baby.

"You know there are no mistakes," he said.

I turned to face the wall away from him. I liked my life drama-free, but that was also lonely. Cam stroked my hair. "Ayana, I know this hasn't been easy for you. I take full responsibility for it though."

"You taking responsibility doesn't make the situation go away."

"I wish it did. I'm going to take care of Yasmin."

I turned to face him. "Cam, don't do anything stupid."

"I promise I have no intention of doing anything stupid. I know that I want you. I want the baby. I want us to be a family and I will not let Yasmin run my life."

His tone frightened me, as if he'd be willing to harm her. I said, "Cam, please don't do anything to hurt her."

"Ayana, people like Yas, you have to deal with them through legal channels. I've always been slightly sympathetic because she is the mother of my son, but that shit is over. You are my wife and I have to protect you against all odds."

It hurt that I wasn't happy about my pregnancy when I should have been, considering my age. I felt full and empty at the same time. Up and down, a roller coaster of emotions plagued me as I lay there preparing to be discharged.

yasmin

I was sitting in the shop drinking a cup of coffee when my cell phone rang. I was shocked to see Cam's number, knowing that I had just dropped Caron off to those thieves. I quickly answered because I didn't know what he could want.

"Yeah."

"Listen, I'm tired of talking about this. I'm just calling you to let you know that we know what you did with renting that house in North Carolina in Ayana's name."

"What the hell makes you think that I want to use that bitch's name for anything?"

"We're pressing charges."

"Haven't you guys done enough to humiliate me? I'm pressing charges too. I'm tired of you accusing me of shit I didn't do."

He laughed and it angered me. I started screaming, "I hate you! I hate you! I hate you!"

I didn't even realize that I was screaming so loudly in the shop until I looked around and saw every client staring at me like I was a crazy woman. Just as I headed out of the shop, I noticed Cam had hung up.

When I walked back in, Tayshawn shook his head. "Girl, you're going to need a restraining order against them, because they are out to get you, girl."

"You're right, Tay."

I went in my wallet and pulled out the sheriff's card. I went outside so I could speak with him privately. "Hi, Jacob, my name is Yasmin Small. We met earlier..."

I could hear his smile. "Yes, Yasmin. How are you?"

"Not so good."

"What's wrong?"

"Well, my ex called and accused me of some things and says they are going to press charges on me for something I didn't do. Can they do that?"

"They can file a civil suit if they have enough evidence."

"What if they don't?"

"They can still file a suit but they'll have to prove it and civil suits are about money. If you have no money to give them, there's nothing they can do."

"I'm so stressed out."

He said, "I'm sorry to hear that, Yasmin. I wish there was something I could do to make it better."

"Dinner and drinks is always nice."

"We'll see about that."

"As my son says, 'We'll see means no.'"

"I'm not saying no, I'm just saying I would probably be crossing professional lines."

"Oh, break the rules a little, Jacob."

He laughed. "You're funny."

"Really, I'm not. I'm just a lady dealing with a little stress and I saw a guy today that made me smile and I'm just suggesting we go out for drinks."

"A'ight, when are you free?"

"Well, I'm free pretty much any evening since I don't have my son."

His voice changed, as if he could sense my sadness. "Oh yeah, that's true."

"Yeah. Unbelievable but true."

"How about tomorrow evening?" he asked.

"It depends on what time. I'm a hairstylist and I'm usually not done until seven."

"Maybe we should do seven thirty."

"Cool. Let's hit Beleza Lounge in midtown," I said.

He laughed. "You're aggressive, aren't you?"

"No, I just go after what I like."

He laughed. I figured it was time for me to get back in the game. I'd been running after Cam because I was the mother of his child. Now I had to switch up the game plan. At some point Cam had loved me, and if a man has ever loved a woman, the only thing that can bring him back is that woman falling deeply in love with another man. That was my plan. Jacob was test case number one.

The next day, Jacob met me at the lounge in midtown. I'd been to Beleza once before but only briefly. I wore a black dress that hung off one shoulder and fit loosely down to my hips, hugging them tightly. My legs were waxed clean and I'd pulled my hair into a bun on top. Tayshawn had done my makeup and applied false eyelashes.

Jacob was already there when I arrived. The host escorted me over to where he was seated. I recognized his chocolate bald head from behind. His shoulders were broad like a linebacker's. I placed my hand on his bulging tricep as I stepped up to the table. He stood and gave me a once-over. His wide smile greeted me. "Wow, you look really different."

"Is that good or bad?" I asked.

"That's great."

I pulled my dress down a little before sitting on the plush chair. Global beats filled the air and I looked around the small trendy joint. Then I turned my attention back to Jacob. "I'm glad you were interested in meeting tonight," I said.

He looked at me. "I am too. I thought you were attractive when I first saw you, but you're *really* attractive."

I lowered my eyes, blushing, and took a sip of my water.

He asked, "Why are you acting bashful?"

"I am really, but I found you interesting and wanted to get to know you."

"I'm glad you did."

"Really?"

He nodded. I looked over the menu and asked, "Do you come here often?"

"Not often, but I've been here a time or two."

"What do you usually get?" I asked.

"I like the moqueca."

I laughed. "Oh my goodness. That's exactly what I was thinking of getting."

A big smile spread across his face as I lied to him. It's funny how simple things like that can blow up a man's ego. "Yeah, it's Bahian seafood with coconut milk. I like it a lot," he said.

"I'm going to try it."

We had dinner and chatted about a lot of nothing. He was actually quite boring and I was ready to go home, but he made a dessert suggestion. My appetite just couldn't resist. I ordered the açaí sorbet with granola and assorted fruit. As I made love to the dessert, he interrupted my climax.

"Are you sure you don't have any more questions for me?"

I shrugged. "I mean, this isn't an interview or anything."

"Most people ask questions when they are trying to get to know someone."

"I guess. Is there something you want to tell me?"

The look in his eyes was suggesting that I ask about his relationship status, which I had failed to do. I didn't see a ring and he hadn't resisted me. He shrugged. "Hey, don't say I didn't put it on the table."

Suddenly it hit me that he was trying to tell me something. While I wasn't necessarily fully into him, I hadn't completely written him off. He was attractive, with a job.

I sensed that he was straight and in the A, that's really the biggest question. I usually don't ask a man if he's bisexual because you usually don't get an honest answer. You have to do your research and find people who know people who know him. I asked, "What's your relationship status?"

He smiled. "I'm married."

A dart went straight through my ego. I didn't like that this man had sat all the way through dinner and waited to tell me this. I was sick to my stomach. Though I'd come on to him, it would have been appropriate for him to tell me when I called. Now I felt stupid and embarrassed. I quickly called the waitress over and said, "We'll take the check."

He asked, "Are you upset?"

"No, I don't even know you that well. Why would I be upset?"

"You just looked like you were mad when I said it."

"Mad. Why would you think I'd be mad?"

If anything, I was irritated. Then again, maybe I was mad at myself for aggressively dragging this married man out. I was just ready to buy a fifth of vodka and go home. He took care of the check and pecked me on the cheek before parting.

I stopped at the store and headed home. When I pressed the garage door opener, something came over me and I began to cry. Fuck my life. I needed to see my therapist twice a week if I planned on getting back on the gruesome dating scene. Ugh! Why couldn't a good man just drop out of the sky?

ayana

I was nauseous from the day I found out I was pregnant all the way through. The one thing that kept me going was decorating the nursery and planning for my baby's arrival. I allowed another therapist to take over the practice so I could focus on the radio show.

Things seemed to be going well. After I'd requested a third extension on my book, my editor pushed the publishing date out a year. That gave me another year before it was due, thankfully. The marriage, the pregnancy, and getting used to being a stepmom were a lot to take in. To my surprise, Yasmin had scaled down a lot. She often caused scenes or arguments about Caron and his upkeep, but no attacks against me. I think it was all a mission to get Caron back. I fully supported his return to his mother. Being a stepmother was more than a notion. It was so challenging to step into a child's life and take a leadership role. That transition is rarely seamless.

We had no difficulties during the pregnancy, except with Cam's business. The real estate market seemed to have crashed overnight. When I'd met Cam, he was selling million-dollar homes nearly every week. Then some-where along the way, after I got pregnant—or better yet, after he trapped me—he'd be lucky to sell a house for one hundred thousand dollars. It was as if a tsunami had come and wiped out the entire industry.

He made smart investment decisions so we weren't struggling, but things were much tighter than they had been when we first met. Initially he wanted to continue to pay all the bills, but I suggested that it made sense for me to help. There was no reason for him to struggle to pay for everything when I made good money too. He'd already proven his manhood to me over and over again. Luckily we'd been able to find reliable tenants to lease my condo so that was off my back and I had more money to contribute to our home.

I peeled myself out of bed every morning, wishing I could sleep through my delivery date. Most days, if Cam was available, he drove me to the radio station. He'd wake up and make me breakfast, then take me to work. He was frustrated by the market, but I felt that it was a blessing while I was pregnant and while he adjusted to being the primary caretaker for Caron. I was confident things would pick back up shortly.

What irritated him most was that several investors wanted to pull out of the Blake's Overlook project. They were frightened by the trends and felt it was a bad time to start development. They wanted to put the project on pause until the economy bounced back. Cam on the other hand believed that Atlanta was the home of enough celebrities and power movers that a luxury complex would thrive. The investors had yet to be convinced. Since Cam had money tied up in the entire project too, he was desperate to make it happen. He had mortgaged the land and didn't want to sell because he'd gotten it for a steal. The mortgage was more than he wanted to be obligated to pay, especially with the investors talking two years before development. Cam called a meeting with all the investors to plead his case. If the building was erected the buyers would come. This was his last song and dance.

He had that meeting this morning, forcing me to drive myself to the station. My poor little Prius often sat in the driveway feeling unloved and underappreciated. I didn't feel like driving the Range Rover or the Audi, so I hopped in my single-chick car and headed to the city. As I approached my exit, I tried to brake. The car was still going fifty miles an hour. I tried to swerve over to the shoulder, but I was afraid I would run into the side rail. My heart was trapped in my throat, and of all the things to do, I closed my eyes. If I was going to have an accident, I certainly didn't want to see it. I heard the speed strips rumble as my tires rolled over them. It seemed like an eternity but I found a section of the expressway with a patch of grass on the shoulder and steered the car in that direction. Finally, the car rolled to a stop. It took me a long time to catch my breath. There had been several Toyota recalls because of faulty brakes and I couldn't believe it had happened to me. My body was shaking and my baby flipped uncontrollably inside me. I was so unsure of what to do. Although I really didn't want to interrupt, I called Cam and of course he didn't answer.

Then I figured it would probably be best if I called Aaliyah. She answered, "Why aren't you at work, fat mama?"

"Well, fat mama's brakes gave out."

"What, the brakes on your car? Are you kidding me?"

"Nope, I'm riding down 400 and I go to get off on the ramp and my car wasn't slowing down."

"What the heck? That's crazy. Toyota better be glad nothing happened to you."

"I know. Right? It was so scary. I sat here for like five minutes before calling anyone. I can't believe this happened."

"Girl, where are you? I will be there shortly."

"Thanks, Sister."

"I know the girls are like, damn, we always going to rescue Auntie."

I laughed but it really wasn't funny. I told her where I was and she said she was on her way. I called Quentin to let him know about the accident and tell him that I was still coming in. He told me to take my time. I called GEICO so it could tow the car and was told a tow truck would arrive in less than thirty minutes.

I wasn't in the mood for anything anymore, least of all car issues. I debated whether I should have Aaliyah take me home or not. There was no telling if Cam was going to be done by the time I was finished and I wasn't sure

I wanted to wait. All I needed was sleep. My feet were swollen. I was heavier than I'd ever imagined I would be.

I knew I should have stayed home and not contaminated the world with my negative emotions, but I'd pressed my way through it anyway. When I felt like this, the worst things happened.

It seemed like forever before Aaliyah came and finally chased away all those dark feelings that were floating through my head. When she pulled up, I looked at my watch and it had only been twenty minutes. But I guess the way I was feeling, any extended period of time alone was too much.

She beeped the horn and cars sped rapidly by. Suddenly I felt a sinking feeling in the pit of my stomach. I was scared to get out. Every car that passed shook my little car. Aaliyah called, "Ayana, what you waiting for? The second coming of Jesus?"

"No, girl. These cars are speeding. I'm scared."

"Well, climb over into the passenger seat and get out on that side."

I rolled my eyes. How did she expect for me to move all two-hundred-plus pounds of me to the passenger seat? Well, that wasn't possible and the only choice I had was to open the door, pray, run in front of my car, and hop in Aaliyah's passenger seat.

Fear mixed with adrenaline forced me to laugh uncontrollably when I got into the car. Aaliyah laughed too. The girls began to laugh also, but absolutely nothing was funny. Maybe I was just happy to be rescued.

I pondered with Aaliyah whether I should go to work or not. She offered to pick me up afterward and suggested that Mandy could also come get me if Cameron wasn't available. I decided to go to work. I found myself giving the wrong advice and had to check myself. Even though a talk show was a form of entertainment, I still needed to be positive and not be overopinionated. Quentin gave me a weird look from time to time and I ignored him.

When my segment was done, Quentin asked, "Is everything OK?"

"What? Besides the fact that I'm irritated and pregnant? Or maybe it's because my car nearly killed me. Or maybe it's because my husband is missing in action, fighting for our livelihood."

"I'm sorry. You do have a lot on your plate. You just seem really angry."

Angry? That was a rather strong description that I had no desire to be associated with. I apologized for anything that might have been offensive. I called Cam and he still didn't answer. It was Yasmin's weekend to pick up Caron so I didn't know exactly where he was or why he hadn't responded to my desperate SOS.

Quentin offered to drive me home and I took him up on the offer because I didn't want to disrupt anyone else's day. On the ride I opened up about my feelings of doubt when it came to the whole relationship. Quentin assured me that it was worth it. He told me that all relationships had their problems, some more extreme than others. He said that as long as Cam and I remained a unit, no one could divide us. He looked into my eyes. "You know all of this, don't you?"

"Yeah, I know. It doesn't mean I don't question a lot."

"I would be lying if I said I wake up every day jumping for joy that I married my wife. Some days I think I made a big mistake, but the good days outweigh the bad days, right?"

"Yeah, mostly."

"That's what makes it worth it. The friendship and partnership that you don't get with any other relationship. Not with your mother, your father, your sister, brother, best friend. They don't feel your ups and downs like a spouse. Your partner is compassionate and in the fight with you."

I laughed. "That sounds like some bullshit I've said."

"Yeah, I probably got it from you. You say all this stuff without thinking but in your own life you want to throw in the towel—"

"No, I'm not throwing in the towel. I'm just saying I have doubts."

"OK, I can take that."

I didn't want to tell him that my doubts were heightened because I hadn't spoken to Cam since he'd left that morning. There was probably no cause for concern, but I was alarmed and I didn't know why. Maybe it was because at eight months pregnant, I had imagined my husband wouldn't allow several hours to pass without returning my phone call.

When I got home, I called the Toyota dealer to see if my car had arrived and to ask about the faulty brakes. The vehicle hadn't been recalled, so they didn't understand the issue with my car. The problem I described hadn't caused any recalls.

"How do you know this is not a new issue that I've discovered?"

"We're not sure but we'll have our mechanics look at it first thing tomorrow morning and give you a call."

I huffed. The representative on the phone sounded compassionate. She said, "Ms. Blue, if you need a loaner, just let us know."

"Nah, I'm good. I have another car. I just want to know what's wrong with that car. I'm expecting a baby and—"

"I know, I'm one of your fans." Maybe she was just trying to flatter me so I wouldn't go off on her. She said, "Yes, when the car came in I was so excited to see your name."

I smiled. "Thank you. So that means you wouldn't lie to me about this recall, would you?"

"Definitely not. They'll look at it in the morning and as soon as they tell me something, I'll let you know."

"Deal. What's your name again?"

"My name is Kiera. Have a good day, Ms. Blue."

When I hung up, I called Cameron back and still no answer. After I grabbed a bag of tomato basil chips from the pantry and a Snapple from the fridge, I put on my Snuggie and curled up on the couch. The housekeeper had come for the day, so it was clean and peaceful. Caron wasn't there to run in circles. I almost immediately dozed off. Pregnancy sleep had to be the absolute best sleep of all time. I was seeing stars before I could even finish drinking my tea.

I woke up to what I thought was the sound of the garage door. My head popped up and I looked around. My eyes shifted left and right. I slowly swung my feet around to the floor, because if Cam was home, he should have come in by then. I walked to the kitchen to see if he was coming and I didn't hear the car running. I opened the garage door. The Audi and the Range Rover were still parked in their spots, the lights were off, and there was no sign that the door had been recently opened. Maybe I was losing my mind. I didn't want to worry Cam, but I began to get concerned. I wondered if he was OK. So I called again and finally he answered, but he sounded slightly snappy.

"Can you bring me some food?" I asked.

"Yeah, I got you."

I looked at the time and realized it was after nine at night. Where the hell had he been all day? And why was our communication only one-directional? I didn't appreciate the insecurity bubbling in my chest. I had to hold it together. This behavior wasn't normal and I wondered if I should take the understanding route.

When he finally came in, he looked as if he wanted to cry. I asked him to tell me what was wrong before telling him about my car. He sat down on our Restoration Hardware leather sectional with me. He sank in and lay his head back on the top. I swallowed my feelings of rejection and rubbed his head.

"Is everything OK?"

"No."

"Do you want to talk about it?"

"There isn't an investor in the whole United States that's interested in this project."

"It's OK. They are just delaying the investment, right? They haven't totally walked away."

"They did today."

My heart sank, because I knew he was paying the mortgage on the five-million-dollar land, hoping to make fifty million. Instead of his getting rich, the investors had pulled out, which meant we'd be struggling to pay the mortgage until we found either another investor or someone to purchase the property from us. I knew option number two was out of the question. The property would eventually be worth a lot more and Cam was convinced that if he could just hold on, we'd make so much money neither of us would have to work again.

I sat there feeling fat and wanting to break down and boo-hoo. Instead I comforted my husband and told him we'd make it work. We'd have to change our spending habits or whatever we needed to do, but we'd hold on to the property until the market turned around.

He kissed me and I could tell he felt lucky to have me. I wondered if I should hold back my feelings about his failure to answer his phone that day, especially knowing that I was eight months pregnant. I contemplated as I rubbed his shoulders and finally I said, "I almost ran off the road today."

"What do you mean?" he asked, out of obligation, but I could tell he wasn't concerned.

"My brakes wouldn't stop. I mashed down to the floor and I was still going over fifty miles an hour."

He sat up and almost looked angry. He said, "Are you fucking serious?"

"Yeah, I got it towed. Aaliyah took me to work and Quentin brought me home."

"Why am I just hearing about this?"

"I called you."

"You should have texted me something that important."

I just shrugged my shoulders. With your wife, a phone call should carry just as much weight as a text message any day. He asked a bunch of questions about the brake failure, but I didn't even know the answers myself. Finally, he held me tightly like he regretted neglecting me.

yasmin

I took the entire day off to spend with Caron. I wanted to plan a fun weekend. Ever since he had been living with Cam, I liked to do exciting things when he was with me. We'd probably seen more in the last seven months than we'd seen in his entire life before. I'd be damned if I would hear him tell me some shit that Ayana was doing for him that I hadn't done. I needed him to always remember that I was his one and only mother. I didn't want him to get twisted and confused because of what she could provide financially.

I got up and started making pancakes because they were Caron's favorite. He was still asleep. We'd gone to the movies the night before and I was humming Beyoncé as I whipped up my baby's favorite dish. He was truly the pancake gremlin. He would be so happy when he woke up.

It was just a little after eight and someone banged on the door like the police. I huffed. Who could this be and why were they here? I had on a short pink terry cloth robe and my hair was clipped with pins all over. My fluffy slippers shuffled across the hardwood floors as I tried my best to be silent. I don't know why I was trying to pretend I wasn't there. Maybe it's because whoever was at my door had no business being there. I stood on tiptoe to look through the peephole.

Cameron. What the hell was he doing here? Maybe he missed being with me and Caron. I opened the door smiling. Cameron busted in the house like a hurricane. He was loud and aggressive, unlike I'd ever seen him before. I didn't even know what he was saying. He yanked my robe with one hand, jacking me up against the wall.

"Bitch, I will fucking kill you if you keep this shit up, you hear me?"

My eyes shifted from side to side. I wasn't sure what he was referring to. I said, "Cam, get the fuck off of me."

"Stop fucking with me, Yasmin. Stop fucking with me and I mean it."

He looked like a lion, as if he could rip me to pieces. My heart jumped out of my chest. I thought he was going to hit me. I closed my eyes, preparing for the shock. Caron came running down the stairs. He had bass in his voice as he shouted, "Dad! Dad!"

Cam let me go and looked like the demon inside of him had temporarily jumped out. He looked at Caron and said, "Go back upstairs."

Caron demanded, "Let my mommy go."

"Go back upstairs, this is grown-ups' business."

Caron ran down the stairs and attempted to kick and hit his father. Cam lifted him by the arm and said, "Go upstairs and let me finish talking to your mom."

Tears rolled down Caron's face and I could tell that he was hurt that he couldn't help me. He headed back upstairs but his eyes pierced his father like bullets. He had turned on Cameron and I couldn't blame him.

Cam pointed at me and said, "I will make sure they don't find your ass. You hear me?"

He stormed out the front door and my nerves were still jumping out of control. I sat at the kitchen table crying and shaking. My baby sneaked back downstairs and looked at me compassionately. He touched my shoulder and peeked through my hands covering my face. He said, "Mommy, don't cry. Daddy didn't mean it."

"I don't know, honey."

"It's going to be better."

"I know."

"I don't want you guys to fight anymore. Why can't y'all just be together like when I was young?"

"You don't remember that."

"Yes I do. He used to love you and you loved him. I remember. I want it like it used to be."

"That's impossible. Your father has a new wife and another baby on the way."

He held me and said, "You want me to be your husband?"

He made me smile and that decreased the trembling in my hands. I still couldn't believe Cam. I pondered whether or not I should press charges. I'd never seen that look in his eyes, not even when I told him I wanted to break up. Cam had always been reflective and patient. He didn't act on impulse, which was one of the reasons I'd wanted to leave him, but the monster that had torn through my home was a stranger. I'd never seen that man in my life. I was concerned for my safety and the safety of my son. Nothing I'd done warranted his threatening my life. I hadn't even bothered them in months. I'd been busy trying to move on with my life and get back on the dating scene. I had been going to therapy once or more per week and I was feeling more positive than I had in a long time.

At that point I felt afraid and harassed. If I needed to, I would run off with Caron again. I refused to drop him back off to those lunatics. The entire appeal process for getting Caron back was taking too long.

I picked up the phone and dialed 911. When the officer arrived at my home, I told him the story and Caron chimed in.

"He was choking her."

The officer asked, "Was he choking you, ma'am?"

I contemplated and I said, "Yes, he was choking me and he threatened my life."

"OK. Do you feel safe here?"

"No, I'm not sure. I'm supposed to see him tomorrow to drop off my son. I don't know if I want to do that."

He basically told me that I had to take Caron back, especially if it was court-ordered. Otherwise I would be in trouble. He suggested that I have someone else take him instead. The court system was messed up. This man could come threaten my life and that had no impact on custody until we went back to court. This was unbelievable.

He then said, "I will issue a warrant when I get back to the station."

"For his arrest?" I asked, shocked. Suddenly realizing what I'd just done.

"Yes. It sometimes takes a day or two to filter down, so they won't immediately go to his residence. I'm not sure if you want to handle this in front of your son, but you can always call the station and let them know where he is if you know. You definitely don't want him roaming around, especially if you feel in fear of your life."

"Is he going to jail?"

The officer nodded in confirmation. I glanced at Caron and his eyes were full of water. It hurt me to see him this way, but why would Cameron come in here like that knowing Caron was here? Why had he put all of us in this situation? I didn't feel good about what I was doing. Did I think Cam would ever hurt me in a million years? *No.* However, the other guy who had come in here was probably capable of a lot. Would I be stupid not to report this? *Probably.* After giving it some thought, I proceeded with signing the statement. After the officer left, I called Tayshawn. He was already in the shop and picked up on the first ring. "You must be missing me, boo."

"You know I am."

When I told him about Cam, he gasped and huffed and continued to do it over and over again without saying a word. I needed him to say something. I needed him to make me feel crazy or confirm that I'd done the right thing. He said, "Yasmin. You are playing with fire. You have tested that man's ego and I think you need to stop. You know I'm ride or die for life, but it sounds like he's tipping. You ain't going to win. Just stop."

"But, Tay, I haven't done anything in a long time."

"Now, Yasmin, you don't have to lie to me. You keep something going on Twitter about Ms. Ayana."

"Yeah, but that's not that big of a deal. Not enough for him to try and kill me. I was scared."

"I bet you were."

"You should beat him up for me," I said.

"Oh, honey, a lady never fights a man."

I laughed. "You are so crazy. You still got strength like a man. Right?"

"Only when necessary. I couldn't fight Cammy-Poo if I wanted to. I would be rubbing on those abs."

"You are so silly. I knew you would make me feel better."

I asked if he would drop Caron off for me so that I wouldn't have to see Cameron and he agreed. I hated that my few days with my son had been tarnished with his drama. It annoyed me. I logged on to Twitter and tweeted: SO TAKING MY SON WASN'T GOOD ENOUGH, NOW YOU WANT TO WHIP MY ASS?!?!?!

Within seconds, people commented. They wanted to know more. Everyone knew that my ex-husband was Ayana Blue's new husband and women soaked up the drama like a sponge. Tayshawn called me back and said, "Yasmin, what is wrong with you?"

"What? I didn't do anything."

"I'm really starting to think you are crazy."

"Why?"

"Take that shit off of Twitter."

"Why?"

"If you don't know why, herein lies the problem! Don't you think that is inciting him?"

"He doesn't follow me. Plus, my therapist told me that posting my thoughts to Twitter was better than acting on them."

"Yasmin!" he shouted as if to shake me through the phone. "I don't believe your therapist condones harassing them on Twitter."

True. Still, he'd told me to express myself and that was all I was doing. So I left the tweet there and took pleasure in reading the comments bashing him, and her for stealing my husband. I loved that women were always eager to take the scorned woman's side.

ayana

The dealer called Saturday morning to let me know the brakes had been tampered with and suggested I file a police report. As I stood there confused, explaining to Cameron what they suspected, he didn't say a word. He just shook his head. It seemed that he was holding back his true emotions—that the pain of the whole situation was about to make him explode just as it was doing to me. A few minutes later, he got up and left the house.

When the police officer came to the house, I felt alone. Here I was being tortured by Cam's ex-wife and he was nowhere to be found. The officer was kind enough to let me know that these types of incidents were not their top priority. He promised they would question Yasmin and ask people in my neighborhood if they'd seen any suspicious activity around the house. I got the strong impression that would be the extent of the investigation. It seemed that someone had to actually kill you before justice was sought. I was sick of the legal system and wished I could take matters into my own hands.

I went up to take a nap, hoping I could just sleep away all my problems. When I awoke, it was three hours later and Cam still hadn't returned. So I gave him a call.

"What are you doing?"

"I went to the gym for a little while. I had to work out to relieve some of this frustration."

"Baby, come home. Let's go to Babies"R"Us and finalize our registry. We need to do something to take our minds off of everything."

"You're probably right."

Not only was Cam's business plummeting but so was his patience with the entire Yasmin situation. Despite everything that was going on I was here for better or worse and I wanted to make it all better. We were five weeks from becoming parents and I didn't want the joy contaminated with all the problems we were going through. We deserved more. Whatever financial problems we were having were temporary. I had faith in Cam's business savvy and I knew everything would come back around.

He walked into the house, looked at me, and said, "I promised to take care of you."

"Listen, you are taking care of me. I know you love me. I know you're committed to me. I know you are a good man and that's all I need."

"I want to give you everything I promised when I met you."

"I didn't fall in love with promises. I fell in love with a person. A man with character and respect. I wasn't excited about your car or your house. I was excited about you, the morals and values that you have. I fell in love with the same thing that everyone sees in you."

I noticed a smile peeking through the cloud hovering over his face. There was nothing bad that I could say about him. Though I had often contemplated giving up, I assured him that I was in this for the long haul. He had shown me what good men were made of. I rubbed his back. We were about to experience something big and I didn't want us to lose sight of that. The most important thing was that I had made it home safely. But I couldn't help feeling nervous about this whole thing. Yasmin was a very sick individual. The fact that she had done something that could have killed me and my baby was unnerving. I didn't plan to leave the house until after the baby was born. Quentin had already spoken to my stand-in host, letting her know that I would be going out on maternity leave.

I needed to take a seat after walking from the parking lot to Babies"R"Us. Cam stood beside me in the registry area, holding my hand. I asked for the scanner so I could add items to my list. The representative nodded in an irritated fashion. It was too hot to even think about suggesting she fix her attitude if she planned to work in sales. Instead, I picked up a pamphlet off the table and began to fan myself. The Atlanta heat was burning through my soul. Even when I was in air-conditioning I was hot and it was just the first week in April. I wanted to just jump into a freezer and stay there until my baby was ripe and ready.

After she took forever to program my scanner, I was back up and on my way. It seemed as if we came to Babies"R"Us nearly every day. It was therapeutic for the both of us. I always felt calm and celestial when I was there. Early on in the pregnancy, I'd started my registry online, but coming into the store was so much better. I imagined how the baby would smell and how he would look. Cam and I created an e-mail address for him as soon as we found out we were having a boy and decided on his name. We'd both send e-mails about our feelings to him. It was interesting to read Cam's messages. He would often say how much he planned to love the baby and how his love for me got stronger every day he watched me grow. That flattered me. We planned to compile the messages into a book when our son was old enough to read it. I always sent a message when I left Babies"R"Us, because I felt more eager then to meet and touch him.

We explored every aisle as if we hadn't seen it all before. Our clasped hands swung back and forth like those of teenagers in love. Cam always scanned Onesies. We'd probably listed a desired quantity of about twenty. I laughed at him.

"I'm telling you. We need all of these we can get. I remember when Caron was a baby, I felt like he used ten a day," he said.

"That's impossible, Cam."

"He had bad reflux so he threw up a lot and all I remember is changing undershirts."

The smile disappeared as I visualized Caron as a baby. I tried to imagine Yasmin as a normal person and how she and Cameron had interacted. Had he been this loving and caring to her? Had he seemed as ecstatic about the birth of Caron? I looked at him and asked, "Did you do this with Yasmin? Were you this supportive?"

He stared at me and raised an eyebrow. His nose turned up as if the sound of her name produced a funk in the air. "Why?"

"I'm just trying to figure out the source of her anger issues."

"I don't know. She could always snap at the drop of a hat, but she could manage it better. She was young and cute and able to pull the wool over people's eyes. Now she sees her good years fading away. I think she's just desperate. I don't think she can find a good man and I'm the only thing she has left to hold on to. You know the saying, 'You don't miss a good thing till it's gone.' Me being with you makes her feel inadequate and miserable. She'll do anything to make us feel like she feels." He leaned in and kissed my forehead. "Misery loves company, baby."

"Yeah, very well said, honey."

After strolling around the store I was ready to go home. My entire body began to feel heavy. Cam could read my breathing as he suggested that he go get the car and I meet him out front.

We stopped to have lunch at a small café in the same shopping center. Cam ordered a dirty martini. I wished I could share a drink with him. He seemed to really relax the more he sipped.

When it was time to pick up Caron on Sunday, Cam asked me if I wanted to go with him. He said, "I know if you're there, I will keep my cool."

"Cam, you're always cool."

He laughed. "Yeah, until someone messes with my baby."

I agreed to go with him although I really didn't want to see an attempted murderer. It really bothered me that I hated this woman with a passion. It actually scared me. I prayed that I had enough sense not to kill her. One thing I knew for sure, if she tried anything with my baby, I would lose it and not care.

As we approached the sheriff's department, I noticed that Cam's shoulders and arms tightened and his eyes narrowed. He couldn't contain himself. It seemed he hated her as much as I did. He pulled into the parking space and we sat there for nearly ten minutes waiting for her. I asked him if he wanted to call her and he shook his head. I reclined my seat because I needed a nap.

Suddenly, Cam mumbled, "What the fuck?"

I sprung up to inquire. He opened the driver's-side door. "This is some bullshit."

"What, Cam?" I asked, looking around to see what was going on.

Cam stepped out of the car and I saw Caron and a guy walking toward the vehicle. The man was smiling hard

and switching his hips even harder. He had muscles popping out of his tank top, and swished his hair back and
forth as he talked to Cam. I saw Cam nodding his head,
as if to say, "Whatever, dude."

Finally he and Caron headed back to the car. He
opened the back door for Caron. I said, "Hey, Caron.
What's up, buddy?"

He looked through me and didn't respond. He was often like that when leaving his mother so I didn't think
much of it. I turned back around. Cam hopped in and we
pulled off.

When we got back home, Caron ate dinner and we
went out to Rita's for Italian ices. Caron seemed to be re-
jecting Cam's affection also. I wondered what his mom
could have told him to make him so cold. Caron's mood
would get better as the days went on, but it was always
an adjustment. As Caron's stepparent, all I wanted to do
was love and encourage him through this period, but it
was hard to connect with a child who didn't want my
love. All I could do was try to make the transition better.

Once we were in for the night, Cam and I were alone
and free to discuss what had been said between him and
the guy who had dropped Caron off.

"That guy works with Yasmin. Here's the problem. Yasmin has had dude pick him up from school before and
I've asked her not to do that."

"Because he's gay?" I asked.

"Partially, but mainly because he's flamboyant. I don't
want my son around that. I mean, dude is like Yasmin's

best friend so of course he's going to see him, unfortunately, but I'm not cool with him picking Caron up all by himself. That shit ain't cool. You know what I'm saying?"

"Yeah, I get you."

I was on my laptop and Cam was lying in the bed beside me. He looked over and said, "For the record, don't have my son around that shit."

"Cam, I said I get you."

He raised one eyebrow, looking up at me, and said, "I'm just letting you know."

He smiled and started changing the channels on the television with his right hand and rubbing my stomach with his left. "You know, it's good to know that you're in love with a good woman and know for sure that that woman is going to always do the right thing for your little man."

I placed my hand on his forearm and rested it here. I wanted him to know that I would, whether we were together or not. I promised him that I wouldn't make his life miserable just because I could. He looked at me as if he trusted me with his life. It was amazing that he had left himself open for love again. Most men wouldn't have after being with Yasmin. But I was sure glad he had.

ayana

I woke up on Monday morning and just wanted to lie in bed and have Cameron's mother bring me food. She'd treated me like an angel from the second she discovered I was pregnant. It was no wonder Cameron was a great man. She would come to stay with us from time to time but she had a social life of her own, so she wasn't planning on moving in. I wished she could be our full-time nanny, but Cam was concerned about her health. He didn't want her to tire herself out ripping and running through the house after a crawling baby. Though I knew it would be a while before we got to that point, I agreed. It was probably best if the nanny we selected was there from birth instead of coming in once the baby was more active.

Ms. Mae made pancakes with cheese eggs and bacon. She called upstairs and asked if I wanted her to bring it up. I told her that I'd come down. I went into the kitchen and we ate at the big kitchen table. Cam had dropped Caron off at school and he had other things to take care of. That left Ms. Mae and me there to have our good girlfriend conversation. She was so sweet and insightful. I loved her perspective.

I sat down to a plate that looked like it had come from a restaurant's kitchen. She'd sliced strawberries to garnish the plate. She grabbed her coffee and carried my orange juice over and sat it in front of me.

She took a seat also. I said, "Ms. Mae, I love you."

"I love you too, sweetie," she said, smiling.

She was doing her unconscious thing of rubbing her feet together and rocking back and forth. She smiled at me. If the whole world had belonged to her, she would have given it to Cam. He was her pride and joy. The sun rose and set on him as far as she was concerned. I often felt that she looked at me with gratitude, that she knew her son had found a woman who would love and protect him forever.

"Ms. Mae, I really appreciate you. You make the best food in the whole world. I wish I could open up Ms. Mae's Soul Food Kitchen."

"Cam said he always wanted to open up a place for me."

"He's faking. I'm serious."

"No, I think he's just too busy doing his own thing," she said in defense of her prince.

"I'm sorry. You're right. If he had time, he would."

"Yeah, but I'm getting too old for that now."

"You're not too old, you don't look a day over sixty."

"There's a bunch of cars on the road that are all shined up but underneath the hood it's some old parts. They might break down on the highway on you," she said, laughing. "My insides are definitely eighty-one years old."

I didn't laugh. Although I got her point and found it humorous, being stranded on the highway was a touchy situation.

"Ms. Mae, can you believe that girl had someone tamper with my brakes?"

"She is plumb crazy. You hear me? Plumb crazy. Do you know that I cried when he married her?"

"Cried?"

"Yes, Hal didn't understand. He would say, 'Mae, you gotta let him be a man.' It just didn't sit well in my soul. I was in pain."

"What didn't you like?"

"She came across as a sweet girl, but I just don't know. You'll see. A mother's intuition is the strongest feeling a woman could ever experience. It can't be explained or justified. Mothers just know."

"I hear that all the time."

"You won't believe in it until you have that aha moment for yourself. And I think it's even stronger for mothers and sons. I don't know why, but when Cam was a teenager, I always knew when he was in trouble. I could feel it before going to one of his football games if he was going to hurt himself."

"Are you serious?" I paused for a moment. "Do you think that because you were older and calmer when you had him that you were more in touch with your intuition?"

She shifted in her chair and frowned. "No. I was always

calm, but Cam was a miracle so we may have just had a strong bond from jump."

"Yeah."

She smiled and shook her head. "Boys are just the best. You'll see."

Whenever I talked to Ms. Mae, I got excited. Everyone close to me had little girls, so this was going to be a new experience for everyone.

Ms. Mae decided to stay for the remainder of the week and said she'd go home after the baby shower. I sure wished she would just make the decision to move in with us. It would make it so much better for Cam and me. And while she wouldn't be the primary nanny, I would feel safe with her in the house to assist. She might have been old but I knew she was tough and that she would protect Cam's son at all costs. Even Aaliyah loved being around her while she and Mandy were in and out of the house, preparing for the shower extravaganza.

Cam and I invited damn near all of Atlanta. This was going to be the baby shower of the year. So many of our friends and acquaintances had felt left out of our wedding and they wanted to be a part of the birth of our baby. We agreed. Our marriage had been sudden and we hadn't wanted anyone to question our decision. Now all our friends were in complete support of our union. We had two hundred guests confirmed.

On Friday night Mandy, Cori, and Aaliyah arrived with huge Michaels bags. I knew whatever they had planned would be fabulous, because Aaliyah had vision like no other person I'd ever met. She could take a blank room and turn it into a palace. She's always been like that. She's a visual artist. I'd tried to convince her that she should be a party planner but she swore she only had time to take care of the girls. I hoped that having a nanny would free me up to do some of the things I had to do. There was so much on my plate. Yet I still wanted to be hands-on with the baby. I knew something would have to give.

I fell asleep on the girls as they organized all their supplies and talked about where to put what. When I woke up on Saturday morning, Cam said, "You are lucky. Your sister and your friends are some down-ass chicks."

I pushed him because he knew I hated for him to talk like that. He said, "No, for real, you have got to see downstairs."

He amped me up as I rushed to the top of the stairs. White tulle was wrapped around our double stairwell from top to bottom. It looked prepared for a bride to enter. A large poster of one of the pictures from our maternity photo shoot was on a tripod in the middle of the foyer. Mandy, Cori, and Aaliyah had created a pyramid sculpture with the party favors, which were crystal clocks in little blue boxes with brown bows. The cocktail tables they had rented were covered with light blue tablecloths with brown sashes wrapped around the legs. The chairs were covered in the same colors. The centerpiece for each cocktail table was three tea light candles with white rose petals sprinkled around. They had placed the circular eating tables in the back, but hadn't put the linen on them yet. The centerpieces for those were lined up on the island in the kitchen. They were tall glass cylinders holding blue feathers, each bunch with a blue-brown-and-white paisley bow wrapped meticulously around the middle.

There was a long table in the dining room that looked as if it would be the dessert table. They had placed four stainless steel cupcake holders and a stainless steel chocolate fountain. There was a large empty space on the table, which I assumed was where the cake was intended to go.

I looked at Cam and said, "Yeah, they are some down-ass chicks."

Everything looked so good and they weren't even finished yet. This was the prep work. I could only imagine what it would look like once everything was finished. I was so excited. There was no way I could wait until four o'clock for this to go down. I was ready for all the guests to come now. I went into the family room and Ms. Mae was there, watching TV. I said, "Did you see everything?"

"You have some good friends."

"I know. I don't know what I would do without my sister and my friends."

"You got to be a good friend in order to have good friends. Those girls worked up a sweat last night. That says more about you than you can imagine."

"You're too kind."

"I know, sweetie. I know."

I leaned over and gave her a hug just because I was

happy. Cam and Caron went out to pick up breakfast. We decided to eat in the kitchenette in the sunroom so we wouldn't mess up any of the decorations. Shortly after we ate, I was of course ready for a nap. I went upstairs to my room and snuggled up with my body pillow and I was out. I had an appointment to get my nails done at one and I woke up ten minutes before that time. I rushed out of the house. My manicure and pedicure were the things that kept me sane. If only for thirty minutes, someone rubbing my feet relaxed me.

By the time I got back to the house, Aaliyah was already there. The girls were coming with her husband a little later. I hugged her as soon as I walked in. I said, "I'm sorry that I wasn't able to make your showers this fab."

"You're right. Maybe I'll have another baby so you can make it up to me."

"Nah, don't do that."

She laughed. "A'ight. Go and get ready. Don't come back downstairs until the party starts."

"What if I'm lonely?"

"I'll send Cam up there with you."

I laughed and headed upstairs. The bed looked so appealing. Having a baby at thirty-six years old was definitely a challenge. It was like carrying a bag of bricks. I didn't remember Aaliyah being so fatigued. I lay down and set my alarm for three o'clock, which was just twenty minutes away, but I wanted to be rested and refreshed for my guests.

I came downstairs around ten minutes after four. I wore

a light blue strapless maxi-dress with thin-strap flat silver sandals. My hair was pulled back in a bun. I went into the dining room to see the cake. It was a four-tier octagonal cake decorated with blue, brown, and white fondant. Each cupcake had a blue-and-brown cup, with white icing and a blue chocolate wafer with a *B* on it. There were balloons floating throughout the house. The DJ had set up outside and there was a speaker inside the house. He began to play a list of slow jams that Cam and I felt told the story of our love.

Cam grabbed me and we danced to Alicia Keys's "If I Ain't Got You." He looked in my eyes as we danced. He was intense and I knew that he felt all the words of the song. People began to pour in around four thirty. As they entered, Mandy directed them to sign the poster with words of wisdom and/or baby advice. This was the first time some of my friends had been to the house. They all loved the place and the decor.

Aaliyah had mixed a special blue alcoholic drink and the caterers passed it around in tall glasses with a garnish of pineapple, cherry, and orange. They also passed around crab cakes, shrimp, chicken skewers, and spring roll appetizers. There were ice cream stations outside. It was more than I could ever have dreamed of. Everyone showed up.

There were so many gifts from happy, encouraging people. Cam was glowing. I could tell that all his friends were happy for him. When men show up to a baby shower, you know they believe in the union. It was the best day of my life. I felt it was the perfect way to welcome our baby into the world.

Dinner was about to be served when Aaliyah ran out in the yard calling my name in a frantic fashion. My sister and I should have been twins because I knew whatever was going on was going to upset me. I read it all in her face. My mouth hung open as two police officers followed behind her. I couldn't form my mouth to say anything. Several of our neighbors were there, but I still assumed there had been a noise complaint or something. All I could think was, *Not today*. Cam headed over to see what the problem was. He said, "Can I help you, Officer?"

I approached slowly, wondering why they were there to storm on my shower. One of the officers said, "We are looking for Cameron Small."

"I'm Cameron Small, sir."

It seemed like all two hundred of our guests surrounded us. Several of Cam's potential investors were there. The officer pulled out his handcuffs. "Mr. Small, we have a warrant for your arrest."

Aaliyah looked at me, her eyes pleading for me to do something. Cameron took deep breaths. I was frozen still. I heard other people shouting. *Why? What happened? Oh no, it must be Yasmin*. I was speechless. My eyes shot over to Morris, Cameron's high-powered attorney friend. He must have been perplexed too, because he didn't move until I shot him a desperate look. Cam handed his cell phone to Aaliyah. As they were cuffing him, Morris stepped up to the officer and identified himself as Cam's attorney. He requested to know the charge. The officers said something about harassment.

Morris looked at me and said, "Don't worry, sweetheart. I'm going to follow them and meet Cam at the station. I'll handle it. I will call you as soon as I know more."

Water poured from my eyes. I had been hoping that Morris could do something to prevent them from taking Cam out of our home in those silver bracelets. Mandy hugged me. As they turned to walk him out, Cam said, "Don't worry, baby. Morris got it. Stay here and enjoy the rest of the shower."

He asked the cops if they could walk him around the side of the house so his mother and son wouldn't have to witness it and they did. He stayed calm and cool as if this were normal. He tried not to startle the guests, but everyone was already alarmed and confused.

The entire crowd followed behind them. Morris walked closer than anyone. Morris's wife touched his back and said, "Go ahead. I'll be fine. I'll catch a ride with someone else."

When they put Cam in the car, I lost it. I didn't know what this was about. And it hurt. Of all the things Yasmin had done in the past year, this was above everything else. She had set it up to embarrass us in front of all our friends and family. I broke down on Mandy's shoulder and she cried too. My mother hugged me from behind. "It's OK, baby. I'm sure it will all be taken care of. It's just an ugly misunderstanding."

"Why today, Mommy?"

"I don't know, Ayana. I don't know."

I noticed Aaliyah crying also and I reached out for her to join our group hug. This was such a disaster on a wonderful day. The shower was over. Guests came out from inside. They were more confused and I heard different people explaining what happened. I just wanted to go up to my room and cry myself to sleep as if I were thirteen years old.

We walked into the house and Aaliyah asked if I wanted to open the gifts. I couldn't have done it if I'd wanted to. I looked at Ms. Mae and she was confused. She had gotten bits and pieces but she didn't know that Cam was off in a police car headed to jail. My mother sat down beside her and explained what had happened. Ms. Mae claimed she had heard someone saying that Cam was being arrested on sexual harassment charges. My head was spinning because I honestly didn't know if that's what the officer had said. I looked at Aaliyah for clarification. She said, "I thought they said criminal."

Mandy said, "I thought they said sexual harassment."

From person to person, everyone had a different story. Cam couldn't have been stupid enough to have sex with her. All kinds of things began to run through my head. What if she had set him up to have sex with someone else? I'd been too tired to have sex and it wasn't farfetched to believe he'd take a piece if it were thrown at him. My neck was stiff and I felt like I could faint. As I sat there watching our baby shower guests run out of the house like roaches, I wished I could disappear. Everyone came over and offered their sympathy and told me they were there if I needed them. I appreciated that. No one really knew all the details of what we had gone through with her, but they were sure that Cam and I were good people who didn't deserve this.

I'd never seen a house clear out so fast. Caron came upstairs unsure of why his company had left. I told him the party was over. He said, "But we haven't even opened the gifts yet."

"We'll open the gifts tomorrow," Aaliyah told him.

I started backtracking in my mind, wondering what could have happened. My mind quickly went to the previous Friday when I couldn't get in contact with Cam. My stomach began to turn. Where had he been that night? Whom had he been with? I prayed that he hadn't done anything stupid. What if this wasn't about Yasmin?

Ms. Mae called Caron over to her and asked, "Did you tell your mother we were having a baby shower today?"

"Yeah."

We all looked at one another, almost sure that it had been her doing. There were so many unanswered questions. Aaliyah gave me Cam's cell phone and I called Morris. He didn't answer. I held the phone tightly, hoping to send vibes to Morris to call me and let me know what was going on. We sat there hoping to hear something soon. Hours passed before Morris called.

"Hey, Ayana, he hasn't seen the commissioner yet. But here's the deal. Cam told Yasmin that he would hurt her if she kept harassing you. She told the police that he said he'd kill her. Since there was already a protection order in place, they take that charge very serious. They have to issue a warrant to make the police department look like they've done their job should Cam actually hurt Yasmin . . . for argument's sake, of course."

"I know. I know. But it's still not right. She is lying."

"And as a precaution, they are going to try to set his bail really high, because they don't want anything to happen to her, but I'll be there to defend him and more than likely they will lower it, but there will be a bail. I need you to call my man Keith. He's a bail bondsman. Though Cam will have to wait to see the commissioner, we still want to get Keith on board."

"How long will he be there?"

"It's likely he'll be here until Monday."

"Monday!" I shouted.

I felt dizzy. Did they realize that I was eight months pregnant and I couldn't take the stress?

"Unfortunately, Ayana. The weekend is the absolute worst time to get arrested."

My father out of nowhere came and put his arm around my shoulder. "It's OK, baby. It will be OK," he said.

I felt as if I hadn't seen him for the entire shower. I looked at him, wondering if he knew the whole story, but the look in his eyes confirmed it. My dad wanted us to have stress-free lives and he had done everything he could while we were growing up to make sure we were drama-free. He looked troubled that he was unable to make this right.

When I got off the phone, I told my family that it would be Monday before everything was resolved. I suggested they go home and I would keep them posted. My mother offered to stay. I knew Aaliyah had to go. She'd been away from her home for two days. The caterers offered to package some of the food up and store it in my freezer. We agreed since we'd already paid for it. Cori and Mandy took the decorations down and began popping balloons. I hoped the photographer had been able to get some good shots before he was unofficially forced out with everyone else.

It was after nine before the house was back to normal and the caterer had packed up everything. When Mandy, my dad, and Aaliyah and her kids left, I was feeling a little better. I was there with Cam's mom and mine and they were extremely comforting. They made me feel that it would be OK. Each of them shared stories about how things hadn't always been perfect in their marriages. My mother summed it up, saying, "There will always be bitter women in the world who want to spread their evil."

I agreed, but at the same time that really didn't make my situation better. I needed to know how to stop this bitter woman from haunting me. My mother suggested we open the gifts to take our minds off of what had happened. We moved into the living room, where the presents covered half of the twenty-by-twenty area. Cam and I had received some really nice gifts. In addition to most of the things on our registry, we got thoughtful keepsakes, like an engraved platinum comb and brush set

and a silver football piggy bank. We got tons of clothes.
My mother's hand cramped as she attempted to write
down the names of the guests and their gifts. I was laughing and talking about the baby and I felt better. That is,
until I took the wrapping off a box with no card. The
box was filled with white foam balls. I reached in and
felt what I assumed to be crumpled newspaper. I pulled
out a torched dollhouse cradle with a miniature doll baby
inside. A sticky note was attached to the cradle with the
following message: ROCK-A-BYE BABY. I tossed the crispy
thing across the room. Ms. Mae asked, "What was that,
sweetie?"

My sadness turned to anger. I was pissed. What type of
person would do that? I looked at my mother and said,
"Did you see who brought that gift here?"

She shook her head. "There were so many people
here, Ayana, I don't know who brought what."

I took a deep breath and lay my head back on the
couch. I was irritated. I wanted to go put a bullet in
this chick myself. I wouldn't be surprised if Cam had
actually threatened to kill her. She had relaunched with
a vengeance. I had tried to psychoanalyze this woman
but she was so inconsistent and I was too emotionally
involved to make sense of her. Her motive seemed to
change every week.

ayana

I woke up in the middle of the night wondering if I should have called the cops about the gift. Maybe they could dust it for fingerprints. I sat up in bed and looked around the room. I felt lonely. I wanted to talk to Cam. Where was he? What was he sleeping on? What was he thinking?

I wanted to talk to him so bad. I wanted us to revisit moving out of state. I'd had a few interviews for a television show that would send us to New York. That would mean he'd have to abandon some of the projects he was working on in Atlanta and I didn't get the impression that he really wanted to move. Plus, he liked being the bread-winner and I thought he'd feel some kind of way if I were in that role, even temporarily until he could launch his business. But he had enough contacts in the entertainment industry to get up and going in New York in no time. Our peace was worth it.

I tried to force myself back to sleep but I just couldn't do it, especially knowing that Cam was in jail. I wanted him in bed with me to hold me and to make this situation seem worth it. Without him there, all I could think was why I was even in this relationship. I stared at an oversize picture of us on the wall, hoping that would make me feel closer to him. We'd taken that picture right after our nuptials. The sun was shining and we were so happy. My entire body ached and I wanted the pain to go away. I started to cry. Speaking to the empty room, I shouted, "Cameron. Why? Cam, I don't understand. Somebody help my husband. Anybody."

I wasn't stronger than these forces against me. When I met Cam, I'd imagined this would end at some point, and though there had been some lows during which nothing occurred, all in all, it had lasted too long and caused too much damage. My bedroom door opened and I jumped.

"Ma?" I called out.

"Ayana," Caron said.

He walked in and looked slightly concerned, but more confused.

Quickly wiping my tears, I said, "Yes."

"Are you OK?"

"Yeah, I'm good."

"But you were crying and calling Dad's name."

I didn't say whether that was true or not. I just looked at him. "I thought he was hurting you."

"Why would you think he would hurt me?"

"He hurt my mommy."

"Yes, honey, he hurt your mommy emotionally, but he's never hit her."

"He did the last time I was at my mother's house."

My heart plunged and crashed into my belly. The baby jumped instantly and began to kick erratically, as if he were begging for us to get out of this situation. I wanted to know all the details, but then again I wasn't sure if I should allow a nine-year-old to give me the information. What if his facts were sketchy? I was unsure what to think, especially since Caron often refused to talk to me. Most times he treated me as if I weren't there. I didn't know if this was something his mother had put him up to or not.

"Caron, don't tell anyone else about that, OK," I said.

"But he did and I had to help her."

"OK."

"Did Dad come back yet?"

"No, he's not back."

"When is he coming back?"

"I'm not sure, but he'll be back. Go back to sleep."

He left the room and I curled up with my body pillow. I cried until the sun peeped in through the windows. My eyes were swollen shut and that was the only reason I was able to close them. I slowly drifted off to sleep.

Monday morning took an eternity to arrive. I dropped Caron off at school and met Morris at the jail so we could get Cam out. I sat outside in the parking lot as Morris had instructed. He'd told me that Cam would come out when they released him and Morris would show him exactly where I was parked. I reclined my chair and relaxed in the parking lot. An hour or so passed and Cam knocked on the driver's-side window. I was so happy to see him, I leaped out of the car and hugged him. He held me tightly, or as tightly as he could with the watermelon separating us.

I hadn't expected to cry, considering I had been crying for two days, but I couldn't stop the tears from falling down my face. It felt good knowing he was OK. I'd had nightmares that he'd been abused or hurt in there. I touched his face and chest, making sure he hadn't been harmed. I said, "I missed you so much." I kissed him again. "I was so scared."

"Why?"

"I didn't think you deserved to be in there."

"Yeah, but they have to do that. It's the system."

I hopped in the passenger's side and said, "Why hasn't she been arrested yet?"

"We have to prove she's doing these things. The sad part about it is that you can't arrest a stalker unless you can prove they are actually doing what we think they are doing."

I snapped, "Why do we have to prove that ourselves? Isn't that what the police are for?"

"Yeah, that's the crazy part about it. Even with her saying that I said I would kill her, they really can't do anything to me. The system is messed up."

I took a deep breath. This was just ugly. Cam had to deal with an unfair arrest and we couldn't get that lunatic arrested even if we wanted to. I couldn't believe she was literally the devil.

Cam said, "But it's all good. Morris got me."

I figured it was too early to bring up moving so I let

that pass. He said, "And guess what? We go to court on June sixteenth."

"That's my due date."

"I know."

"I asked Morris to see if we can get it postponed."

"Does he think he'll be able to get a postponement?"

"He's going to try. That's all he told me. Where's Caron?"

"He's in school." I paused. I wasn't sure if I should bring this up, but I did. "He told me something disturbing. He said you hurt his mother the last time he spent the weekend over there."

He looked at me without an inkling of a smile. "What if I did?"

I completely understood his anger but it didn't make sense to hurt her and mess up our lives. "Did you really threaten to kill her?"

"I told her to stop playing with my life."

Anger trembled in his voice. He didn't waver or hesitate in his statement. His eyes pierced through me, demanding that I understand him. I said, "Baby, even after all she's taken us through, I don't want to see her hurt."

"Why?" he snapped. "After she basically tried to kill you. The legal system ain't going to help us. I may have to take this into my own hands."

"And miss out on your children's lives. You don't want to do that."

"That's the only reason I haven't done anything yet. I'm so sick of her crazy ass."

"Have you given any consideration to New York?"

"Not at all."

I knew that he wasn't sold on New York and I knew this wasn't the right time to talk about it. He had spent the weekend in a jail cell with a bunch of angry men and was fired up. I figured I should probably wait until he simmered down before broaching that topic.

When we got home, Cam went in to talk to his mother. She said, "Are you OK, baby?"

He said, "I'm cool, Mom."

"I love you, Son."

"I know. I love you too."

"Sometimes you need to make sacrifices and I think you need to give up the battle for Caron. Let him go back with his mama and stay as far away from that woman as you possibly can."

"Listen, I'm not going to have my seed in the same town and don't deal with him."

Ms. Mae shook her head. "That is the best thing for everyone involved. At least until it all calms down."

"Ma, I'm not that dude. I'm not going to do that to my son."

She said, "See, you New Age men put up with more than the men in my day. They would act like she don't exist."

"Ma, you're talking crazy."

She curled her lips. "If you want to continue dealing with this, keep on fighting that girl for custody. Give the boy back and let that girl be."

His eyebrows wrinkled. "Ma, it's not about Caron. She wants me back."

I stood there speechless at Ms. Mae's suggestion that Cam give up his firstborn. Even I didn't think that was a good idea. I could tell that Cam was irritated by her suggestion, but maybe she was right. It seems that women give a harder time to men who are trying to do the right thing, as opposed to if he would just leave her and Caron alone. I didn't love the whole stepmother thing but I was dealing with it just fine.

yasmin

For the past few weeks I had been letting Tayshawn drop off and pick up Caron. It was burning Cam up from what I was told, but I was honestly scared of him. I really didn't know what to expect. He had been acting really flaky. I had the feeling there was trouble in paradise, because he seemed to always be enraged for no reason. He probably realized that Ms. Ayana wasn't all she was cracked up to be. She was expected to have that baby any day now. When I first heard she was pregnant, I cried because that meant we were likely done forever. But then I realized that people always love their firstborn more than anything in the world.

As I dressed for court, I wondered why it had gotten to this point. Cam and I had been fine until he decided to go fall in love with the wrong person. Although we weren't a couple, we were cordial and this chick had ruined it all. I hoped she wouldn't be in court so I could get him alone and talk to him. He was a stranger to me, definitely not the same person I married. The way he talked, the way he acted...everything about him was different. If he were as happy as he claimed to be, he wouldn't look so miserable each time I saw him.

When I showed up to court, I looked around and Cam wasn't there. I wondered where he was and why he hadn't shown. Finally, he arrived looking like he hadn't slept since the last time I saw him. He just didn't look right. We had court orders to stay away from each other, but I needed to talk to him. I needed to get to the bottom of what was going on with him.

When our case was called, Cam's friend Morris stepped up as his attorney. The judge said the case had been dismissed because the charges were dropped. He looked up at me. "Ms. Small, is that correct, you want to drop the charges?"

"Yes, Your Honor."

Both Cam and his attorney looked at me suspiciously. The judge went on to say, "I hope that you are not in an abusive relationship and dropping the charges because you two have made up. I can't protect you if the situation flips for the worst."

"Your Honor, I am not in an abusive relationship. I have been divorced from this man for over a year. He has never put his hands on me. We had a misunderstanding and in that moment, I was afraid, but I do not fear for my life and I apologize for involving the legal system."

The judge nodded as he if appreciated my apology. He said, "Thank you, Ms. Small. Case dismissed."

On the way out of the courtroom, I looked at Cam and I knew I had touched a soft spot with him. He gave me a nod, as if he was proud. The same way he used to do when we were young and in love. I mouthed, "I'm sorry."

He raised his thumb at me and I smiled. For the sake of Caron, I wanted us to start communicating again. I took responsibility for ruining the relationship and I didn't know how I was going to repair it but I was. It was all over the blogs how he was arrested at their baby shower. I'd never wanted it to go down that way. In fact, I'd never really expected they would arrest him at all.

Out in the hallway, he and Morris stood there talking and I kind of lingered around, hoping to speak with him. Morris stayed by his side the entire time and they ended up leaving the courthouse together. I was a little sad because I wanted to say something to him. I wanted to talk about how we would proceed and how we could fix our communication.

Two days later, I showed up to pick Caron up from the sheriff's department. Cam looked shocked to see me when I stepped out of the car. I waved at him, but he sent Caron across the parking lot alone. I looked at him and asked, "So when is the baby coming?"

He got back in his car and didn't respond. I felt rejected. It frustrated me that I had put myself out there and acknowledged his new baby and he'd treated me like some trick off the street.

I wanted to run over and knock his windows out and ask him if he was hard of hearing. Instead I took long, deep breaths like my therapist had suggested I do when

I got angry. By the time Caron got in the car, Cam had peeled off. Caron shook his head. I could tell that our lack of communication was taking a toll on him. He seemed to be getting angrier every week. Maybe it was just a part of his growing up but there was something else going on with him. It could be the new baby that was making him feel neglected. I couldn't put my finger on it. No one in that house seemed happy. Maybe Ayana had them both in a trance. Maybe that was a part of her psychotherapy.

Caron sat in the car and I asked, "What's wrong with you?"

"Nothing. I don't see why I can't go to school at my old school next year."

It was his last day of school and he was already thinking about the next school year. "But I thought you liked the new school."

"I like my other school better. I don't know why Dad and me can't live in our old house. I don't like Ayana's house. I want to go to school with my other friends."

"That's your dad's and Ayana's house."

He snapped, "I don't care whose house it is. I don't want to be there."

"I thought you told me that it was so big and you had your own arcade," I said with a little exaggeration, as he had when he'd told me about it.

He said, "I don't care. I don't want to be there anymore."

"OK, Mommy is working on you moving back with me. Is that what you want?"

"Yeah."

"You don't want to live with your dad anymore?"

"I do."

I said, "So how are you going to live with me if you want to stay with your dad?"

"I want us all to live together."

"What about Ayana?"

He hung his head, like he knew he was wrong. He said, "I don't care."

I wanted the same thing he wanted and neither of us had a clear plan to get there. The fact that Cam wasn't even talking to me meant that we had a long road ahead if we were going to get to our destination. I looked at Caron. "I'm going to do my best."

ayana

Seven days after my due date I was ready for the baby to drop. My doctor planned to induce me within the week, but he wanted me to have a sonogram first just to check the baby's size. He called us to come in the next day to discuss the sonogram charts.

When we sat down in his office, I felt a little nervous because he started talking like something was wrong. He said, "I had every intention of inducing you on Friday and had no reason to think you couldn't have the baby vaginally, but..."

There was a long pause and my mouth dried. Cam reached for my hand as if he could sense my fear.

"Your baby's shoulders are disproportionate to his head."

My eyes shifted from side to side. The doctor was talking about my son as if he were some kind of abnormal creature. "What do you mean?"

"His shoulders are wider than his head." He demonstrated with his hands spread far apart. "If his head comes out and we're unable to get the shoulders out, we may have to break his collar. If there is any nerve damage, it's possible that arm will not grow."

Cam said, "So what are our options?"

"The safest option is a C-section."

I'd been planning for the birth for so many weeks. I wanted to have the baby naturally and this was really blowing me. I said, "So are you saying I *need* to have a C-section?"

The doctor clarified, "No, I'm not saying you need to have a C-section. The decision is ultimately up to you. I will tell you this, if the head comes out and the shoulders get stuck, I will not break his collar, we will do an emergency C-section."

I looked at Cam, unsure of what I wanted to do. Should we press our luck? The gamble was just too risky, it seemed.

The doctor said, "It looks like he's around eight pounds, nine ounces. This is not completely accurate, give or take a pound. Either way, he's a big baby. If he were a little smaller, I would probably say we'd be OK, but with that size and the width of his shoulders, I'm just not confident it would go smoothly."

Cam interjected, "Doc, if it were your baby, what would you do?"

"C-section. No question about it."

Cam looked at me. "That's what it is. I don't want to live with regrets."

Still not completely convinced, I asked the doctor to explain again what we'd do if the baby got stuck. Cam looked at me confused, as if I'd undermined his decision, but I needed to be clear. The doctor said, "I will not do any tugging and pulling. If the baby doesn't come out, we'll do an emergency C-section."

Cam looked at me and said, "Are you serious? You're really not considering taking that route. Are you?"

"I'm just trying to understand everything."

"What more is there to understand than it may be dangerous to have the baby vaginally?"

"What if everything is fine?" I asked.

"Optimism is good in some cases, but not this one."

Wondering if I should just accept what was being handed to me, I covered my face and took a deep breath. It was a little too late for a second opinion. So I agreed to a C-section. We were scheduled for two days later.

I checked into the hospital at six in the morning. Cam carried the baby bag. My mother and Aaliyah met us there. They put me in a pre-op room that seemed too small for me and my three people. It was like the projects of labor and delivery. The nurse hooked me up to the IV. The anesthesiologist came in to discuss the procedure and had me sign the releases.

Shortly after eight in the morning my doctor showed up. "Are you ready?"

"As ready as we're going to be."

Close to nine they rolled me into the operating room. I was only allowed to have one person with me, but because my doctor had delivered Aaliyah's kids, he said she

could come in also. I was grateful he allowed that since
I was missing out on the rest of my family being there to
experience labor with me.

The anesthesiologist put the needle in my spine and
within minutes, I was numb from the neck down. The
doctor then began the procedure. Cam was videotaping,
and once the doctor cut me, the nurse instructed Cam
to only shoot from the chest up. That was a little scary.
What were they doing down there that they didn't want
on camera?

Suddenly I felt a tugging. I couldn't actually feel the
pain. But it was like someone was pulling on my body.
The doctor said, "Wow, he's really high up there." Speaking to me, he said, "Ayana, he's coming."

The baby came out with a little mousy cry. It was almost as if he were struggling. Aaliyah said, "He's here,
Ayana."

The nurses took the baby to clean him up and the doctor continued to put me back in place. As I lay there, I
felt nauseous. I couldn't sit up and vomit. I was scared
that I was going to throw up and choke. What if I died
on this table? The anesthesiologist must have recognized
the struggle in my eyes. He said, "Are you OK?"

"I feel like I have to throw up."

He lifted my neck up and rubbed my hair. He was so
gentle. I could hear Aaliyah and Cam adoring the baby.
I was anxious to see him too. The nausea went away almost as suddenly as it had come. Minutes later the doctor
was done patching me up and the nurse brought the baby

over to lie on my chest. It was love at first sight. I kissed his head over and over again as they rolled me into the recovery room.

My mother came in shortly after we got there. My little Ethan lay calmly on my chest, as if he knew I was his mommy. The nurse picked him up and listened to his breathing. Her frown let me know something was wrong. She told me to let him lie on my skin to see if his breathing would catch the rhythm of mine. She explained that when a baby doesn't come through the birth canal, he often doesn't get prepared to take that first breath.

After a few minutes of his lying on my chest, she checked again. His breathing was still too fast. She sent him to the Neonatal Intensive Care Unit to be safe. Why did I have to part with my son so soon? My mother and Cam were able to go up to the NICU with the nurse. Aaliyah stayed with me while we waited to get a room on the labor and delivery floor. Another nurse came to let me know that Ethan was doing fine and he'd be coming to the room shortly after I got there.

An hour or so had passed when the nurse came in to tell me that Ethan's breathing was still too fast and he'd be spending at least one night in the NICU. Cam had been back and forth and I was jealous. The nurses didn't want me to ride in a wheelchair so soon. They suggested that in a few hours I would be able to visit. When my friends came, Cam took them up to see the baby.

My mother left to pick up Cam's mother. There were so many people there but they kept leaving to see the baby.

I felt alone. I knew it was for his safety, but I didn't want him upstairs in the intensive care unit.

At close to midnight, the nurse on duty asked if I had been up to see the baby. She got a wheelchair and called up to let the nurses know we were coming. I woke Cameron up so he could tag along. When walking into the unit, we had to wash our hands and present identification. No one was getting in who didn't belong.

Ethan was in a little subunit where the bigger babies were, but on our way to him, we passed itsy teeny little babies. Some you could tell were as small as two pounds, with tubes and monitors all over them. That made me sad as I imagined what their parents were going through.

When I rolled up to Ethan's little plastic crib, they told me it was time for him to eat. They had been feeding him by bottle but the nurse asked if I would be breastfeeding. Since that was my plan, she suggested we try it now. She picked him up to wake him and he squirmed a little and began to cry. After changing his diaper, she handed him to me.

I had taken a breastfeeding one-day course so I was familiar with all the tricks they used to help the babies latch on. It was foreign to me but the nurse instructed me in how to hold him and position myself while simultaneously opening his mouth. Mr. Ethan latched on right away and sucked for dear life. Cam laughed. "Go ahead, man. Tell Mommy you missed her."

This was the first time that I'd really gotten to look at him. He was so precious and calm. He clung to me. His eyes began to close and the nurse suggested that I move him to my other side. It had been challenging even in my class to try to feed with the left breast, but just as the instructor had, the nurse said I shouldn't get too comfortable with one breast, because when he really started eating I wouldn't be able to produce enough milk from just one.

After he ate, Cam sat down in the rocking chair beside me and held my hand as I held Ethan. Ethan was wearing a cute little undershirt that read ADORABLE. That was an understatement. I asked the nurse where his Onesie had come from. She told me the hospital had tons, that some were donated and some were left, and that they were kept clean for all the babies coming in and out. I looked in Ethan's crib and noticed a white Beanie Baby. "Do they all get these?" I asked, reaching to pull it out.

The nurse said, "Hmmm, I didn't notice that. One of your family members must have put it in there with him."

I looked at the card tied around the little bear's neck: ROCK-A-BYE BABY. My mouth hung open and I took long, slow, deep breaths as I passed the opened card to Cam. I was angry and I snapped at the nurse, "Is there someone here monitoring who comes in and out all day?"

The nurse adamantly said, "Yes. No one's getting in here without identification or one of the parents."

Cam said, "Well, some unauthorized person obviously came to see our baby and we have proof."

"What kind of proof do you have?" she asked.

We ended up telling her that Cam's ex-wife had been

harassing us and had made a statement or two in the past similar to what was written on the card. The people who had visited that day knew that ROCK-A-BYE BABY was a touchy subject. None of them would have put that on the card.

The nurse went to the front desk to get the visitor log for us and there were no random names listed as visitors for Ethan. She then called security to discuss the issue. They asked if Cam was willing to look at the footage to see if we recognized anyone. Cam agreed and I stayed with the baby. I didn't want to leave Ethan's side. If that meant I had to sleep in a damn wheelchair all day, that's what I'd do to protect him. This whole experience had let me know that anyone can get to you if they are really determined to. It was frightening. As I sat there with Ethan on my lap, I was really rethinking the whole idea of being in the public eye. I just wanted to be a good mother and a good wife in peace. Everything else could fall by the wayside at this point.

Cam returned with no resolution. Cam looked at me and said the unthinkable: "Could it be someone we're close to?"

I shook my head. "I know my family and my friends. They would never, ever do anything to hurt me."

I could see that Cam doubted that in that moment, but I knew it had to be his ex-wife. She was the only person who wanted us to fail. She was the only person threatening the life of our child. The legal system was bullshit. A restraining order was senseless when you ordered a crazy person to stay away. The law doesn't mean shit to a person determined to make your life miserable.

Cam did not leave the NICU for the next twenty-four hours, until they finally brought Ethan down to stay in the room with us. We were there three more days, and I was so happy to be going home I didn't know what to do, but I felt safe because there would be no intruders in my home.

ayana

After being home with Ethan for four months, I wasn't sure that I wanted to be an overachiever anymore. When Cam landed a group of investors prepared to proceed immediately with development for the Blake's Overlook project I was ecstatic. If things worked out as Cam projected, we would walk away from this project fifty million dollars richer. It had been extremely tight over the past few months for us. And while I didn't make nearly as much money as Cam, all his income was going to retaining the land. I wanted him to sell the Bentley, but he felt that investors wouldn't take him seriously if he were driving a less expensive car. I decided to give him a year to work things out. If there was no return or at least another investor I wanted him to sell the land. He had a bunch of other properties that had gone into foreclosure, but he was committed to this land. He believed the project was big enough to sacrifice everything else. We butted heads on that a lot.

As we dressed in preparation for the groundbreaking party, I was happy he hadn't listened to me. He kept saying that we were doing well but we weren't wealthy. I felt differently, but his plan was to leave wealth for generations to come. This project alone would guarantee that, but knowing Cam's mind he'd be looking into the next big thing now that this project was going well.

I wore a black fitted one-shoulder dress. Of course I had on a tight girdle underneath to bind my baby weight. Once I was dressed, Cam looked at me the same way he had when we first met. My hair was pulled over into a side ponytail. I'd had a makeup artist come to do my hair and makeup. This was the first time I'd felt beautiful in over a year and Cam looked as if he really noticed and appreciated my effort.

On our way to the party, he touched my leg and smiled. He said, "This is what it's all about."

"Yeah, I agree."

He was dressed in a black tux and we were headed to the Hyatt in midtown. When we got there, we were among a small group of investors and contractors. Groundbreaking was scheduled for the following day. It felt so good to be out, drinking wine and conversing with new people.

At one point people began to make toasts, thanking others for their involvement and faith in the project. Finally the group shouted, "Cam, Cam, Cam, Cam."

I smiled as my baby stood there blushing. Before he started speaking, he motioned to everyone to be silent. He began at the moment he'd discovered the property was up for auction and described how he'd gone to sleep and had a vision. He said even with the real estate market being in the dumps, he'd known this was what he was born to do. He thanked all the investors and promised that everyone would walk away in the black, repaid ten-to twentyfold. Then he turned to look at me. "They say behind every good man, there is a good woman. I have an amazing woman." Everyone clapped. He continued, "When I met this woman, I told her on our first date, I felt like God sent her to me. I think she thought it was just game. But I knew from the second I laid eyes on her that she would be a partner and friend unlike any other. This past year has been hard. There have been times when I didn't think we'd ever break ground on Blake's Over-look, but she had my back with a smile and encouraging words. You can't invent a person like that with all the sci-ence in the world. Ayana Small, you are my dream."

My eyes watered and I patted them with my fingertips. I didn't want to mess up my makeup. Cam came over and kissed me on the mouth. When I looked at him, I noticed that his eyes were watery too. He was so good to me.

After the party was over, I wanted to make passionate love to him. He held me tightly in the elevator. I felt his penis and it was rock-hard. I wanted him to take me right there, but I knew it would be too much to peel off my un-dergarments. On the ride home, I pulled his penis out of his pants. I was proud of him and I wanted him to know it. I was impressed with the man he had been to me over the past year and a half. He was everything, and I wanted to show my appreciation. I bent over and put his penis in my mouth. He smelled so good and tasted even better. He moaned, and I could feel the car slowing down as if he couldn't concentrate. My head bobbed up and down as we rode down the freeway. There would be no mess in the Bentley, because I swallowed his pleasure with joy. He thanked me and told me how much he loved me.

The next day was the groundbreaking ceremony. Cam had to leave a little earlier, so I had to drop Caron off at the bus stop. Cam and I were running late because of our long night of lovemaking. There were other kids at the bus stop when I got there. Cam usually waited until the bus came, but if I did I would be late for the ceremony. I wanted to be there to stand by my man. He deserved my support. I rushed Caron out of the car and sped off.

When I arrived at Blake's Overlook, I was just in time. The mayor, Cam, and the contractors wore hard hats as the bulldozer dug into the ground. I knew that Cam had dreamed of this day so many times. I was so happy that it had come true. As I watched him in admiration, I knew he deserved it. So many women would have walked out on him, but I'd known I had something good. Once the ceremony was over, he came over to hug me. I stayed around for a while, but he was so busy talking to reporters, I figured I'd head back home to get a manicure and spend the rest of the day relaxing. This was the beginning of my pampered life and I was ready to get adjusted.

When I sat in the car, my phone rang immediately. The Bluetooth in my car picked up the ring because I had my phone on silent. It was the nanny calling from the house. She said, "Ms. Small." The hesitant sound in her voice scared me.

I said, "Is everything OK with Ethan?"

"Ethan's fine, but I got a message from the school saying that Caron never made it. Is he with you?"

"No, he's not with me. I dropped him off at the bus stop."

She said, "The principal said the other kids saw you drop him off and then you came back to pick him up."

"I came back to pick him up? I don't get it. From the bus stop?"

"Yeah. That's what the kids say."

"Let me go to the school."

I sped down the highway trying to get to the bottom of this. Had Caron walked away from the bus stop? I was so confused. I decided not to ruin Cam's day with the news and headed to Caron's school on my own. An unknown number called and I quickly picked up. The voice was disguised.

"You've finally gotten rid of the one nuisance."

"Who is this?" I shouted.

"Your helper. You never wanted Caron. Now that you have your new baby, you can get rid of him."

"No. That's not true. Who is this?"

"Ha ha ha." The laughter sounded spooky with the voice distorter. "Whatever you do, don't call the police. Because I will take Caron out with one shot and it will look like you did it. Remember, you picked him up from the bus stop."

I said, "What do you want from me?"

"Meet me at your grandmother's house."

"My grandmother's house?" I asked, confused.

"Yes, asshole. Your father's mother's house."

My face frowned. Who could this be? We'd decided to keep my grandmother's house in the family after she passed. My father was mainly responsible for the upkeep. We'd gone back and forth on whether to rent it out. My father had reservations and I think preserving it helped with his grief so we all went along with it. He often went there to relax alone. He kept the electric and cable on. This person was someone who knew me well. A part of me thought it was Yasmin, because she was a certified stalker.

But why would she threaten to kill her own son? I didn't know, but I sped to my grandmother's house to save him.

I got out of my car and suddenly felt that maybe I should call Aaliyah. Then again, I was running on adrenaline and wanted to get to the bottom of this. I was down for a tussle but I really wasn't feeling murder on my hands, especially the murder of my stepson. My motherly instincts kicked in for Caron. I wanted to protect him, and whoever this lunatic was trying to harass him had to be exposed, even if it was his mother.

Using my key to enter, I called out, "Hello."

Caron's voice trembled as he said, "Ayana, we're down here."

Before heading down to the basement, I went to the

kitchen to grab a knife. My curiosity overpowered my fear. I slowly walked down the stairs. It was dark but there was enough light peeping through the small window for me to see Margo, my patient who had threatened to kill her father. Caron sat tied to a chair. He looked helpless and scared. She held a gun to his head. His eyes begged me to do something to fix this.

"Ayana, are you going hurt me?"

"Why would you say that, Margo?" I asked, placing the knife on the floor. "I didn't know it was you when I came down here."

My mind raced. I'd called the psychiatrist treating her several times after she was admitted and he hadn't returned my calls. While I'd prayed that he had taken my advice to keep her for an extended period, I often wondered if she had been released.

She said, "What do you mean you didn't know it was me? You don't know me? You don't care about me?"

"I do care about you."

"You don't!" she snapped.

"OK."

"You made me feel like you cared about me and you could give a shit about me. You tried to send me to jail."

"No, I just wanted you to get help."

"I was talking to you in confidence."

Using my hands to talk, I said, "Margo, I told you that I am mandated by law to call authorities if I believe you're going to hurt someone."

"Bitch, you didn't tell me and you didn't even have

the decency to take me to the hospital yourself. You're a sorry motherfucker. And then you just got rid of me. They told me I was released from your care at the hospital. You're a goddamn coward. I guess it's in your blood."

I should have taken her case more seriously from jump. The first day she came in, I'd thought she needed a psychiatrist, but I overestimated myself. Here I was being terrorized by this woman and wondering if there was anything I could have done differently. Regret wasn't going to help me at the moment. All I could do now was keep talking to her. I said, "I'm sorry if you felt like I betrayed you. I shouldn't have. I really shouldn't have."

"You're not sorry," she said. "You're only worried about yourself. You got the police to come to my house and you never even called to see if I was OK. I got evicted and was on the street. You didn't care."

"Listen, Margo, I told them to keep you in a residency program. You needed their help."

"They threw me out on the street to be homeless."

"I'm sorry."

"Don't be, because I got a place as Ayana Blue. Don't you like how easy it is to be someone you're not?"

My mind flooded with all these questions, wondering if she'd been doing all these things to me this whole time. As I was stumbling over the timeline in my mind, she shouted, "Why should you have all the luck? Why do you steal the man and live happily ever after?"

I said, "Margo, I didn't steal the man and I swear I have problems too."

"Bitch, don't patronize me. How are you going to feel when they lock you up and you lose everything?"

"Margo, please. Don't do this."

"Why? Why shouldn't I? You have hurt me my whole life. You! I want you to feel my pain."

Her hand was trembling with the gun and I was trying to think of a way to get it away from her. "I never meant to hurt you. What can I do to change it?"

"How would you feel being a child and your father treated you like you didn't exist?"

"I'm sure that would be very hard."

"You and Aaliyah would come here every Sunday, wearing the best clothes. Our father would usher you inside so you couldn't play with the neighborhood kids. Do you know why?"

Before I could answer, she snapped, "Because he never wanted you to see me! He wanted to act like I didn't exist. He treated me like a piece of shit. The same way he treated my mother when she told him she was pregnant."

I started putting all the things she'd told me about her father together. It all added up. This woman was my sister and it had been my own father's life I'd saved.

"I'm sorry, Margo. I'm really sorry. I don't know why he would do that."

"You're not sorry. All he cared about was making sure his little princesses were fine. I was treated like a mistress my whole life."

"Did you have any contact with him growing up?"

"No."

"Did he and your mother have a relationship?"

"Yes, they were in love and then he went to More-house. My mother wasn't good enough. Your mother took him from my mother and she knew my mother was pregnant and didn't care. She married him and they pretended that me and my mother didn't exist."

"Margo, that wasn't right."

"Duh! You're the fucking psychologist. Say something smart. You fucking quack!"

Caron cried loudly and she pushed his head. "Shut the fuck up, you little brat. Your father is in your life."

Caron sniffed back his cry. I said, "I understand why you're upset, Margo, but it's not his fault. Let him go. If you want to take it out on someone, hurt me."

She pointed the gun at me and I instantly wanted to swallow my words. I said, "Margo, you know me and Aaliyah didn't know. We would have loved you anyway."

"No, you wouldn't."

"Yes, we would have."

"When I first starting seeing you, I believed you were a good person. Then you left me to rot just like your sorry father."

"I'm so sorry. Is there anything I can to do make it better?"

"It's too late. You've forced me to do this."

"I wish you would have told me before," I said, still very confused and shocked by what she had told me.

I heard footsteps over my head and Margo smiled. "She made it."

My eyes questioned and she said, "Yasmin, we're down here."

There was no way Yasmin had been working alone, and this explained it all as I heard her anxiously approaching. Her neck snapped back. "Margie?"

Margo pointed the gun at her. "No, bitch. It's Margo. I fucking tried to tell you my name a million times and you keep calling me Margie. My fucking name is Margo!"

Yasmin said, "OK, I got it, Margo."

Yasmin was even more confused than me. I realized that Margo had been working solo, but how did she know Yasmin?

"Why are you making them pay for my mistakes?" I asked.

"Number one, this bitch talks too damn much. Tells all her business in the salon. I got my hair done to snoop and she told me everything. I knew every move you made because she couldn't stop talking about you. And I couldn't stand the thought of you just storming in and doing the same thing to someone else that your mother did to my mother. I hated it!" she yelled.

She looked at Yasmin. Tears welled in her eyes. "I was trying to help you. And you looked right through me like I was invisible every time I came into the salon."

Yasmin shook her head. "I'm sorry. We went skating together a few times. I thought we were cool. Whatever I did to offend you, please forgive me."

"Fuck you. You dumb bitch. You're so self-centered you didn't even know I was trying to reach out to you."

I said, "Let's start over. Let's be sisters. Now that I know you're my sister, I will never leave you. I'm sorry that my father abandoned you. I'm sorry that my mother did what she did. No one will hurt you again."

She looked to be softening and turned the gun to Yasmin. "Do you want me to get rid of this insensitive bitch?"

My eyes shot at Yasmin. As much of a pain in the ass as she'd been, I didn't want anyone to hurt her, especially not in front of Caron. Yasmin was confused. Margo was bitter and she didn't care who it was, she wanted to kill someone, anyone, so they could feel her pain. Yasmin said, "Please, Margo."

"Now you know my name?"

"I'm sorry, I have a bunch of clients. I just..."

"You just care about your own stupid problems. You spend all day talking about this bitch instead of getting to know the people who pay you."

Nervously I watched as Yasmin approached her and Margo cocked the gun. Yasmin didn't seem to be afraid at all, probably because she was equally crazy. She said, "You're right. I hate her. I hate that bitch so much that I want her dead. And Margo, you hate her too. She doesn't care about you. She only cares about herself. She's a selfish, self-centered bitch and she'll abandon you like everyone in your life."

Margo nodded and tears rolled down her cheeks. I

couldn't believe it. Yasmin was connecting with her with some bullshit. Were they in this together?

Yasmin continued, "She has a sister. She can't be your sister, but I can. I promise I won't hurt you."

She stepped closer to Margo, whose hands shook. She looked almost as if she no longer had control of the gun. I closed my eyes and shifted to the right, thinking that if she inadvertently fired I didn't want to be in her path. She aimed at me. Yasmin kept getting closer to Margo. My eyes shifted back and forth. I wasn't sure how this would end. In a flash, there was a struggle. Yasmin tackled Margo and started beating her.

"Get the gun, Ayana!" Yasmin yelled.

I was frozen and afraid. I didn't want to touch the gun but I knew I had to in order to save everybody. Suddenly the Atlanta Police Department busted in and took control of the situation. Yasmin hugged Caron, and I just stood there as Margo was arrested. I was still stunned by everything she had told me.

Yasmin hugged me, and I said, "How did you know we were here?"

"She called me and pretended to be you, saying you were about to kill Caron. I knew that was a lie. I just knew."

To my surprise, I reached out to hug Yasmin. She had saved my life. When we walked out of the house to all the police cars, I asked Yasmin, "Did you call Cam?"

"No, I just called the cops and came straight here."

"Thank you."

"No problem."

"And I think I owe you an apology because I've blamed you for a lot of things that I now believe Margo was doing."

"No big deal. I'm not totally innocent."

"I guess we should start over," I said.

ayana

A year had passed since that fateful day and a lot had changed. Caron and I had gotten extremely close. Yasmin and I had built a respectable relationship and Cameron and I were finally at peace. We joked that our relationship was the opposite of most: it had started out hard and now we were enjoying the fruits of our labor. I closed my practice and focused on writing and the talk show. Ethan was running around the house like a big boy. It was a good thing I had gotten so many extensions on my book, because I changed the entire second half to discuss the blended family. It was tougher living through the situation, but it made me a better psychologist. Instead of just understanding the theory behind it, I now had my own real-world experiences.

My father felt horrible about the Margo experience and admitted that it had been the wrong thing to do. He'd felt that he had to deny her because he didn't want to hurt my mother. He said my mother didn't know anything about Margo or her mother and he thought it was best to keep it that way. He claimed his love for my mother blinded his judgment. He had been my hero, and to say that knowing he had a child that he never claimed didn't taint my image of him would be a lie. I didn't understand, and the illusion that we were a perfect family was shattered. Aaliyah blamed Margo, but I knew better. I blamed my father. So in the blended family section of my book, I discussed conceiving a child with someone other than your spouse. It was important for people to know how to approach it. Most people are more afraid of hurting their spouse than they are of hurting the child. They don't realize that kids carry the burden of rejection longer and feel it more deeply than adults.

To promote my book, Quentin suggested we have Yasmin on to discuss how far we'd come. Cameron was nervous, because a part of him always felt that Yasmin could revert at any time. Based on conversations we'd had, I thought her therapist had really helped her change her behavior.

I started the show by saying, *"Love and Marriage* hits bookstores today and I expect to see all my listeners at my mega book release party tonight. And I want to thank you all for your support and encouragement." I paused. "Today I have a special guest, my husband's ex-wife, Ms. Yasmin Small. You all may be familiar with her as ShearGenius08 on Twitter." Yasmin smiled and shook her head. I said, "Thanks for being on the show."

She said, "You're welcome."

"I think everyone wants to know how we can be in the

same room together. I will let you answer and then I will answer that question myself."

Yasmin shifted her body sassily and curled her lips. "Well, it's hard to accept that someone you love is in love with someone else. For me, it was hard and I just didn't want to accept it. I figured that if I could make your life miserable, I could win him back. I was committed to it. But it took a lot of therapy to accept that life doesn't always work out the way you plan. So for me, I'm here because I finally accepted that Cameron moved on."

I was slightly stunned by her rendition of how we'd arrived at this cordial point. I didn't speak immediately, and Quentin waved his hand as if to say, "Hurry up and respond." I said, "And I guess for me, forgiveness is a crucial part of life, and holding grudges and anger is no good for anyone. I've seen the growth in you right before my eyes. And who am I to judge by past mistakes? I can sit here because, as a human and more importantly as a therapist, I believe that people can and do change."

Yasmin said, "Wow."

"Can you tell me your thoughts on raising kids in a blended family? Especially from the perspective of being the first wife and having your biological child integrated into another family without you?"

After a deep breath, she admitted, "It's hard to hear your child talk about family bonding activities and you're not included. Or when I may miss one of his basketball games and he says, 'Well, Dad and Ayana were there so I'm cool.' That hurts. It makes me sad sometimes."

I felt her pain and I knew that it would probably hurt if I had to be on the outside looking in with Ethan. I asked, "So, as far as you see it, are there any benefits to having a blended family?"

"Well, I never thought I'd say this, but I think Caron likes having two mothers. You give him something that I don't and I give him what you don't. I mean, now that we get along, I think he gets the best of both worlds. But when we were fighting, I think he felt like he had to pick sides and he seemed to be very insecure and uncertain of himself."

"Yes, I definitely notice that he's a lot more confident and happy. And we often don't realize how our issues are evident in the child's personality. The lines are open for questions."

I answered a call: "*Girlfriend Confidential*."

The caller said, "Yasmin, are you seeing anyone, because I can't imagine how you could be completely at peace with everything. It's almost unbelievable."

Yasmin said, "Yeah, I see what you're saying. I am seeing someone, but I think I started working on myself first, because I wanted to get my son back. And I think that's why someone came into my life, because I was at peace. So it wasn't like I came to peace after I met someone, it was the other way around. But to be honest, having someone definitely makes it better."

The caller said, "Did you get your son back?"

Smiling, Yasmin said, "I certainly did. We have joint custody and I have him four days and they have him three."

She seemed so happy to say that. The caller thanked Yasmin and hung up. The next caller directed her question at me. "Ayana, do you harbor any negative feeling toward Yasmin? I mean, she trashed you on Twitter, like, every day. That was crazy."

Yasmin looked at me and said, "You can say, 'Yeah.' I would understand."

"No, I don't have any negative feelings toward Yasmin. She saved my life. I have never discussed this on air, but I was being stalked by one of my patients last year and the patient had lured me to a location," I said, suddenly getting choked up.

Yasmin looked at me sympathetically, knowing that was the situation that had really bonded us forever. Her eyes encouraged me to continue.

"And this person had me at gunpoint and Yasmin wrestled her down. I will forever be grateful to her for that. Nothing she did to me prior to that point even matters. When I look at her, I see a good person."

Yasmin looked as if she wanted to cry too, as a tear fell from my eye. I was happy, but also sad about Margo. I felt I had failed her. I felt my father had failed her. Yasmin reached out for my hand and spoke for me because I was lost for words. "Thank you, Ayana. You're a good person too."

We took several more calls before closing the show. I

finished by saying, "Things aren't perfect between us, but we are a work in progress. Life is a work in progress. And as long as you are progressing, you are living. Thank you for tuning in to another segment of *Girlfriend Confidential*. I am your host, Ayana Blue Small. Until next time..."

BOOK CLUB DISCUSSION QUESTIONS

1. What was your initial impression of Ayana? How did you feel about her actions on the first date with Cameron?

2. Should Ayana have found a new Realtor after Yasmin called in to the show?

3. Do you think Cameron was worth the drama? Why or why not?

4. What do you think he could have done to mitigate the situation with Ayana and Yasmin?

5. Do you feel that Cameron had a bit of sympathy for Yasmin? Why or why not?

6. Do you think Yasmin really loved Cameron?

7. Did you ever feel sorry for Yasmin?

8. Do you think Ayana should have tried to reach out to Yasmin, considering she was a psychologist?

9. Would you have married Cameron, believing that his ex-wife was crazy?

10. Did you believe that Yasmin was acting all alone?

11. What did you think when you discovered the truth at the end?

If you enjoyed *The Ex-Wife*, then be sure to
grab other novels from Candice Dow—

Now available from Grand Central Publishing

(06/11)

London Reed needs lots of cash fast, and
when handsome tycoon William Thorne
shows her just how to bend the rules, she
becomes addicted to fast money until she realizes it could be the most dangerous gamble
of all.

(09/09)

Their passion burned hot and intense, but
also tore their lives apart. Now Devin Pat-
terson and Clark Winston once again can't
resist a dangerous—and sizzling—temptation
in this RT Book Reviews Award–winning
novel.

(01/09)

Candice Dow and Daaimah S. Poole tell a
steamy, scandalous, no-holds-barred tale
about one irresistible man, two women with
only one thing in common, and way too
much of a good thing.

For information on GCP African American titles, please
visit http://www.facebook.com/#!/GCPAfricanAmerican